PATRICK KEALEY

Patrick knew he wanted to be a storyteller from the age of six, when he discovered that a rich interior life was a lot more fun than everyday life.

He has worked as an actor and theatre director, producer, drama lecturer, workshop leader and playwright. His theatre work has taken him to America, France, Eastern Europe, Scandinavia and Colombia, as well as theatres and festivals throughout the UK and Ireland. He performs two solo shows, including the award-winning adaptation of *The Life and Times of Archy and Mehitabel*.

Patrick also worked as a tour guide all around Ireland for over twenty years and, somewhere along those winding Irish roads, Bogboy was born. This is a true story in everything but the detail.

bogboy

bogboy

patrick kealey

Constellations Press

First published in 2025

Typesetting by Constellations Press
Print Management by Biddles Books, King's Lynn, Norfolk PE32 1SF

A CIP record for this book is available from the British Library

ISBN 978-1-917000-08-6
e-ISBN 978-1-917000-14-7

In memory of my two mothers

Bogboy

Bogboy has been trailing Hawk for hours in his kingdom of desolation. He loves the way she swoops and sails across the sky. He runs to keep up with her dark speck. He is always running. Backwards and forwards through tussocks and sedge, skirting pools of brackish water; a little hopping dance through his kingdom of sludge and stone. Here, he is prince of all he surveys; here, he is home. Here, no-one is coming for him, calling out for him. 'Bogboy, do this, Bogboy, do that.' The piss-stained hills rise, rusted gold along the skyline.

There's a movement in the distance. Bogboy stands stock-still, borrows Hawk's eyes to gaze upon a slow farm cart, drawn by an old nag, trundling down the snakelike twist of ancient road that cuts across his kingdom. A mound of bright-green cabbages has been tied down with tarp and old rope. Beyond those hills lies the market. Tante used to take him there when he was younger. Now, once a month, Molly and he load up the jaunt and head into the village for market day. The journey takes him to the farthest reach of his world.

Bogboy eyes the stranger's cart. Not really a stranger. O'Donnell is a grumpy, neighbouring farmer, a widower who, years ago, had had the temerity to tip his hat at Tante. Bogboy had once strayed into a small hillside pasture, strewn with slabs of rock, to observe a young calf suckling its mother, and the red-faced, old sod had appeared out of nowhere to yell at him for trespassing on his land and disturbing his livestock.

Bogboy whips two fingers to his lips and emits a piercing, lapwing shriek. The startled nag rears. It's enough to tilt the cart and the load leans perilously sideways. O'Donnell jolts upright, clasping the reins tight. Too late. Cabbages cascade to the earth to roll and scatter. Bogboy can hear the farmer's curses carried on the wind.

Bogboy grins. His heart blazes in his scrawny, mud-stained body. His tattered jersey and rough leggings are nothing but layers of filth, begrimed from his deep scurries into the world he loves. He whoops and leaps skyward to shake a fist of triumph at Hawk, still circling: predatory. He races towards a familiar cluster of trees – yew and rowan and wind-blasted ash. Arms outstretched, he flies towards the dark shadow-world of the dead heroes, the sons of his father, the great chieftain of the maggots.

Here is where the ancestors abide. Bogboy likes to crawl into dark places to lie still and listen for them. Jaws split apart, blackened stumps of teeth, they whisper their secrets in his ear. They are heroes from the ancient times, brought forth from a cauldron of fire beneath the great crust of the earth. Once flesh like him, now bleached bones. Bogboy likes to listen, while beetles and ants crawl across the landscape of his limbs; to listen and listen, even as cold winds cut him like a knife and rain drenches him to his marrow. Here, he is happy. Here, he belongs.

Hawk

Hawk sees everything. Hawk: eye of heaven, eye of evermore. Sees past, present, future. Hawk knows everything to come.

The dream of love that consumes and destroys. Floating serene, caressed by warm currents of air that ripple her wing feathers and stretch to infinity. Hawk above. Bogboy below. Ascended spirit and earthbound clod. Hawk, shot forth as if from Bogboy's skull, ascends and ascends with sheer force of will that lifts her higher and higher. She sees Bogboy, a mere dot below. Sees granite mountain, sees each rock and stone. Hawk is talon, beak and feather, light and air and fire. Her gaze pierces all, burns like the sun, scorches all she sees with fierce desire. Hawk soars into celestial cobalt: electric blue. Hawk is flux and flame and flow. But Hawk is also hungry. She is hunter and harrier, scouring earth below for prey, itching to shred raw flesh and hot blood, tear skin from bone. Her cry fills the valley and bounces off the looming shadow of the mountain top. Stillness and silence enfold the earth.

Tante

She keeps rooms heaped with memories. She lights the lamp in her private chamber, the room she still insists on referring to as 'the boudoir' and draws the thick velvet curtains against the encroaching blackness, while the moths gather to dance in the light, finding a ballroom of iridescent, dusted wings. These are the same moths that cocoon and then consume the once-fine silks and cashmeres of her trousseau, all still folded carefully in layers of tissue in trunks but rotting nevertheless. She refuses to throw her past away. It's all she has left. She catches a glimpse of herself in the ornate, bevelled-glass mirror – another wedding gift she cannot bring herself to dispose of – and stares at the apparition she's become. Stern. Ramrod-straight in defiance of the illness that wracks her body and leaves her prematurely aged, sometimes bent double with pain. She grimaces. She's only too painfully aware of what a foolish woman she's become. She read her Dickens as a young girl. There's an old leather-bound set of her father's somewhere in the attic still. Mildewed, no doubt, by now – like her and everything else in this damp, mould-infested prison. She takes in the photos above the huge, carved Connemara marble mantlepiece. Two sisters, side by side in matching oval frames. Both lovely. But only one a true beauty: Rose. Rose, the good; the pure; the kind. Her exquisite face, framed by her cloche hat, stares back, amused. Her seductive, bee-stung lips, so fashionable for the day.

'You should be in the pictures,' one failed beau had told her – a chat-up line Rose had cheerfully related to her sister.

Tante glances back towards the tall, long-curtained window. It's not yet dusk, but she likes to shut away the outside world at the first hint of night. Pain shoots through her. An owl is hooting in the distance. Where is the boy? The strange, uncaged creature that was her sister's last gift to her. Pregnant Rose, sweating on her deathbed, delivered a startled, squalling, tiny, unwanted bundle of screeching flesh into the world. How could the filthy, semi-feral, burrowing, skunk-like creature she can barely bring herself to look upon have emerged from the delicate, porcelain beauty of Rose – the princess, the fashion plate, the slut? The boy, born of betrayal, her sin made flesh. Rose, fatally weakened by her confinement, was still able to produce new life, something Tante's own body has never managed.

Now, her grim face glares back at her from the mirror, and reminds her of the arched eyebrows on the powdered, chalk-white mask of an actor she once saw in a pavilion in Kyoto. She remembers a tranquil pool of lilies by moonlight, and fat, guzzling carp flicking golden fins lazily through the reedy depths. The owl hoots again. She wraps her nightgown more tightly round herself. No. Not a happy memory. Tainted by all that came later.

And the father? It could have been the butcher's boy, or a handsome Canadian airman, or any one of an ogling gaggle of farmers' sons who would whistle as Rose cycled past or stepped out haughtily with her parcels on market days in her lovely, pale-blue woollen coat, straight out of a magazine. But Rose, stubborn to the end, felt no shame. All Tante could recall was her imploring face, begging, 'You'll keep him. Please. Don't let them take him away, promise me.' And she had promised. Even though she knew the truth. Despite it. She made the vow.

Bogboy: the bastard son who would never know his father. She would never tell. What does he have? Neither father nor mother. Just her. And a mutual loathing that binds them together in the tight twine of fate. She dreams sometimes of stuffing all her hate and repulsion down his throat like petrol-soaked rags and lighting them until his face melts like wax. What she can barely admit even now to herself, is that in his huge, expressive eyes, she occasionally snatches glimpses of a playful amusement at the absurdity of life that is all his mother's. It is as if Rose lives on in him just to haunt her.

Joseph

A figure approaches the tarn. A man-boy, barely seventeen, but already built like a young bullock. He approaches the edge, fringed by bulrushes and tall reeds. Wades forward, naked. Sends disturbed ripples across the sheen of silvery mirror. The ice-cold water slaps at his flesh, slides down his skin, pours off him. He wades further in. Deeper. The last warm rays glint off his dark hair tufted like a crown of antlers on a young stag. He surrenders to the depths and ducks all the way in. Plunges and disappears.

Joseph holds his breath, kicking down into the silky, silted depths until he feels his lungs begin to burn. Kicks fiercely and explodes up to the surface. The water erupts and splashes all around him. His exposed marbled buttocks curve out of the water; he holds dripping arms aloft to the sky, exposing the tufts of jet-black fuzz sprouting under his arms and over his chest and around his nipples, and a tell-tale bush of hair floats free of the water just above his barely concealed cock. He stands straight and tall, the statue of a young prince, a warrior god, and offers himself as a sacrifice to whichever goddess is watching over him. He closes his eyelids to sense the play of fire inside his skull. He luxuriates in every inch of his growing male power. His hand slides down to grasp his stiffening cock and he strokes at it lazily until the urgency is too much and he cascades a stream of spunk over his fist and across the shimmering water and lets loose a high, hoarse, youthful yell at the heavens. The echo from the granite scree slope bounces back at him off the rock wall and the note explodes all the way down the valley in a ricochet of sound. Finally, he douses his head and body in a last exultation of baptismal immersion.

Bogboy

On the shore, Bogboy watches, entranced. Electrified, his throat tightens, his mouth is dry. Sick to the pit of his stomach, Bogboy is consumed by desire.

Joseph

Joseph turns and spots Bogboy on the shore, not fifty yards away. His pleasure switches to rage in an instant. 'Feck off you little animal, you filthy little pervert. Piss off.' The boy vanishes into the bushes like a wraith with a snap of twigs and a trembling of leaves. Joseph scampers to the slippery bank, gathers up his rough work shirt and pants and hurriedly dresses, aware that suddenly it's turning cold. He feels an odd mixture of venom and complicity; a bile of shame rises in his gorge, yet it's mixed with a perverse pleasure at the intimacy of being witnessed. He feels invincible. Ten feet tall. Like Cuchulain holding off the armies of Maeve at a narrow mountain pass. He heads for home the same way the boy went, crashing through the undergrowth.

Molly

Molly's fat fingers tear at the shallots, skinning and slicing each purple-pink bulb and plopping them into a big, white china bowl. It's an affront. She could cook a perfectly good onion pie if asked, but no, Madame insists on these fiddly, garlicky things she orders from a special greengrocer in Westport, and then demands Molly prepare for a special *tarte tatin* which, at best, she'll nibble at with her birdlike appetite. Madame and her old French recipes. Still clinging to her past. 'Her non-existent past,' Molly sniffs. Tears prickle behind her eyes. Enough crying in this house to last a hundred lifetimes, she thinks, sourly.

Joseph will have finished for the day. He'll be swaggering back home soon enough. He's taken to washing off the muck of the day with a dip in the lake at dusk since he's started filling out and grown too self-conscious to wash in the cast-iron tub in front of the range. She misses the times she used to scrub his sweat-soaked back for him, while the turf and coal blazed away, and they'd enjoy a good catch up on any local gossip. Gone are the days he'd drop to the kitchen floor to do a rapid set of press-ups, eager to show off his prowess, straining every sinew of his coltish body. 'Look, Mammy, twenty, and I'm not out of breath at all,' he'd lie, straight-faced, panting like an old farm dog. She worried he'd cut his hands on one of the cracked terracotta tiles but he'd just grin. 'Ah, whisht, Mammy, I'm not a babby anymore.'

She still keeps the stove stoked just in case, even though the kitchen gets uncomfortably hot and Madame complains about the waste of good turf – turf her Joseph will have been out on the bog cutting for the house. The cheek. And Madame wasting good housekeeping money on shallots. If her ladyship can afford fancy vegetables, she can spare a bit of extra turf. And with that, Molly chops viciously at a few more of the offending onions.

But her son has grown wary and secretive. He's at that awkward age. She boils up his sheets and doesn't comment. He's all she has left. He'll be a giant of a man like Paddy, his da. And she feels the familiar, feathery catch in her throat. Her man, snatched away too soon, all because of that pointless accident, one stupid moment of negligence. The sharp blade nicks her finger and she winces. A tiny jewel of blood wells. Now she's giving blood for the blasted shallots, as if sweat and tears weren't enough.

Bogboy

Alone. Angry. Afraid. Bogboy goes to the wood to shelter in the mantle of resinous gold-green. He lies beneath the storm-blasted tree where Hawk has made her nest. His mind is whirling, full of visions of captive bodies, pinioned, entwined like serpents, sliding in and out of each other, in pain or ecstasy, he can't tell. The figures remind him of a painting he saw once in one of Tante's art books. But they were meant to be saints. He doesn't feel much like a saint. He drifts in and out of sleep. He senses movement in the leaves and the violent flurry of powerful wings above him. He is wide awake in an instant. Hawk is glaring down at him with a baleful, pale-yellow eye. There's a hint of fire in her stare.

'Who am I?' asks Bogboy.

'Chwirp,' says Hawk.

'What am I?' asks Bogboy.

'Chwirp,' says Hawk.

'Why am I here?' asks Bogboy.

'Chwirp,' says Hawk.

'That's not an answer,' mutters Bogboy. 'Who loves me? Nobody, that's who. I'm just shit, shit, shit. Where do I even come from?'

'Chwirp,' says Hawk. And vanishes.

It's cold. A damp chill from the soil is seeping into his skin. He's smeared in mud and there is a moist patch at his crotch. He aches in every limb as he trudges homewards to the gloomy house of hate and silences, cold soup and colder stares; the house of shadows and dead things.

He had once yelled at Tante, 'You're not my mother, you're just fat, old Aunt Joycie.'

'I forbid you to ever use that name again,' she'd hissed back at him. 'You will henceforth refer to me as Tante.'

Thereafter, neither ever referred to the other by name if they could possibly avoid it. He was Bogboy or sometimes just 'the boy'. 'Give the boy his supper,' Tante would order Molly. 'Tell the boy to wash himself, he looks like a dirty tinker's son,' or, 'It's market day. Take the boy with you.'

Fat droplets of rain splash off the leaves onto Bogboy's head. He doesn't care.

Tante

Her arrival back in the parish all those years ago had been a triumph. The happiest day of her life, happier even than her wedding day. The shock on the faces of the villagers had been delicious. The images flicker in her memory as if an old newsreel is stuck on an endless loop in her head.

Like royalty descending to grace the common people with their presence, Alphonse, Duc du Comte Rochefoucauld, had appeared in their midst, at the wheel of his gleaming chrome and burgundy Hispano-Suiza, driven all the way from Paris. And she alongside him, haughty and proud, still dressed for the sun, lightly sheathed in a primrose-yellow, silken summer dress and a hat of palest gold straw that spoke of joy and young love, despite the dankness of the day.

The entire village had come out to gawp, amazement and disapproval in their eyes, particularly those of the envious crow-black widows. How could she have known that all too soon she'd be joining their ranks – and worse? On that glorious day, she was just an adored and adoring young bride by the side of her handsome, moustached husband with his gleaming Marcel wave, the very picture of a Hollywood Latin lover, as they made their slow progress along the narrow high street, home from their lengthy honeymoon. Delhi, Bangkok, Shanghai, Tokyo, Kyoto,

Kuala Lumpur: passport stamps accrued; a litany of exotic postcards, with breathless descriptions, sent to Rose, home from Italy and ready to be impressed; a trunkful of gifts and souvenirs to show for their efforts.

Travel had been wonderful, but also wearying, and now married life and new responsibilities were beckoning. For her, it was the estate, already tumbling into rack and ruin, while he was to turn around the fortunes of the family vineyards. All that remained after settling in would be to pay a call on Father Diamond, the parish priest, to arrange the church's blessing on their civil French marriage. They had known it wouldn't do to offend the Church, particularly out here. But Alphonse was a charmer; she'd had no doubt that between them they'd smooth away any moral qualms the old dinosaur might be harbouring.

Tante reaches across for a small phial containing her sleeping draught, the powerful night potion that is her only recourse when the bad dreams and black memories take over. She swallows it in one gulp and lays her head back against the hard bolster that she needs to support her aching neck. Strong as it is, the drug takes time to work. Not soon enough to overcome the tidal wave of anger and grief threatening to engulf her.

Fifteen years ago, to the day, the vintage Hispano-Suiza H6 Cabriolet had purred into the driveway of Coolhooley, drawing up to the front terrace steps where Rose was already waiting at the half-open doorway to meet and greet the happy couple. She had been relaxed and insouciant, smoking a cigarette, a habit she'd picked up shockingly young, and smiling that inscrutable smile of hers as though she was the only one there who'd been let in on some secret of vital importance. Back then, her beauty bore an ethereal, ivory glow highlighting the intensity of her amused, dark eyes. Alphonse, ever gallant, had barely suppressed a gasp of wonder; in that moment, the planets re-aligned, the heavens shifted, and a whole new cosmos came into being: an entire parallel universe. Next to her sister, pale as the palest pink rose at dawn, Jocelyn's flame had reduced to a tiny flicker. All her own prettiness had dulled into insignificance as Rose, still smiling, had come forward with a lazily outstretched hand to greet her brother-in-law.

Bogboy

Bogboy suddenly feels ravenous. He makes his way up the bank of furze and fern and gazes at the huge house silhouetted in the distance.

The blow to the back of his head is swift and sure: a chop to the base of his skull that sends him flying.

'That'll teach you to spy on me, ya little fuck.'

Sprawled on the ground, he feels utter dislocation, seeing stars, but tries to lever himself up to face his assailant. Before he can raise his head, it's smashed back down into the earth and the metallic taste of blood fills his mouth. He struggles again to rise. Big mistake. He feels the sudden shock as he receives Joseph's full body weight – brutish, animal – land on him from above.

'Oh no, you don't. You're going nowhere 'til I'm done with ya,' the harsh voice rasps in his ear. The breath is hot and moist, full of menace, yet intimate at the same time. It's as if an electric current passes between them. Joseph's body is burning hot. Trapped beneath the older boy, Bogboy wants to cry out but already knows better than to plead or resist. Instead, he lets his body go limp. Joseph shifts his weight so he's kneeling across Bogboy's narrow thighs. The momentary relief Bogboy feels is followed by a sickening dread, as he hears his tormenter pull off his thick leather belt and knows what's coming next.

'Liked what you saw, pervert? So, what about this?' Joseph holds Bogboy's head down with one huge paw and, with the other arm, doubles the belt over and swings it, buckle-side outward, with all his might, across Bogboy's spine, protected by nothing but his thin jersey. Bogboy can't help but emit a muffled scream. Blows land one after another until Bogboy feels his entire body is nothing but pain. He's aware of himself floating up out and away from his body, as though he were Hawk looking down on the scene from above. The furze and heather tipped golden, the whole landscape alive with soft light, and – far, far below – two small human figures bathed in the day's last glorious radiance. Bogboy is now flying high above himself, staring back down at his poor, cowed, brutalised body. And from this vantage point he is suffused with a moment of tender, rapturous compassion for his enemy.

Joseph

Joseph catches his breath. A power greater than his own possesses him. Astride the boy, he acknowledges his dominance. He feels as though the entire universe has chosen him to fill with its endless force and power. He looks down at Bogboy's limp body, and for a second thinks him dead, but then feels his ragged breathing and realises the younger boy is sobbing. He's aware of a new, even darker impulse, a wholly different craving – to control this wild, arrogant creature at his mercy. His hands itch to choke all life out of the little runt, yet his fingers are stroking the soft, vulnerable skin at the nape of the boy's neck.

Suddenly overcome with fury, he rips down Bogboy's leggings, exposing the narrow, curved buttocks. Then he tears at his own pants, freeing up his angry, semi-tumescent cock and slams himself against Bogboy's arse, in a series of short, sharp thrusts, as though trying to stab the very innards of his victim. It's an act of desperation: manic and uncontrollable, a relentless, rhythmic, dry-humping back and forth. Eventually, he spends a trickle of sperm in the small hollow of Bogboy's back and hurriedly wipes the moist tip of his penis in a silvery snail trail from top to base of Bogboy's moon-shaped bum.

He gets up in a daze, gathers himself together, picks up his belt and re-inserts it, all the time looking down at Bogboy who doesn't move and is no longer making any sound. Joseph's elation evaporates. A sense of futility steals over him; the carefully prepared ambush, waiting patiently for the little bastard for what seemed like hours, has turned to ashes in his mouth. He leans over Bogboy's prone body and hisses, 'Say nothing.'

It's getting late. Mam will have prepared his supper and will be worried if he's not back before dark. She'll have got a good fire going and there'll be a plate piled with spuds and buttermilk waiting for him. Without another glance, he heads homewards.

Bogboy

He lies still for the longest time. Listening. To the wind in the grasses and tussocks. To distant birds returning to roost and owls just beginning their nocturnal forays for food. It's a crisp, crystal-clear night.

Finally, he grits his teeth and manoeuvres himself inch by inch up onto his right elbow. If he died out here, who would even mourn him? A tear wells and he angrily brushes it aside. No pity. No pity. He's the Bogboy King, son of chieftains and warriors. A calm descends despite the fresh welts on his back.

Diamond-bright stars are coming out, and, above the dark outline of the mountain, a sliver of new moon. He stares into the firmament and sees Hawk, circling, watching, and knows that he and Hawk are now irrevocably connected. He feels at one with himself and the source of all things. As though what happened had to happen, had to unfold exactly as it did. Now, he no longer sees with paltry, human eyes but with the eyes of the ancestors and of the gods, deep into the mystery of things.

He struggles to rise, coaxes his poor body forward on hands and knees, and looks straight into the expressionless eyes of a rough-haired billy goat.

Bogboy stares at the goat and the goat stares right back. It is like staring at the devil. The small bell round the goat's neck jangles. Suddenly, he feels safe and secure. Nothing else bad can happen to him out here now, amongst the goats. Cautiously, he crawls towards the herd. The goats simply move aside to let him through, then close around him.

Molly

She glances out of the window. She's grateful for the heat inside the kitchen, takes a couple of turf logs from the basket beside the stove and throws them at the low flame. 'Damn the expense', she mutters, then hurriedly crosses herself and clutches at the small, gold crucifix around her neck. She'll ask for forgiveness for her cuss word and the waste of good turf at midweek confession. Her old friend, Bridget, God rest her soul, used to laugh at her and say, 'Don't be getting yer knickers in such a twist. Sure, it's better to have a few good sins to tell the Father. What other excitements does the poor old cratur have in life?'

Joseph should be back any moment. He's been working in the upper pasture, clearing the ragwort that gets worse every year. Backbreaking toil. He'll be wanting his feed as soon as he gets in. It's nearly eight already and this is late, even for him. She feels a rising anxiety in her throat as though a small fluttering bird has lodged there.

She'll pile his bowl with the heavily salted, mashed spuds soaked in buttermilk he loves so much, plus a slice of the thick bacon she's saved for him. He won't touch the *tarte*, she knows that much. 'All that foreign muck yer one likes,' he'll say, with new-found contempt. He's growing up. Just recently he's been so moody and taciturn, she barely dares to open her mouth for fear he'll snap at her. Like a young bullock kicking out at being stalled. He needs a fine girl, she thinks. And where around here will he find himself such a one? Nobody stays in these parts if they have a bit of a spark about them.

In his room the other day, she found a brochure he'd sent away for from the agricultural college in Maynooth. But she hasn't brought it up. Hasn't found the right moment to broach the subject. She's torn between wanting the best for her son and losing him to the big, wide world out there. And if he went, what on earth would become of them here? No-one left but herself, Madame and the little divil.

She glances once again outside at the gathering darkness. The little divil is still somewhere out there too. But, unlike Joe, he could be anywhere, miles away. He might stay out all evening before he slides back into the house at midnight, filthy and bedraggled as a tatterdemalion. She's had dogs that were better trained. He's out and about at all hours in a world of his own, a wee slip of a thing, all skin and bone beside her man-mountain of a son. Watchful, skittish as a wildcat, barely able to string one word after another. As if he isn't quite all there. A fairy child, hardly even human, like a changeling out of the old tales, and with those eerie, dark, fathomless eyes that sometimes make her shudder when she catches him staring at her. She knows he likes to creep around the house after dark, won't let her anywhere near his pigsty of a room. And yet... and yet. She's always had a soft spot in her heart for the poor wee mite. She's known him since he was a babby. A blue baby. No-one believed he'd survive a week. His mother barely survived the night. An orphan from the moment he was born. The pain and suffering it cost to bring him into the world.

He rarely comes and eats with her in the kitchen anymore. But she often opens the pantry door in the morning to find he's helped himself to a plate of leftovers, some cabbage and spuds, a bowl of cold chicken soup, or nibbled at some of Madame's pies. She now deliberately leaves a plate of bits and pieces she knows he might like. It's an arrangement that satisfies his scavenger nature and, to be properly honest, suits them both. Her train of anxious thoughts is suddenly interrupted by the tread of heavy boots on gravel and her heart leaps with relief. Joseph pushes at the kitchen door and enters. Raw animal health and vitality. She goes to hug him but remembers in time how much he hates it.

He nods curtly, mutters, 'Ma,' and throws his old tweed cap on the kitchen table. She's asked him in the past not to do it – 'It's a filthy old habit, son' – but the cap was his father's, and he wears it in all weathers and she hasn't the heart to keep scolding him. She's heard him get mad, almost panicky, on days when he's in a rush to head out to the bog to turn peats or help with haymaking in the lower pastures and he can't find it. 'Ma, have you seen my cap? Have you?' And she'd calmly point to the kitchen dresser. 'There where you left it, ya eejit.' He even wore it to the village school in the early days after his da had died, although it was way too big on him then and he got jeered at for looking like a peasant's son until he dealt with the offender, an older boy who fancied himself the cock of the schoolyard, by smashing in a couple of the lad's front teeth, and was roundly thrashed for his pains. But no-one ever dared taunt him again.

'Your food is on the table.' She's gruffer than she intended. She softens and points to the bowl. 'There's a bit of that bacon you like, too.'

'I see it.' He sits himself down and she perches opposite, watching him. He wolfs down the food, then looks up suddenly. 'What are you staring at?'

It's like a slap to the face. 'Joe, don't speak to your mother like that.'

'Well, then, don't be staring at me with them eyes goggling out of your head.'

There's something amiss, she knows it in her bones. 'Is everything all right, son?'

'Sure, and why wouldn't it be? That field is a bastard of a job is all.'

Silence stretches awkwardly between them.

'That's me, I'm done. I'm off to my bed. It's been a bitch of a day.'

Before she can utter another word or remonstrate at his foul language, a whole new provocation, he's scraped his chair back and then, to her surprise, he offers her a peck on her cheek before thump-thumping upstairs.

She misses her young boy. Her lively mischief-maker. She

doesn't recognise the surly giant he's becoming. But men will be men. At least she has him here still, in the light and warmth of her kitchen hearth. What will happen to them all? she wonders. How much longer can they carry on like this? And what if Madame were to take a turn for the worse? She takes the plate and scrapes the remains into the swill bucket, and rinses it in the big, old, chipped Belfast sink. Everything is falling apart but she won't allow herself to think unpleasant thoughts. She picks up one of the left-over shallots at random, slices it open and grimaces at the black mould. Rotten to the core. She's not a superstitious woman, but she hopes it's not an omen.

Tante

Restless in her canopied, four-poster bridal bed, Tante lies tense and exhausted. She hasn't heard the boy return. Usually, a creak on the stairs announces he's creeping his way to the top of the tower, a tiny space he's turned into his own den. He insists on sleeping on the floor, surrounded by rocks, pebbles, feathers, dried leaves and various skulls and bones amassed from his never-ending expeditions to the wild places into which he disappears for hours – sometimes whole days on end. He furiously refuses all furniture, throwing out any chairs, drawers or mattresses she's tried to introduce into the room, leaving the place looking and smelling more like the temporary nest of some predatory bird than an actual human habitation. She long ago gave up trying to tame him, finally surrendering and accepting that she wasn't bringing up her nephew, but keeping a wild animal as a not-so-amusing pet.

Unlike the boy, who seems to revel in maximum discomfort,

she feels the cold acutely. The bed is swaddled in blankets and on top of them lies a magnificent counterpane of heavy, blue silk with an open-jawed, embroidered, gold dragon which sinuously ripples as her restless body tosses and turns awkwardly. The magic night-potion hasn't done its work. When she can't get to sleep under any circumstances, she often pulls out her Tarot deck, unfolds the cards wrapped in yet more silk in a box of inlaid ivory, and shuffles and cuts, shuffles and cuts, trying to empty her mind of all anxieties, most of them to do with how to make ends meet and what on earth is left to sell off. She makes three piles and chooses a card from each to study. Past. Present. Future. She lays the chosen cards before her. She turns over the images one by one.

The past: Queen of Cups reversed. She was never to be the nurturer: all the tests with specialists, expensive quacks, mountebanks and self-appointed healers: all useless, a litany of disappointments. Barren. The word so hard, implacable, cruel.

Once she had been quick to laugh, flirtatious, high-spirited. But, in the end, her cup was empty. And with her dried-up womb came the shrivelled feelings, the griefs and longings and – yes – rage that couldn't be expressed. She was disposable. Her love was never enough. He had a family name and titles that stretched back to the 13th century. He'd proudly shown her the chateau built upon the foundations of the original fort that had stood there. Had actually said, 'One day all this will be our son's.' The family motto, 'Evolution et Continuité', meant everything to him. But she had failed him. The family required a brood mare. And she wasn't it. Fortunately for him, her lovely sister was all too ready to step into the breach. What proud, red-blooded male from a long line of bad faith, bad blood, treachery and betrayal, scion of pillage, plunder and privilege – what man – could have resisted the fecund charms of the delectable Rose? Well, not Alphonse Henri Gaston Laurence Christian Meriveaux, 17th Comte du Rochefoucauld, for starters. In like Flynn he leapt, into her open arms and legs. And the result of this heart-stopping betrayal was now out roaming the bog-lands beyond the crumbling, walled estate, like a mad dog it would be a mercy to shoot in the head.

She turns over the second card. Present. And laughs! The Fool. Of course. What else could it possibly be? The journey of life had begun with such high hopes and gay abandon, only to face betrayal and heartbreak: the chatelaine locked away from the world, a virtual recluse, subject to every juicy scandal and rumour imaginable, never again able to show her face in respectable society. Weren't they all fools? Herself, Alphonse, Rose. A holy trinity of fools. It had ended with Alphonse storming out in a fury, clambering into the Hispano and roaring off at high speed on the day of their marriage blessing, the day Rose chose to announce, coolly, that she was carrying her adulterous brother-in-law's child and was also dying. The child was Irish and should be brought up in his homeland where he belonged, whatever it took, whatever his father's thoughts on the matter. They'd had their fun, she'd made a mistake but they were all adults and '*C'est la vie, n'est-ce pas?*'

Irish country roads being what they were, particularly in the west and particularly after rain, and simply not built for high-speed roadsters, the beautiful piece of precision engineering had shot over the parapet of a narrow bridge on a tight bend and landed its aristocratic owner head first in a gulley, breaking his neck (and her heart). She can still picture, in her imagination, the near front wheel spinning like the wheel of fortune, thus bringing the direct noble line of les Comtes du Rochefoucauld to an ignominious end. Well, unless you count the boy. And he will never know who his real father was. She will make sure of that. That is one secret she is most definitely taking with her to the vault in the family chapel.

And lastly: the future. She stares at the card, then grimaces with satisfaction. The burning tower, the falling figures. Sure. Let it all come tumbling down. She sweeps the deck away from her and the thick cards scatter to the floor as if acting out the image of the Tower card. Yes. Perhaps it's time. She's held on to the estate too long. Has kept going herself for no discernible benefit to anyone. What is to be is to be. She notices one card hasn't fallen – the Queen of Cups again – and an old Spanish proverb pops into her head: *'Amor loco – yo por ti y tu por otro.'* Who loves her? 'No-one,' says the voice in her head. What good does it do anyway? Who will miss her when she's gone? She's startled when the image of the boy – urchin, waif and ragamuffin – appears to her. She feels a tight clutching at her chest, breathes heavily and moans, lifts the bell on the nightstand and rings for Molly.

Hawk

Hawk stirs in the high canopy, all her senses alert to the sounds and sights and colours of the morning that surround her. She ruffles and preens her feathers, tilts her head this way and that. It's time to rise up from her perch. Yesterday's tiny field-mouse hasn't satisfied her. Her appetite is sharp. Soon she will glide and swoop across her terrain to hunt. She feels her connection to Bogboy. She calls to him with her shrill, piercing cry that sounds out like an alarm, and feels his body stir within her own, stiff, aching and cold. She sends him her message. 'Be bold of heart, child of the universe, and embrace your destiny.'

Bogboy

Bogboy wakes to a steel-grey, pre-dawn light. The earth is cold and hard beneath him. The goats have moved further up the stony hillside, but Bogboy doesn't feel alone. In the distance he hears Hawk's cry, and his spirit lifts. It's as if he is barely flesh at all any longer. He has no further need of aunt or father or mother. He will never return to his cage. Better to die or starve among the rocks, the goats and the stars.

The wound to his head hurts, but with immense effort of will he stands himself upright. He licks his parched lips, then spots a small waterfall, a narrow trickle of a mountain stream dribbling over an overhang of vivid moss on the rock face. In the distance he can see the outline of Father Goat and family, while the chime of their bells is getting louder and louder as though he was the mountain and they were all grazing inside his head, somehow. He feels the pulsing of the light, the pumping in his veins like a deep, whooshing noise. His brain is reeling. He blacks out again.

Molly

The village postman almost never comes to the house. Once a week, Molly takes the pony and trap the five miles down to the village to pick up the mail. There's never anything but bills to pay, requests and, more often than not, final demands. So, it must be important for Declan to have made the detour on his old bike.

She won't indulge him in conversation. He hands over the aerogramme like a tissue-thin, pale-blue hand grenade. Molly turns it over. New York. A name from the distant past. A florid, manly hand in black ink. But it's not a telegram, so not a death, at least. Illness? She itches to know, but daren't risk steaming open the fragile paper. Instead, she places the almost weightless letter onto a small, silver salver kept for the purpose and adds the mother-of-pearl letter opener.

Will Madame share the contents? Hard to say. Her moods are so unpredictable these days, and letters, real letters of any kind, are as rare as unicorns. Molly carries the unexpected post up the staircase towards the room that has known nothing but sadness, grief and loss, and wonders if Madame will be awake. She'd had another bad night of insomnia. Molly had mixed up a strong concoction of valerian root, chamomile and passion flower in warm goat's milk for her, so there's a chance she'll still be asleep, although it's past nine. Joseph was away this morning with barely a word to say for himself and there's still no sign of the boy. Apart from the tick of the grandfather clock and her footsteps on the creaking stairs, the house is as quiet as the grave.

The bedroom emits its familiar aroma of stale camphor, lavender oil and eucalyptus as she pushes open the door, which creaks despite her best efforts. Madame is wide awake and sitting in her old, winged armchair with a leather-bound volume open on her lap. She's pinned up her waist-length, greying hair in a lopsided bun.

Molly passes across the wafer-thin envelope.

'What's this?' It's purely rhetorical, since Madame is already reaching for the letter.

Madame raises herself further up the chair with a groan that feels like a reprimand and Molly steps forward to rearrange the pile of cushions at her back but is waved impatiently away. Instead, Madame holds out her hand for the paper knife and for one instant Molly thinks how satisfying it would be to stab her mistress in the eye with it. She watches meekly as Madame slips the knife into a small gap in the corner of the fragile paper.

Madame indicates her bedside table. Molly instantly leans across, retrieves a delicate pair of tortoiseshell spectacles and hands them to her. Madame doesn't bother with any courtesy or acknowledgement. She betrays no emotion as she scans the letter, throws it aside, picks it up and re-reads.

'Michael.' She turns to Molly. 'Coming here.'

It's as if an icy draught suddenly blew around the room. Molly feels a shiver all the way down her spine.

'May it bode well,' she says, without conviction, crossing herself at the same time. Madame purses her lips, and says nothing. The letter falls to the carpet.

Michael. The gangster, the vagabond, the rogue, the black sheep of the family. The brother from America is coming home.

Jenks

At first, Jenks had stared in disbelief. What from a distance had looked like a puzzling bundle of old rags turns out to be a barely breathing body. He must have been lying there out in the open for the best part of a day. It is a miracle he is still alive. His body is ice-cold. The boy's skimpy jersey clings to him. Dark patches have soaked through the material. There is a nasty bruise, a real humdinger, the size of a pigeon's egg, at the back of his head.

Even more distressing, when Jenks turns the boy over, as gently as he can, there are deep scrapes and cuts across his forehead and cheeks, and his mouth is a bloody mess.

Have the goats attacked him? It's plausible. The boy is small, and a riled adult billy, using his curved horns, could inflict a lot of damage. In that case, his goats – and, by extension, he himself

– would most likely be held out as the culprit, thinks Jenks. This would be a very bad situation indeed. He is regarded as an oddity in the neighbourhood; the locals refer to him as 'the quare Englishman.' He can just imagine the accusing voices in their soft brogue, as they gossip together, breaking immediately into Gaelic the moment he comes into their vicinity, as frequently happens when he drops by the village-shop-cum-post-office for his modest weekly supplies or to post a brief letter home. He's been the subject of fearsome speculation from the first moment he set foot in the parish a couple of years ago. A loner, some kind of artist, and – worst of all – a Protestant, and an atheist to boot. This incident would confirm all their doubts about him. 'Letting his herd run wild,' people would say, accusingly, and that had not been his intention at all; they'd broken out of the home-made pen he'd fixed up for them, and then gone for a nice ramble up and over the mountain. 'Sure, what do you expect?'

In the few moments it takes for these thoughts to race through Jenks's head, the boy has started groaning. The goats can wait. He'll deal with them later. The boy needs shelter and treatment, and fast.

The big house is nearby, but he knows little or nothing about it apart from local rumours. The housekeeper, Molly, a plump, friendly sort, comes by in a cart to buy a bit of goat's cheese and milk every week, counting out every last coin diligently from a worn black purse, but apart from exchanging a few pleasantries he's never learned much about what goes on there. A loner and recluse, he has no interest in a dutiful social call. The chatelaine is rumoured to be a bit mad, and virtually housebound. Molly seems ordinary enough and has a strapping son whom Jenks has seen out working the peat bogs or tending to a few stone-fenced fields. But they've never had occasion to pass the time of day.

There is talk of another lad, too, supposedly some kind of a half-wit, but Jenks has never come across him.

He looks down at the boy, who's come round again. If Jenks doesn't act quickly, pneumonia is going to set in and the wounds could turn septic. He kneels down next to the boy, whose eyes have now taken on more expression, and whispers, 'My name's Jenks. I'm here to help you. Let's get you back home, eh?'

The boy stares at him and then, to Jenks's alarm, thrashes violently from side to side which causes him once more to scream out in agony, so that Jenks has to hold down his arms to stop him hurting himself further.

'No. No. No. No. Please.' The terror in his eyes is absolute.

'No? You sure?'

'Well, in that case, we'll get you back to my place. But you'll have to let me carry you. It might take us some time.'

The boy relaxes, and allows himself to be lifted into Jenks's arms, and holds his own loosely and trustingly round his rescuer's neck, like a child being carried up to bed by his father. Whether it is the comforting strength of Jenks's arms and body or the sheer physical and emotional effort of their last conversation, he is out again like a light almost at once. Jenks manoeuvres him into a more comfortable fireman's lift and has a sudden jarring flashback to another time and place, carrying a similarly frail body – Kenny, his brother-in-arms – along a lethal stretch of the Libyan desert, the scream of the German panzers ricocheting around them. He had watched in horror as Kenny had taken a hit to the chest, a small spurt of blood erupting from his ripped-apart tunic, and then pitched forward into a quagmire of blood-soaked sand. Carrying Kenny back the hundreds of yards to the British encampment had been an insane, suicidal act of bravado, and one he should never by rights have survived, but his angels were watching over him. Besides, he'd already nursed Kenny through months of the horror show that was Tobruk, and wasn't about to leave his friend out there to rot in hell, not after everything they'd shared. No matter that Kenny died two days later, Jenks received a Victoria Cross for his gallantry. He'd not been much more than a boy himself. And now, again, he is acting out of pure instinct.

He braces himself for the mountain, which is really nothing more than a boulder-strewn, rocky outcrop of glaciated granite and volcanic schist, not more than a thousand feet high. He is glad, for once, of the Irish habit for embellishment. Still, what the mountain lacks in scale, it more than makes up for in mass, and an air of gloomy menace in all weathers. When the Atlantic gales come tearing across the ocean on winter nights to buffet the shoreline, you can well believe it is the howl of the banshee calling some doomed soul to their final rest.

His cottage is nearly all the way down the other side, perched just above the strand and the great, rolling Atlantic breakers. There is a path of sorts to the top and he knows the way down like the back of his hand. This is already getting to be a matter of life or death. It is a calculated gamble. But the day is still bright, thank goodness. As for the goats, they'll heft close to the mountain; there is enough here to crop. He takes a deep breath and begins the slow ascent, while at the same time trying to keep at bay the insistent bombardment of cannon fire and the desperate cries of men inside his brain.

Molly

The house is in a complete uproar. The boy is missing. He's never run off for so long before. It's already been over two days since any of them saw him. And now the weather is on the turn. Last night, a storm front broke. The morning is eerily calm again. But more is coming. Where in God's name can he be? She constantly fingers her gold cross and sends up a prayer, 'Dear God, please keep the poor, wee mite safe.' There are bothies and fishermen's huts, of course, and the ruins of an abandoned cottage, so he'd surely have the wit to make shelter for himself, but is anyone else thinking what she's thinking? What if he's had a fall and smashed his head or got lost in the dark and stumbled into the waterlogged places? Madame has taken to her bed in a state of high dudgeon and seems to regard his vanishing as a personal affront. She's more tense and furious than ever. First the letter, now this. And things always come in threes, thinks Molly, scattering the last of the grain for the hens out by the back yard. And now the Gardai are on their way. She'd taken matters into her own hands, in spite of Madame's angry injunction, 'Leave him be, he's just playing the cod. He'll be back through that door any minute now with that look of his, cute as the divil.'

But Molly's agitation could not be stifled. 'No. I'm not leaving him out there lost and maybe hurt. I'm hitching up the trap and going to fetch Dessie.' Desmond Doyle is the only member of the Gardai within a twenty-mile radius.

As good as her word, Molly had headed down to the village post office to make the call. She's several times tried to persuade Madame to have a phone installed but the reply has always been delivered in the same implacable tone. 'And why would we want to do that? Just think of the expense. Besides, they only ever ring to bring bad news.'

All the way, Molly's mind had tormented her. Joseph had been acting so strangely, more furtive and uncommunicative than ever. When she'd asked him if he was sure he hadn't caught sight of the boy somewhere in these last couple of days, he had answered, 'No,' but then looked away much too quickly. Then, when she had sent him out with an old torch yesterday evening to have a look out for the boy and check around the grounds, his response had seemed even more callous than that of the mistress of the house.

'What's the point? Fat lot of difference it'll make.'

'Joseph!'

'No, Mam. It's a complete waste of time. If he doesn't want to be found, he won't be, and there's an end to it.'

It had been on the tip of her tongue to snap, 'Just do what you're told. You're not so old I can't give you a good hiding for your cheek,' but she'd just said, 'There was a time he was like a brother to you.'

Joseph gave her one of his long, hard looks and his eyes seemed genuinely cold.

'Aye, well, that was a long time ago, Ma.'

She sighed and softened her tone, passing him the torch. 'Do it anyway, Joe. He might have just worn himself out and fallen asleep nearby.'

She heard the lack of conviction in her voice. Searching was a mere formality. He was back within the half hour, with a cursory, 'No sign of him.'

Molly's heart had sunk into a bone-deep melancholy she can't express, let alone shift. Not for the first time, it crosses her mind that maybe she doesn't very much like this taciturn man her son is turning out to be. She wonders now if the two lads have had some sort of a fight and the younger has run off in a sulk. Perhaps Dessie will be able to shed some light on it all.

Tante

Oh, Desmond Doyle, what a great, galumphing clown of a man you are, Tante thinks, staring at his bulbous, red-veined nose. He's standing, half to attention, clearly ill-at-ease, on the shabby Persian rug in her icy drawing room, having refused her invitation to sit. She can't bear the room and its memories of happier times. One wall displays, against the faded, hand-stencilled wallpaper, the bright, empty spaces where the family's collection of the finest, eighteenth-century, Irish watercolours – long-since sold at auction in Dublin – once hung.

So, now, here's Desmond Doyle ('call me Dessie', which she has absolutely no intention of doing) with one of his great fists twiddling his peaked cap while the other is awkwardly clutching a fragile, porcelain cup from her best tea service. He stuffs the cap underarm and looks at the Lapsang Souchong she has just poured for him from the tarnished silver teapot by her elbow.

Tante herself, taking a delicate sip of the smoky tea, is seated on a stiff-backed uncomfortable-looking horsehair settee opposite him. She has dismissed Molly's suggestion that they retire to the warmth of the kitchen, insisting that it's an official visit by a member of the constabulary so the drawing room it has to be. But she has to admit, if only to herself, that the spectacular view – through the tall windows onto the front terrace and down to the trees by the lake and the rocky crags beyond – hardly compensates for the freezing atmosphere.

Dessie opens proceedings with a mumble about having, 'Just a few questions, like, to get a bit of a picture of what we have here.' Do they know the youngster's favourite haunts? Does he have places he likes to hide? Maybe a den of some sort?

She realises she can't answer. She's faced with how strange

and bizarre the boy's life actually is. He's lived a semi-feral existence for so long now, a law unto himself, that neither she nor Molly have any idea where he might choose to go. He's a boy who can disappear at a moment's notice. He could be halfway up a mountain, down by the lake, across in the bog lands, burrowed under the earth even. Anything is possible. Now her neglect is out in the open for all to see, as if an electric light has been switched on in a room only normally seen by the glow of candlelight, exposing piles of dust in the corners and cobwebs on the ceiling. The balance of power in the room has subtly shifted. It's as though Dessie's awkwardness has transferred to the household.

'He likes a bit of a swim in the lake there,' is Joseph's sudden contribution. Tante has been unaware of him. Now here he is, skulking by the door, half-in half-out of the room, with a wary expression on his face. Dessie turns to look out over the water, glittering in the mid-morning sun and says, 'Well, we'll go down and check it out for sure.' The implication of his remark is clear. For all his shambolic demeanour, there's a shrewd glint in Dessie's eyes; he suddenly appears a lot wilier than his provincial, oafish exterior might have at first suggested. He pulls out a scuffed black notebook and a squat nub of a pencil, and proceeds to make some notes with painstaking care. Looking up again, it's evident he's hitting his stride. Has Alfie, Alfred, done anything like this before? The boy's Christian name exposed in this clinical fashion makes Tante flinch as though she's been struck. Might he have gone to stay with friends, perhaps?

'No,' Tante replies, somewhat tartly. '*Alphonse* doesn't make friends easily.'

'I see.' Dessie jots down another note. 'And you... took him out of school?'

It is almost an accusation.

'Yes.'

'Was there a particular reason?'

'It didn't... it wasn't... suitable for him.' Tante, tetchy at this unnecessary line of questioning, is certainly not about to admit that her sensitive nephew is entirely unsuited to a rough-and-ready Irish village school; indeed, probably to any educational institution. 'We prefer to have him educated at home.'

'He has a tutor?'

'I have undertaken to educate him myself.'

'Could he have run off, d'you think?' Dessie meets her glare and ploughs on regardless. 'You know, at this age, the young ones do be getting some quare notions. Stuck out here, he maybe got it into his head to see a bit of the wide world and not think too much about the consequences.'

The idea is so outlandish, she finds herself laughing.

'I really don't think so, Constable Doyle.'

'Well, the chances are he'll turn up of his own accord.'

'Exactly what we thought,' she says, stealing a sidelong glance at Molly, who adds, 'But as a precaution, we thought it best to let you know, what with the fierce gale that was blowing up last night and more bad weather to come.'

'Very wise, very wise and all the more reason to crack on. You've searched the whole house and grounds, of course, though 'tis a mighty big place you have here,' says Dessie. Tante can't be sure if there isn't a sly dig in his remark. She pauses to regain her composure – it wouldn't do to fly off the handle with the man – and replies, frostily, 'The house has been thoroughly searched from top to bottom.'

'Every nook and cranny,' Molly adds.

'Well, I might have a look in at his room, if you don't mind.

See if we can pick up any clue that might help, if one of you wouldn't mind showing me the way?'

He's a better strategist than she gave him credit for. She and Molly exchange another hurried glance but before she can think of a good enough reason to stall him, Dessie has moved out of the room with surprising alacrity for a man of his mass and is heading towards the staircase with the words, 'This way, I presume?'

Before anyone can hold him off, he's clumping up the stairs. They scurry after his receding figure.

'Just keep going to the very top of the house,' Molly, ever accommodating, calls up to him, as he takes a glimpse into Tante's room with shocking informality.

They make their way up the tower: Dessie, visibly out-of-breath, followed by Molly, then herself. There's a moment's pause, then she hears, 'Jesus, Mary and Joseph, what in hell's name is all this? You're telling me this is where he sleeps? He has no bed?'

Molly's reply – 'He likes to sleep on the floor' – doesn't seem a particularly satisfactory response. 'And you just let him?' There is a much sharper edge to Dessie's voice now.

She joins the two of them to peer into the boy's private world. It's as though they are gazing at his very essence. The world outside has been brought in, piece by piece, and built into a shrine or sanctuary. There's something both immensely beautiful and terribly sad about it: a personal treasure trove, an accumulation of utterly banal objects. The room reeks of death. The objects take up the entire floor space – bones and stones, feathers and strands of fleece, beetles and other dead insects, shells and lobster claws, dried flowers and twigs, broken glass and bits of rusted metal: amassed and carefully arranged in intricate delicate spirals in a mandala around an old mattress, as though to protect the dreamer within, and in such a way that enhances both their individual essence, colour, shape and texture, as well as their inter-connectedness, so that the whole has a strange beauty beyond the sum of its parts. She has to remind herself that this is her sixteen-year-old nephew's work. It touches something within her that she can't quite name. How had she been so blind?

She gets a distinct sense of Rose, still laughing at her, saying, 'You fool. See all the damage you've done? And only you can fix it again.'

For the first time in her life, Tante understands what it is to stare straight into the soul of an artist.

'So, would you say he was a happy lad?' Dessie asks.

She pauses for what seems an age before answering. 'I wouldn't say so... no.'

Molly blinks at her sudden candour.

'Has he seemed particularly unhappy recently?'

'No more than usual.'

Once again, out comes the little black notebook, and Dessie adds a few more scribbles.

'I think that wraps it up for now,' he says, snapping the notepad shut with an air of a man who knows a job well done when he sees it. 'We'll round up a few of the fellas from the village and thereabouts and get a bit of a search party out. Oh, and we'll take along a couple of keen dogs, so would you have an item of clothing we might bring with us, by any chance?'

Once again, it's the ever-cooperative Molly who comes to the rescue. 'I managed to get an old shirt off his back the other day that's still waiting for the wash. Will that do?'

'It will indeed. Grand. Grand. Best be getting on my way. I wouldn't be worrying too much at this stage. As I say, chances are he'll turn up; sure, I had a heifer once ran off for days –'

'Thank you, Constable Doyle, your assistance is most appreciated,' she cuts in before Dessie can regale them all with the tale of his lost cow.

Hawk

Hawk soars from her solitary nest to ride the air bristling with currents only she can feel. She spirals, then hovers, her senses honed by a magnetism that calls from the earth's core. She is pure vibration, every particle alert. She feels the boy's soul calling to her, his physical body weak, barely pulsing. She resists a moment, stubbornly determined to rise to the heavens, where there is music in the high spheres, harmonising with her own call, and from where she can fly out beyond time and space, into the void of voids, the nothingness from which all is born and is returned to be reborn. A change is coming from the west. In the uneasy silence before the storm breaks, Hawk cries out.

But the lure of the human is too strong and the breeze buffets her body as she bullets earthwards.

Jenks

'Clifford's mad escapade.' In three words, his father had summed up his son's idea of living a simple, self-sufficient life in the far west of Ireland with the same dismissive tone he had used for eviscerating defence counsel's closing arguments. He refused point blank to offer any financial support. Even though the dilapidated cottage had cost Jenks next to nothing, there were renovation expenses. And his invalid war pension was no more than a pittance. It had barely sustained him in Cork, where he had spent the best part of two decades trying to eke out a living with his paintbrush. His mother had been sympathetic, sending him occasional, modest sums from her own personal allowance, no doubt sacrificing a visit or two to Covent Garden or the Royal Ballet. He'd been her favoured son. Robert, the first-born, had proved much more amenable to his father's wishes. Robert had gone into the City. But one good and dutiful son was not sufficient for his father, a man who had no time for an artistic vocation.

'Even the bloody Church we might have understood, Clifford,' was his reaction to Jenks's pursuit of truth and beauty and a place at the Slade at the expense of mammon. Clifford. He always detested the name, which honoured his father's younger brother, some colonial adventurer who'd disappeared in darkest Africa on his own mad escapade, up the Limpopo River. Jenks had preferred Christopher, his second name, which had been his mother's choice. His father may have won the tussle over naming his child, as he invariably won most arguments, but at school Jenks simply took his initials, C.C., and reversed the name order. It was the first of many battles for supremacy between father and son. At Cambridge, when he won his rowing blue, his crewmates acclaimed him as Jenks, and Jenks he remained thereafter, although his best friend and roommate at Trinity, Jack Protheroe, had handed him an ironic St Christopher medal as a parting gift before he set off for Ireland.

Jenks had, on a brief visit home before he left Cork for Connemara, confided to Protheroe that, now that he had to accept that he was not a Royal Academician in the making, he was going to make art for its own sake, and planned on growing his own vegetables, raising goats and selling their milk and cheese for a living. He'd avidly devoured the radical writings of

Edward Carpenter and his back-to-the-earth philosophy of the simple life. Carpenter spoke of a new vision and a new breed of men, brothers sharing in everything; his sort were pioneers for a better, kinder world. Clean and healthy. Not the stifling, clubby atmosphere of nods and winks and secret handshakes that had been his father's world. Protheroe hadn't pretended he approved – he was much too decent a man to lie – but he'd at least recognised and understood the impulse that drove the decision, and his reaction was typically good-humoured. 'Well, old man, you'll need this then,' he said, pressing the medal and silver chain into his friend's palm. 'You'll be up at all bloody hours rescuing baby kids and baa-lambs from snowdrifts and carrying them across your shoulders through hailstorms, just you wait and see.'

And with it a generous loan – 'Just to get you started, eh?' – that they both knew was really a gift.

Jenks was no papist or high church Anglican but he chose to wear the medal as a talisman. He liked having something of Protheroe's close to his heart. Protheroe and he had been close at college and had remained so in later years, even though his friend had long since become a respectable, happily married man with three almost entirely grown-up children.

What would his father have made of all this? Well, the fearsome Jenkins senior of old was now long gone, his piercing, merciless intellect slowly reducing via senile dementia in a care home in Eastbourne.

Jenks thinks about this now as he struggles further up the scree. St Christopher indeed, with his sacred burden. As the crow flies, it can't be more than a mile to the cottage but it is a steep slope. And the same, maybe even more perilous, down the other side. He is grateful at least that his lungs are holding up well so far. He has never felt cleaner, healthier. In the pure air of Connemara, he breathes more easily than he has for years.

He settles into a comfortable rhythm. He is conscious of how light the boy is and he feels a surge of confidence that he is doing the right thing. He reminds himself to breathe, recalls times he'd been exhorted to equally great efforts in his days as a competitive rower – early mornings on the Cam, having been drinking 'til late the previous evening, then back to his rooms to complete an overdue essay, and snatch a few hours' sleep, then up before dawn and onto the river in all weathers, the crew hoisting the shell of the boat into the welcoming, limpid water beyond the college boathouse. Most of the crew were bleary and barely half-awake; they suffered a few cursory muscle stretches, then the bracing shock of early morning air, and an exhilarating, sudden surge of energy in their young limbs, the rhythm and team spirit kicking in, the bonhomie, the rude jokes. Someone nearly always let rip an explosive fart which always brought giggles. Then all limbs were straining at once, defying the body's resistance, as the cox screamed, 'Pull! Pull! Pull!'

They were hardly more than boys really, little knowing the grim man's world that awaited them just beyond the horizon.

Fewer than half his teammates had made it through the war, he recalls, as he opens his old coat and wraps it like a blanket as best he can around the boy. It makes the going more awkward. He is barely halfway up the mountain when a gusting breeze from the ocean starts to bring tiny droplets of rain, a soft skein of mist which saturates him. Where is the legendary luck of the Irish when you need it? Although this is probably it – when you think about their history.

He ploughs on doggedly, step by step, stone by stone, crunching over the chipped layer of rock beneath him, pushing onwards against the elements that seem to mock him. He won't surrender.

A renewed sense of urgency drives him on. The boy's skin is cold and clammy. He is feverish. Jenks had done his best to clean up the wounds with a strip of his shirt, back at the rock pool, but he is anxious to get the boy to warmth and safety quickly. He feels a rising panic that he tries his level best to hold down. He's been in much tighter fixes during the war. He'd survived against the odds as fires raged, buildings collapsed and whizz bangs exploded overhead; he'd pulled dead and dying out of the rubble, sometimes with flesh charred to a crisp.

But he is weakening. He is reduced to a painstaking trudge while the voice in his head yells, 'Too slow! Much too slow! The boy's dying on you!' The path is getting more treacherous by the second, as the soft rain thickens into a white curtain rolling ominously down towards them. The best he can manage is one foot in front of another, feeling his way along animal tracks, perilous if he were to lose his footing. At this rate, he'll need a miracle to make it.

The boy's narrow stream of hot breath against the side of his neck is the only reassurance he has that this madness is not yet all in vain. A sudden whoosh like a gust of wind across the top of his skull makes him cry out in shock. It happens a second time. And then he hears it. A harsh bird cry.

The boy stirs in his arms and whispers, 'Hawk.'

The bird calls again. A series of rapid cries, almost as if the bird was calling them. And again Jenks senses the bird strafe him. He can almost feel its talons scrape along the hair on his head.

'Hawk,' the boy whispers again. The thick, curling mist becomes finer, patchy wisps for a few moments and Jenks sees a small hawthorn, leaning inland against the prevailing westerly winds, and with shallow roots wrapped around a massive glaciated boulder. On the highest branch is a bird, perched like a guardian spirit.

'Hawk,' murmurs the boy, contentedly, for the third time, and falls back onto Jenks's shoulder.

The hawk has risen up and is soaring in spirals above them, but not flying off, definitely keeping a mark on them.

Jenks sees that he is just a few hundred yards from the summit, and that the onshore wind, that in winter blows so fiercely it sometimes traps him in his cottage for days on end, is dispersing the mist and clearing a route.

'Don't give up,' he murmurs to the boy or to himself. Then he hears the faintest whisper, 'Hawk', and he says, 'I know.'

All sense of panic, stress and anxiety has lifted. He feels at peace with everything. He takes longer, more confident strides, knowing exactly where to place each foot as he heads home.

Mickey

A woman walks into a bar. Holy moly, but she is a looker. He watches her from the moment she steps in. And he knows she is aware of him too. He likes that in a woman. Plus, she is shapely in all the right places. He likes that too. He's always had a thing for brunettes. He's had his fill of blondes. She is just his type. Class with a touch of sass. Foxy. He likes the way her short, tight-fitting skirt reveals shapely legs and stocking seams and dainty feet in expensive high heels. What is a gal like her doing so far down town? And in a bar like this of all places. She looks like she's been around and knows the score. Yeah, Mickey likes that too.

He's already lost all interest in the Tuesday night poker game.

He's been on a losing streak all night long. He had a couple of queens last hand but nothing to keep them warm. Up until now. And here she is. A vision. Destiny. If he's learned anything, it's that life is all a game. Sex, too. And he knows how to play that one. The trick is knowing when to play your hand. He is never wrong. Time to enjoy the ride. Who knows where it might end? The night is young and things are definitely looking up. There are rules here too. Just like poker. One wrong call and you fold. Get it right and the pot is yours for the taking.

Should he offer her a smoke, light up for her? The old Bogart/Bacall routine? No. Best wait. Jeez, she knows how to knock 'em back. Give it a moment or two more. See which way the wind is blowing. He'd learned that at sea. Take your time and get your bearings first, or you'd be overboard and in the swell before you knew it. To win at this you have to enjoy the thrill of anticipation. Too many men go charging in. Women hate that. They want to be reeled in slowly. Foreplay. There is an art to it.

They'd been sitting around in Paddy Mac's one night after listening to the game – the Boston Red Sox flaming out to the Yankees yet again and throwing away the game in the ninth after holding their own and going toe-to-toe for eight innings – and they'd ordered another round and Mickey had put it on his tab. He was feeling flush, he'd had some overtime on the docks, and someone led the whole gang in a burst of the Irish baseball song to cheer themselves up – you could never keep the Irish down for long. The bar rang to a rousing chorus that got louder and rowdier by the second –

The Flannigans and the Branigans, the Caseys and the Flynns,
The McIntyres, McFaddens, McGinnitys and Quinns.
The Sullivans and the Dalys, the Hogans, and the Burkes.
The Comiskeys and Loftuses, the Walshes and McGuires.

The Hagans and Dugans, the Daughertys and Byrnes,
The Halihans and Hanrahans, the Haleys and the Hears.
We could name a raft of Os and Macs, but maybe that'll do.
They were playin' ball in Ireland in the days of Brian Boru
– until they started mixing up the words and it all descended
into the usual banter, insults and smut, typical locker-room jibes,
bragging and bravado – but then Tom, who liked to imagine
himself as a bit of a thinker, started holding forth, complaining
that the Sox were always too desperate for the quick win, a big
hit out of the park, whereas the Yankees always knew how to sit
it out and wait to pounce like they had in the ninth.

Poker. Women. Horses. They're all the same. You need to
calculate the odds and know how to play the waiting game.

Meanwhile, your woman has already ordered her second
shot, wasting no time. A confident, warm voice. A woman of the
world. Something foreign. That's okay. She's definitely giving him
the eye. And now she's pulled out her cigarettes. That is the green
light right there. He feels the old, familiar surge of excitement. As
she lifts the glass to her lips, he notes she has no ring.

He turns to look at his cronies, who are still all gaping at her
like she is the Virgin Mary here to announce the second coming.
He tips them the wink as if to say, 'Watch this,' and prepares
his famous, killer grin. Not one of them would have the balls to
do what he is about to. Time to step into the ring. It has been
too long. He feels for his silver Zippo lighter in the pocket of
his sharp-pressed slacks. Women told you who they were with
jewellery; men with accessories. He'd learned that as a young
con, from some old insider who'd taken him under his wing,
when he'd been a callow, terrified first-timer. 'Never show fear.
Always put your best foot forward even when you got holes in
the sole of your shoe. Keep 'em shined good as new, anyways. Tie

pin, lapel badge and a good lighter that lights first time. It's the little things people notice.' He'd made it his credo and has stuck to it ever since.

The little things. Her nails. A shade of vermilion. Subtle. Ever the ladies' man, he takes pride in picking up on that kind of detail. He is already imagining those nails clawing down his back. 'Down, boyo!' As he comes close, he catches the heady fragrance of her. And signalling to the barman, he moves in for the kill.

Jenks

Whenever the yips strike, like presently, Jenks takes to his bed, sometimes for days on end. But he now has a guest in his bed, barely visible, burrowed under a mound of bedclothes. Having installed the boy there, he has had to find his own rest and comfort on the old chair. So, he does the second-best thing and sits himself in front of his hand-built loom that takes up an entire far corner of his kitchen.

As a boy, Jenks had loved stories. His childhood favourite was a much-thumbed, cloth-bound copy of *Tales of the Greek Heroes*, a last birthday gift from Grandfather Hugh. It had been loved to death. He can still recall the faded, cursive, gold lettering on a deep-purple background and the embossed outline of a fierce warrior launching himself straight into battle – impetuous Achilles preparing to do battle against noble Hector to vanquish the Trojan prince and avenge the death of his loving comrade Patroclus. Jenks had felt Achilles' rage and, even as a child, knew that he would have done the same and fiercely fought to the death for a dear friend. He still feels a sharp pang of loss for Kenny, the would-be poet, his sweet, shy, sensitive young friend, a loss which only adds to the physical symptoms, the shakes that descend without warning and leave his entire body shuddering for hours on end. Theirs had been an intimacy forged among scuttling rats, in a wasteland of fire and sand. At these times, his mind would be forced to recall his season in hell, the savage noise of warfare and the even more terrifying silences when the body, already twisted into knots of fearful anxiety, awaited the next cavalcade of destruction. He carries all of it inside him.

But the story that had fascinated him most as a boy was that of the three fates, daughters of Zeus, when he understood for the first time that true power lay not with the glorious warriors, but with the crones who held life and death in their implacable hands as they unspooled the thread of destiny for all living creatures, men and gods alike. This story had coincided with the unexpected death of his beloved grandfather. He understood then that to risk love also necessitated risking loss. And that moment had sparked a fascination with weaving, as though, in some way, to weave was to thread together the broken heart, the shattered universe and pull it back towards wholeness. One of his earliest memories was watching a little spider construct a web between a fence post and a large rose bush. Weaving is healing and entrapment, fate and creation: the world crafted into something more beautiful than before. It is a divinely ordained skill. The highest art. The fates decreed who perished and who survived, moment by moment across the universe. And time and again he had survived. As he has now, and the boy with him.

He'd brought the boy into the two-roomed cottage, and had gently laid him on the rug in front of the embers of the turf fire that he now replenishes and stokes. Next, he had lit his old oil lamp, and only then unpeeled the boy's pitiful rags and tactfully begun to sponge at the terrible, red gashes and wounds along his spine and the back of his legs that stood out against the paler than pale skin. The boy had barely stirred, sucking in and out, expelling short, shallow breaths. Ned, Jenks's old collie, watched proceedings with sharp-eyed curiosity. Jenks had always kept a useful supply of bandages and first-aid materials to hand, a habit born of experience; the nearest doctor was miles from here, in Ballykineen. He'd hesitated before removing his grubby underwear – after all, there was no appropriate etiquette for such a situation. But Jenks had seen enough to know that this was no time for middle-class qualms over decency. So off they came and he softly washed him before turning him over and wiping down his buttocks, noting that bathing was not a regular part of the boy's routine and noting also that, although not apparently conscious, the intimacy of the act had stirred the boy into a state of arousal. He found a clean pair of his own long johns to clothe him. Jenks attended to his cuts with an antiseptic mixture of alcohol and iodine, before carefully wrapping him in a fine linen parcel of bandages, making a slow, winding motion, criss-crossing the slender torso as tightly as he dared.

The sight had reminded him of the lads he'd seen stretchered across the desert in North Africa, still within earshot of the tanks. Images of faces blown apart, or pitiful severed stumps of hands and legs, were seared into his brain. He thinks frequently of those young men, scarred in mind, body and spirit, broken for life.

The strain of making it over the mountain had left Jenks's nervous system much more depleted than he'd realised. When he'd first moved to Connemara, it had seemed that remoteness and solitude were the perfect antidote to his memory-demons. But no, they were always lying just below the surface, waiting for any sign of weakness.

He had felt the tell-tale signs of a migraine beginning to tighten his head, sending bolts of pain across the inside of his skull. Nevertheless, he had managed to complete his task and carry the boy, wrapped in one of his own cotton shirts, into the bedroom and to the big brass bed that takes up most of the space. Jenks recalled how his mother would sometimes carry him up to bed in similar fashion when he'd worn himself out. She had been tactile where his father had been distant, except on the irregular occasions when he read to his son, the closest he could ever come to a paternal show of affection.

Looking down at the boy lying peacefully, Jenks had felt a temporary relief from his own physical distress, and a powerful paternal feeling had stolen over him. Impulsively, he bent and kissed the boy's forehead and tucked the thick, comfortable blankets around him.

Bogboy

He wakes suddenly – shocked out of a dream of places he'd rather not remember – into fierce light. He blinks rapidly, closes his lids against the glare, and opens them again more cautiously.

Am I in heaven? he wonders. He's bathing in an effulgence of pure white, floating in calm and stillness.

As his ears adjust, he can hear waves sucked and sloughed off pebbled shingle and beyond that the roar of the ocean, a low susurration. But there's a tight, stiff feeling across his chest. He feels around himself gingerly, poking under a weight of heavy bedclothes. He's been closely bandaged all the way from back to front, as though his body has been entombed. Now he can feel a burning throb in his torso and the back of his head. He fingers coarse material turbaned round his skull, secured by a large safety pin.

'How did I get here?' He recalls a pair of strong arms, a gentle voice, a feeling of being scooped into the air and a comforting, musty, masculine smell of tobacco and hay and damp. He feels new-born. Overhead is a casement window. Molten gold light streams down onto the bed.

He experiences a feeling of lightness as though his body has melted away like butter in a dish left out too long on the table on a warm day. For a moment, the stabs of fire deep in his back surrender to the sensual pleasure of warmth on the surface of his skin, one cancelling out the other or maybe creating within and without one pure flame. Beyond the room, he can sense an intense radiance that stretches from the bedroom window in front of him as far as his eye can see.

'Blue,' he thinks.

The world is intense and distant at the same time, as though a general view is missing. All that remains are edges, peripheral visions. He's conscious of objects coming into sudden sharp focus for just a few seconds. He's acutely aware of any movement in the room. A dance of shadow across a lime-washed wall, the flight of a seabird crossing the sky through the window, and the prism of colour cast by panels of stained glass: vivid night-sky purple, purest gold, iris-blue and crimson, all suspended by fine threads from an oak beam and lazily scattering jewelled colours across the ceiling and down the wall.

The rapture is so intense it is dizzying; the vividness of coloured flames lit from within stirs something too deep for words. He feels as if he's falling – on the verge of panic. Memory returns, more painful than his physical wounds. He calls out but no sound emerges.

Jenks

At the loom, he sets up his threads, all the time trying to quieten the storm now raging in his head. As he begins to work the loom, the sensation at the tips of his fingers draws him back into his body and the present, gradually replacing the scream of the panzers, the howls of pain and the insistent ceaseless pounding in his head. He begins to lose himself in the task at hand, breathing slowly and sinking into a state of automatic repetition that is as close as he ever comes to a feeling of true peace. Time passes; it could have been minutes or hours, he can barely tell, but the migraine has begun to ease to a sullen throb. He feels a sudden draught at his back and Ned gives one low, warning growl. The bandaged figure of the boy appears framed in the doorway, his eyes scanning the room. Jenks watches his gaze hover over the loom, the kitchen and the embers of last night's turf fire burned to a soft, grey ash, and says, softly, 'So you're up?'

Finally, the boy points at the tapestry Jenks has begun – inspired by his vision on the mountain, the shape of a bird rising towards a fiery sun – and emits an unearthly, piercing shriek somewhere between triumph and rage.

Tante

A year. Maybe eighteen months if the treatment works. But it isn't a tried and tested protocol. She stares hard at the x-rays. The machine has exposed her inner workings. The great hulking contraption showed no fear or favour. This is who you are, it proclaims. Blood and skin and soft tissue and bone and organs – heart, spleen, pancreas, kidneys. Here she is, lit from behind and clipped to the screen on Dr Bentley's wall in his fashionable Dublin consulting room. Ovaries. A miracle and a terror – one's inner workings exposed to the harsh light of day. The doctor's voice, so soothing and kind, pronounces her death sentence with practised clinical precision. She has been unwell so long that finding she now has a fatal condition is almost a relief. And there is still a chance the treatment might work, but the tumour has advanced in malignancy – obviously, it would have helped if she'd had her symptoms checked out earlier. She detects the implied criticism. Well, she's always been stoic by nature. Cramming the evidence of her bleeding beneath the mattress until Molly had come across it and demanded she see a proper doctor, a specialist, not the country bumpkin who passes for medical treatment where they live. And, wearily, she had succumbed to reason.

Her exhausted body is giving up on her at last. Her mother's motto rings in her ears: 'If it is God's will, sure, there's nothing to be done.'

God's will. What kind of God is it who inflicts such suffering? Hers and that of everyone around her. Too late. Everything is too late. It always has been. They've always been a family who left things too late and they have paid the consequences.

Dr Bentley is still talking. His soft brogue is suddenly an irritation. People have been known to survive, he tells her.

'And if not?' She can hear how her voice sounds.

'Well,' he pauses. 'It's... unpredictable.'

She's always been good at reading between the lines. It could take her at any time.

'Thank you,' she says softly. A small mercy, a silver lining.

Now she knows the worst. It is time to make provisions for the future. Not hers, obviously. She'd had no future since...

but there is the boy. And a cloud on the horizon. That cloud is Michael. After years of silence there has now come a flurry of excited missives, each one more effusive than the last. America has been the making of him but he can't wait to see the old country again, be part of the family, make amends. Plus, he's met someone and can't wait to introduce her to the family. They are planning to marry. What a blessing to find love so late in life.

It is a fishing expedition. No doubt about it. Coming home to see what he can salvage, to pick over the leftovers at a feast where there is nothing but scrags on the bone. She knows him through and through. He's failed to make a go of it, so this is his last desperate throw of the dice. Well, over her dead body, if need be. Her grim resolve gives her a momentary comfort.

Ghosts

Rose is back, smoking in her bedroom. Tante wakes, choking.

'What about Alfie?' Rose asks, bitterly. 'You failed him. You tried to steal his joy. But he's a bird flying high. He's already free of your shackles. We grow and we bloom and then one day we're just compost for worms and maggots. But my son will live. My son will escape. My son will live out the life of his dreams.

'Help him, Jocelyn. Give him back what you owe him. Give him his rightful inheritance. Do that for all of us.'

Tante

The boy has miraculously survived the storm and been rescued, against the odds, by their neighbour, the mysterious Englishman, who has appeared at their door now the storm has abated, to give them the welcome news. However, it appears he has suffered more than just the weather. When Jenkins discovered him, he was in a parlous state, covered in blood and bruises. Immediately, they hitched up the pony and trap and have headed round the coast road, leaving Joseph waiting while they make their way the last few hundred yards down to the Englishman's cottage.

Alfie emits a terrifying, high-pitched scream at the sight of them. It rings round the tiny kitchen and sends chills up and down her spine. Molly reaches forward, but he pummels her and clings to the big Englishman with fierce possessiveness. The affection and trust the boy already has for this reticent, solitary individual is evident. She notes the way Jenkins reassures the boy, gently stroking his head and shoulder, like one might calm a highly-strung young colt. While Molly continues to look alarmed, the Englishman appears embarrassed.

Tante thinks, Oh, the absurdity of life!, feeling unexpectedly amused by the utter ridiculousness of the situation. Hysterical laughter threatens. To spare her the possibility of a wild bout of merriment making her appear like a total madwoman, she glances over at the Englishman and says, 'Let's you and I step outside for a little chat, shall we?' The boy just stares at her with undisguised contempt.

They duck outside of the dark, cosy interior into the harsh light of day where she can get a closer look at the man for the first time. He stands a little apart from her now, out of wariness or politeness – she's not sure which – and stares out towards the small field that leads down to the ribbon of strand beyond, waiting for her to make the first move. When she says nothing, he takes the initiative and suggests, in his quiet, diffident way, that maybe Alfie could stay at least until the wounds have properly healed? That perhaps the effects of the fall, which appear also to have rendered him temporarily speechless, would be healed more quickly if he simply stayed put. That he seems happy just resting in this little cottage, and Jenkins gestures back towards it as though to confirm the fact. She doesn't know the best way to respond to this unexpected offer and, to give herself time to gather her thoughts, suggests, 'Perhaps we could take a stroll?'

It's not entirely clear who has the upper hand, or for that matter whether they're on opposite sides or the same one, but he has the advantage here of being on home turf. Nevertheless, he nods in assent, and they move towards a small path that leads down to the shoreline fringed by a rough-hewn wall on one side and a tangled hedge of gorse, fuchsia and blackthorn on the other. She glances over and observes how he holds himself stiffly upright as he walks, the remnants of military discipline and a starchy English upbringing she guesses. He appears to be in his fifties, but he has the kind of face that can appear both unexpectedly boyish and, simultaneously, older than his years. He's somebody who's had more than his fair share of suffering, she thinks. Not unlike herself then, and she feels a moment of unspoken connection as though she'd found someone who would understand her own sense of loss and loneliness. It's an odd situation they've both found themselves in, to be sure. As they make their way down the rocky, uneven path, she offers her opening gambit.

'I really must thank you for all you've done for my nephew.'

He merely nods, and answers the implied compliment with an almost apologetic half-smile. The fine lines around his eyes and mouth deepen. Across his face flashes something not hostile, exactly, but certainly wary. She realises he doesn't trust her and given Alfie's reaction to her arrival, she can appreciate why. He's undoubtedly handsome and he'd be a fine catch for any woman, if he were that way inclined, which she somehow doubts. He's not a ladies' man, of that she's certain; she's come across such quiet, rugged bachelor types before, self-sufficient and entirely uninterested in the opposite sex, and it adds another layer of difficulty to his current proposal. Both of us have reason to be distrustful, she thinks.

He now gestures to a slab of rock, smoothed and hollowed out by wind and wave, where they can take a moment's breather. A gusty breeze is blowing up now from the beach, but despite all the physical strain she's under, she's determined she won't let him see the effort all this is costing her. When he finally does speak again, there's something quaint and formal in his manner.

'I've done what I can to help your young man but, of course, if you want to take charge now, I do understand. You have every right, although –'

'Although?'

'Forgive my speaking frankly but, as I've already said, it might be in everyone's best interest if he were permitted to stay where he is for the present.'

'You think us incapable of giving him the care he requires? That we have been in some way... neglectful?'

He looks at her gravely and his reply is barely audible.

'I think he himself has made his feelings plain. He has been through some kind of terrible trauma. In my opinion, his wounds may well have been inflicted, not accidental –'

'Are you accusing someone of beating him?'

She turns on him her steeliest gaze. Lesser men might have shrivelled, but not him.

'How or why he ended up like this none of us can guess, until he chooses to speak again. But he likes it here, and I think I might be able to help him.'

'You?'

'Possibly. If you agree to trust me.'

'And why might I do that, Mr Jenkins? It might be considered an unconventional arrangement, to say the least.'

'I understand. All I can say is that he's been badly hurt, and he clearly doesn't want to leave. It might be unwise to force him.'

She pauses to consider where the discussion might be leading them. She'd noted the slightest suggestion of a limp in his gait as they came down the path.

'You were in the war, I take it?'

'Yes.'

'And you saw action?'

'Yes. I was a medical orderly during the Blitz, and later I served in the desert in North Africa. In Libya.'

'I see.'

'I've had some experience with... let's just say I know about men who've been through terrible physical ordeals. The mental scars are the worst. It takes time and patience to heal them.'

And there it is. He's talking about himself, she realises. She admires his willingness to reveal his own pain while pleading the cause of the boy. They stare at each other with a new knowing.

'And were I to permit this?'

Behind the ghost of a smile, the shy boy he once was peers through.

'Of course, you will have complete access to him whenever you wish and I'll update you on his progress. Give him time. That's all he needs right now.'

That Alfie has been saved, and is now being well cared for by this man, is obvious. Without Jenkins' intervention, who knows how it might all have ended? They're all in his debt. What harm could it do? Alfie's life has always been a chaotic one. And the thought comes to her, with a guilty start, that the boy has never known a father's care.

There hasn't been a man about the place since Big Paddy. In her head, she hears a sentimental ballad that was popular a few years back. She once came across Molly singing it along with the radio, accompanied by Joseph and Alfie, all three joining in the chorus with cheerful gusto, which felt oddly inappropriate given the lyrics. But it was the year after Paddy's death and grief took many strange forms, as she knew all too well.

Nobody's child,
I'm nobody's child,
Just like a flower, I'm growing wild.
No mommy's kisses and no daddy's smile,
Nobody wants me,
I'm nobody's child.

'Shall we head back?' She proffers an arm and they make stately progress back to the cottage. She takes pleasure in the look of astonishment on Molly's face. Alfie is also there, crouched low on the front step, his face buried in the matted hair of an old sheepdog. He seems to have calmed down but at their approach he looks up, and his body stiffens. A familiar shadow crosses his features. She and the Englishman come to an abrupt halt.

Some kind of predatory bird wheeling about overhead draws her attention with a harsh cry, and she thinks: it's a sign. She regards her nephew and observes: he's just like a bird himself. It's something about the alert way he holds his head as though always keeping a weather-eye out for danger, ready to fly off at a moment's notice. It's as though she's seeing him properly for the first time in years: a raw-boned, malnourished thing, yet alive with a fierce energy that blazes through green eyes flecked with gold and amber, and she stares into those eyes, full of undisguised enmity. Yes, she thinks: watching me like a hawk. Then there's the stubborn set of his jaw, just like his mother's. She imagines wild and wilful Rose as a ghostly presence, watching them all from a distance, taking rapid puffs on her favourite Turkish cigarettes. She's neglected her sister's child so long that he'd almost died as a result. She's withheld her love and duty of care. She can almost hear Rose's scorn. 'So, this is how you keep your promise?'

'We must talk,' she says to him. He shakes his head. Trust him to make this more difficult than necessary. She is tempted to order Joseph down to the cottage from where he's waiting on the road above and simply to bundle the boy into the cart and let him rant and protest all the way home, but immediately dismisses her angry thoughts. Isn't that how she's always dealt with him? Where was this urge to curb him first born? She'd once overheard Aidan McSweeney, a successful horse-trainer and family friend, explain to her father, after yet another particularly egregious display of bad behaviour by her brother, that there were two ways to get any animal to do your bidding: punish disobedience or reward co-operation. While both were equally effective in the short term, only one had a satisfactory outcome if you wanted a genuine relationship with the creature. She had punished Alfie his whole life, not because he was disobedient, but simply for being who he was: the living embodiment of her sister and husband's betrayal. And here was the result staring back at her with silent hostility. She has to quickly rein in the wave of grief that threatens to overwhelm her. But she won't be deterred. Maybe the whole situation isn't yet hopeless. This accident, or whatever it was that has plunged him into this state of mute trauma, might turn out to be a blessing in disguise. Maybe, for once in his short life, she could show him some understanding. It's worth a try.

She tries again. 'Alfie, look at me. Please.'

He has been studiously ignoring her and petting the old dog, but gives her a sidelong glance at her unexpectedly gentle tone.

'Alfie, I only want what's best for you. Are you absolutely certain that this is what you want? We have to be sure this is wise, that you'll be safe here. I'm happy, of course, that you've made a new friend in Mr Jenkins, but you do realise you're asking us to entrust you into the hands of a virtual stranger?'

Now she has his full attention and sees him slowly turning her words over in his head, looking for the catch. To reassure him, she adds, 'Your mother, on her deathbed, asked me to promise to keep you but you're nearly grown-up now and it's time you made some of your own decisions in life. If this is what you really want, I won't stand in your way. We'll call it a temporary arrangement and Molly can drop by and keep an eye on you from time to time, to see how you're getting on. What do you say?'

It's the longest conversation, albeit entirely one-sided, she can ever remember having had with him. He looks up at her in apparent astonishment. The Englishman might be a stranger, she thinks, but for Alfie this affectionate version of herself is probably even more strange. She holds out her hand, which he ignores, but he slowly nods his assent, just once.

Tante is acutely aware of the watery-blue sky, the hum of the sea at her back, the neat cottage, the velvet-green hillside speckled with gorse. Yes, it will do. It's her duty now to let him go free.

It's as though she's suddenly being afforded a glimpse of the future and has been given a chance to do the right thing at long last. Alfie's road will always be a hard one but it will be his and his alone. Furthermore, she will now do everything in her power to make that road easier. Who is she to stand in his way? What's one more unconventional arrangement in the life of a fatherless and motherless child?

She makes her announcement. 'Yes. Let Alfie stay. He's made his choice. He obviously likes it here. If it's God's will, sure, there's nothing to be done.'

Nothing more needs to be said. She holds out her hand once more and, this time, he takes it, and they seal their agreement. Let the healing begin. For all three of them: her, this singular man and her troubled nephew. A lost boy now rescued by an apparently equally lost man.

Bogboy

In his dream, they're walking a desert road together. Spindly trees in the distance are extending twisted, imploring branches to heaven for the rains that never come. She's the porcupine woman in her prickly skin of quills and thorns. He's the boy in blue, his arms and torso coated in thick woad. They approach the place of sacrifice. The deed must be done for the rains to come. He tugs hard at the chain noosed around her neck and she stumbles forward. The tribe stands in expectation. The blue people. His ancestors. On a dais is her red, velvet chaise longue.

He strips her of her porcupine cloak, observes in disgust her wrinkled flesh, distended belly and shrivelled breasts.

'Bury her alive in the earth,' he announces to the assembled multitude, his people, who whoop and holler and raise their spears. One handsome, young warrior brother leaps forward like a blue-painted gazelle and prods her in the back. Moaning weakly, she scrambles up onto the sacrificial altar to seat herself on her blood-red throne. The chant begins low and deep, growing in power and volume as he proclaims the sacrificial prayer.

The tribe bows in reverence. Bogboy climbs up onto the altar in his chieftain's headdress of golden-tipped hawk feathers, and, staring deep into her eyes, captures her terrified gaze. Her bony hands clutch at him as he tips her with deliberate slowness backwards, chair and all, into the grave-pit already dug for her. As she tumbles earthwards, the light of life and morning and stars flares up one last time and is then extinguished.

'No loss!' he cries, brandishing the cloak. 'She was born old.'

With a rolling crash of thunder, the heavens open. Torrential rain rinses away the body paint which runs down him in rivulets, smearing and streaking his skin from head to toe. The blue people are melting into puddles at his feet. He's the blue boy no longer.

Bogboy wakes from this disturbing place to one of happiness, where morning light pours into the room, to the sound of surf roaring in his ears. This momentary state of bliss swiftly vanishes. Tante has been temporarily vanquished, it's true, but it doesn't feel like victory. What remains is not triumph, but a feeling of loss and desolation deep inside his belly.

Is hate so different from love? Bogboy wonders. He'd known how things stood, the battle lines clearly drawn between them. But now all he can see in his mind's eye is her face contorted into every shade of sorrow. He hates her self-pity, her endless complaints, her hungers no-one can fill. And he realises that he wants to extinguish her pain for good. Kill, kill, kill, kill everything in her because he feels it inside himself too. His own loss and longing. If only he can let it go, then maybe he will know what it means to become a man.

Mickey

Back then he'd been a man's man. In his world it was the highest compliment you could earn. Yes, he had been a boyo alright. He'd once been the golden boy too. The son. The family hope, outshining his two sisters. Born to go far. And he had. Sailing the seven seas in the merchant navy. After his great disgrace, he'd run away to sea. It had been the easiest option by far. He'd circumnavigated the globe – endless days on board ship and jaunts ashore to all-night bars with upstairs rooms. Santiago. Havana. Valparaiso. Yokohama. Panama. Cartagena. Shanghai. Malta. Singapore. But distance didn't bring with it amnesia, not even in his youth in shadowy, back streets with nearly always a drunken brawl to round off the evening, and an easy lay with one of the local chicks to lick his wounds, heal his bruises and fuck away his cares. Plenty of those. Gambling and risking everything. Losing streaks in back rooms. Always the same wily card sharps. But the lure of the game had never left him – a fool and his money were soon parted. Well, there were worse ways to squander his dough. Picking up lazy Americanisms en route.

Respectable Michael from good stock is now plain Mickey O'Brien with nothing to show for thirty-four misspent years. Up here, the breeze on deck blows away the past and clears his head of the self-pity and the bitter tang of failure.

His recklessness had been his undoing. Always chasing the quick buck. Rounds of drinks and rounds of golf. Sure-fire ventures. Gambling the family inheritance. His partners had seen him coming a mile off. Mickey the mug. He'd never been a great judge of character. Too trusting. Sign here, Mr O'Brien. And here... and here. Men in neat suits and ties had handed him thick, gold-nibbed fountain pens to sign away his life. He had imagined coming to Joycie in triumph when the profits started rolling in.

The downfall of what was left of the family fortunes had been swift and shocking. He'd been embezzled by a slick accountant and his cronies, but his was the signature on the bank loans, using his expected portion of the inheritance as collateral.

More men had come, to size up the estate and reclaim monies owed with interest. Banks could be ruthless bastards. Sharks in suits, sitting in rooms with deep, plush, fitted carpets. The best of what was left of the land had gone under the hammer, to be snapped up greedily by local farmers in a fire sale auction. Land that had been carefully stewarded by over nine generations, land that had even survived the Cromwellian invasion: gone overnight. More fool them, was the opinion thereabouts.

As for Joycie, she was more ruthless even than the banks. Her vengeance had been swift and sure. She'd fought tooth and nail to hang onto the deeds of the house and a modest acreage. Husbanded carefully, it would see her and the boy through the worst. Mickey had all but ruined them. Her eyes bored through him. The golden boy, nothing but tarnished silver.

'All you ever cared about. Swank. Looking good in front of your so-called friends. Showing off in front of your drinking buddies. You'll never be welcome in this house again.'

Admittedly, he'd been young and foolish but he'd more than paid his dues. We all get to make mistakes, surely?

He thinks of the boy he once was. Standing on the western shore, watching this very ocean with hungry eyes and dreaming of Manhattan and the cloud-capped towers of Tír na nÓg. But for all its bright lights and promise, no gold-paved streets lay in wait. There'd been foolish mistakes: he'd paid a high price for his misdemeanours. He'd barely made it out of Rikers alive.

So now he is coming home: black sheep, cunt-chaser, hollow man, just another prodigal son in need of forgiveness. Now there are no more big dreams, just bad dreams. Now there is one last throw of the dice, one last hand to play, one final ocean to cross.

So, a fresh start in the old turf, to suckle at Mother Ireland's shrivelled old teat one last time. Set up a little bar somewhere and tell tall tales of the seven seas to gullible, wide-eyed country lads. Forget the dark days, just a little pot of gold to set him back on his feet again. He can see it now. Mickey's shebeen, out in the boondocks. A place for the locals and a bit of good craic. A couple of old fellas on accordion and tin whistle. Why not? It isn't much to ask, after all he's been through. There must be a bit of family silver to cough up, even now. The thing is, will Joycie even let him back over the threshold?

He watches the sleek liner plough its way through the bottle-green, froth-capped Atlantic swells.

'It could get rough later,' the slim-hipped, young purser had informed the first-class passengers earlier. Carolina had retired to their cabin, saying she could feel a storm rising and had a headache coming on.

Carolina. Even now, he still can't quite believe his luck.

That first evening, on the way back to his walk-up, he had been nervous. He was never nervous. He'd had more than his fair share of women. Passing fancies. But she had been different from the start. He'd had no illusions – the way she hit the bottle back in the bar was far from ladylike and yet, somehow, she had still managed to maintain her poise. She was a cool customer, no doubt about it, even when modestly drunk. As he'd pushed open the splintered door to his tiny room and switched on the harsh, overhead bulb, he'd felt a wave of shame. What had he been thinking, bringing her back here? The dingy appearance and stale air gave off an impression of utter neglect. The one exception was the rail of neatly pressed, perfectly creased pants and meticulously ironed white shirts.

As she'd crossed to the window that gave onto the street below, she'd been bathed in a glow from the garish red and green neon sign of the all-night bodega beneath them. She'd looked so out of place, a gleaming crystal laid on a piece of old hessian sacking. Dressed for Fifth Avenue, not the Bowery. And yet she'd also managed to look totally at ease amidst the squalor, even as she'd turned away from the window and caught him staring at her, entranced. A high-pitched wail of sirens had sounded above the general cacophony of traffic and night noises. Carolina had appeared to be unfazed by it all, even sardonically amused at the whole situation; had appeared to find the circumstances exactly as she had expected.

'Nice place you've got here,' she had said, and he'd looked at her to try to discern the true, hidden meaning of her words. But she'd been smiling. He'd seen how the corners of her eyes had creased in genuine amusement and, in that moment, they had both laughed. He'd started trying to shove empty bottles away, suddenly aware that yesterday's underpants were soaking in the tiny sink opposite the bed, that the bed itself consisted of an old mattress pushed up against a wall of peeling, yellowed rose-patterned wallpaper and that his one seat was a cane-backed, broken rattan chair he'd come across in the street.

She had come up to him, brought a hand to his face and in her deepest, whiskey voice, had half-whispered, 'Relax, honey, I've seen a whole lot worse. Maybe you could fix us a drink?'

She was in control and he loved it. It seemed only right and natural that he should do her bidding. He'd eagerly scouted out a couple of reasonably clean tumblers and poured out generous measures from a half-full bottle of Jack Daniels. She'd sipped it, and eyed him like a sloe-eyed vamp, and he had felt himself slip into his old self: beautiful, cocksure, able to strut down any street.

They'd toasted each other and in seconds their bourbon-laced lips had collided – hungrily, greedily devouring one another until nothing else had mattered but the moment.

Bogboy

He watches intently as Jenks's slender fingers begin their deft shuttling of the bobbin and the delicate back-and-forth threading of warp and weft. The clack of the loom soothes him, a rhythm that matches his heartbeat. Each action has its appropriate sound that has grown familiar to him. The first morning he'd been startled by the unfamiliar noise beyond his bedroom door, but now it's become a welcome part of his world. Now he loves the song of the loom, and the way Jenks strums the threads as if he might draw music from them. He likes the easy flow and ripple of the older man's muscles as he works the loom. The confidence of his ease and skill. The sense of stillness he exudes, even in motion, that says, 'Feel free to be here with me. I ask nothing of you and need even less.' He likes most of all that Jenks respects his reluctance to talk, that the two of them have developed their own language of gesture. It reminds him of Hawk.

'I am Hawk now,' thinks Bogboy. 'I can never be tamed, in spite of your kindness.' And yet some part of him knows that that's not the whole story either. That sometimes lives can become woven together and entwined before a person is fully aware of it or understands the reason why. This is a new idea and he feels a moment of trepidation that might also be excitement.

At the big house he was subject to Tante's bell, imperious and impatient. But in Jenks's cottage, he can do as he pleases. Time is fluid, and goodness is possible. Here, Hawk has come to rest inside him. He is attuned to the sensual, elemental world around him and the possibility that tenderness can heal. 'I came here to reclaim my kingdom of light,' thinks Bogboy.

Just then, the sun breaks through the small kitchen window to bathe Jenks's head in a halo of silver. He looks like an Old Testament prophet. His fingers too are dappled with threads of light. Bogboy's heart fills with love. For the light. For the scene unfolding before him. For this man.

'Show me how to create my new life,' prays Bogboy. Jenks turns and smiles at him and invites him over. He stands next to the big man. Bogboy looks closely at the new creation. A sunburst of red orange gold rises like the rapture of dawn above a jagged peak, and the unmistakable, open-winged outline of Hawk flies towards it. He wants to say something, but can't think how. There is a feeling he can't name, let alone describe.

Jenks makes room for him at the loom. Bogboy hesitates, then sits. Jenks places his hands, warm and firm, over Bogboy's, and shows him how to place his feet, how to square himself up, how to move the shuttle back and forth, how to keep the threads from tangling, and how to build the next row. Nothing is said or explained. Jenks calmly tutors and corrects by example. Bogboy feels his way into the process, renewing and revealing the vision, and they move more and more in unison.

He begins to appreciate the mystery of it. How each thread and knot is part of something new being created, something from nothing but the imagination. It reminds him of his circles of stones and feathers.

Joseph

He surveys the wall with a critical eye. Around him lie rocks of varying sizes and shapes that have rolled down from the mountain. Now embedded in stretches of grassy pasture, they provide the raw material for the wall that stretches, snakelike, towards the summit, and that had once marked off the grazing ground for their flock of sheep. When they'd had a flock. In the days before it had all came tumbling down.

He sits back on his haunches, surveying the stones he's painstakingly assembled to mend the gap. It is a job he's been putting off for months; he hasn't had the heart to come back here since Big Paddy's accident, nearly ten years ago. But the wall separates the last remnants of what had been the estate's sheep farm from that of O'Donnell, the neighbouring farmer, and the old man's cattle have now taken to squeezing through the break in the drystone wall to help themselves to the tillage on the other side. 'Apparently, the other cows' grass is also greener,' Joseph grunts, as he strains to lift one of the larger boulders into place.

But the reality is no joke. O'Donnell is an irascible old bastard who's taken to hollering at Joseph from a distance to 'Fix that bloody wall of yours.' His main complaint is that his heifers are choking on the ragwort that now covers the pasture that Big Paddy had tended with such diligence and care. Most of what had been an estate had been squandered by the master's foolishness back in the day. All that remained were these few dozen acres. Marginal land. Fields that Big Paddy had brought back to life, largely cleared of stone, and kept clear of hazards to the livestock. Now they are an unkempt and weed-infested mess.

'Fix it yourself, you old bastard,' Joseph had yelled back and O'Donnell had threatened to set his dogs on him with, 'Is it

Paddy's sprog that speaks? Ya little whelp – you're not a tenth the man yer da was,' and had stormed off to complain to her upstairs. And Madame had hauled Joseph into the drawing room and informed him, in front of his mother, that from now on he was to keep a civil tongue in his head when speaking to the locals and didn't they all have enough to put up with without making any more enemies in the neighbourhood?

'To hell with the whole bunch of them,' he says aloud, and smashes down on the boulder with his sledgehammer, which jars every muscle in his arm. And it is too late to repair the damage done, in every sense of the word.

'Serves those idiot cows right if they're stupid enough to eat the ragwort in the first place,' Joseph thinks, furiously, as he tries to bash the boulder into place again. It wobbles. He strains with all his might to lift and reset the flat slab of granite to wedge it more securely.

'Not a tenth the man.' He won't surrender, even though by rights it is a two-man job at least. No chance of yer one bringing in a hired hand, the stingy oul' bitch. He is a man. He won't succumb to the dark, guilty thoughts in his head. He will be all he needs to be. Get away. Far away. Like Michael, yer one's brother she can't even bring herself to mention. He'd been a fecker right enough, but he'd had the right idea. Escape. Joseph's own plans aren't fully formed yet. Not agricultural college. The army maybe. A bit of travel and adventure. Anything has to be better than this muck-heap.

'And this should be our land.' He feels a flare of rage, but whether at O'Donnell, the wall, the aforementioned eejit cattle or the equally stupid accident that snatched away his father's life so prematurely, he cannot tell. The sheer unfairness of it all burns him up inside. Why do some people who do feck all have everything, while others who do all the work have nothing? It is an anger that now lives permanently inside him and can be stoked from ember to uncontrollable rage within seconds, at the slightest provocation.

His mind goes back to Bogboy for a split second before he catches himself and, instead, squares up the boulder with one last mighty grunt and heave.

'Turn it round the other side and it'll go flush for ya.'

Joseph nearly jumps from his skin. It is Big Paddy's low voice, clear as day at his right ear. He spins around, knowing the foolishness of the notion, only to see the big man standing there, feet apart, briar pipe – filled with his favourite sweet tobacco – in hand, regarding him with that quiet, penetrating glance that misses nothing and brooks no resistance.

'There's yer cross piece. Fill in around it and cap it off.'

He sees a wedge of stone, half-obscured by clover and thistle, next to the bit of damaged wall. A perfect flat top to lay horizontal.

The main surprise is that he felt none whatsoever at this apparition, as though it was only right and proper that his da was still watching over him. But better men than he have been known to quake before that gaze. It is on the tip of Joseph's tongue to reply, 'Right y'are.' He'd never been one to cross the da. When Big Paddy spoke, in field or house or local bar (and he didn't often), men listened. Whether the subject was politics, the best lures for trout fishing or the best means of breaking in a skittish colt, Paddy got respect. Joseph had grown up eager to please his father and win approval. It had never been an easy task. A lashing with Paddy's thick belt for cheek or an occasional rebellious show of stubbornness had been as much the norm as quiet pride.

''Tis well enough done,' or a quick grunt of approval were

the height of praise in his books for a rare, good school report or a victory by the local GAA boys, where Joseph, always big for his age, had proved a reliable stopper in defence. Joseph had never felt prouder than when his da came out to support him. He would bask for days in the glow of his father's praise.

He had never understood, therefore, the tenderness Paddy reserved for Bogboy. Harsh as he could be with his son from time to time, Paddy had treated Bogboy like a fallen sparrow with a broken wing – with a gentle, tender indulgence. They had shared a mutual understanding and love of the wild, untameable land that lay all around them, whether mountain or meadow, peat bog or pasture, stream or trout lake. Then, one day, Bogboy had been out assisting Paddy dipping the sheep and made the mistake of boasting about it. Joseph had been cooped up all day behind a desk at school, bored senseless. He'd grappled Bogboy to the ground and hissed, 'Keep yer distance from Big Paddy, ya hear? He's my da, not yours, ya filthy little tinker.'

Molly had overheard and had had to tear the boys apart. She'd told Paddy. Joseph had been thrashed to within an inch of his life. After that, Bogboy mostly had kept himself apart, increasingly lost in his own world, roaming the land hither and thither like Wandering Aengus. But it had been all too short a triumph.

'Not a tenth the man,' says Paddy at Joseph's ear. He spins around again. But this time, there is no sign of his father's ghost or hallucination or whatever it was.

These stones are soaked in his father's blood. It wasn't lost on Joseph that if Bogboy had still been trailing after Paddy like a faithful puppy, he might have raised the alarm. But Paddy had died alone out here. He felt the familiar lump of grief in his throat. Paddy's terrible, pointless end, the big presence that had towered over him all his life, a crumpled heap on the ground, his head fatally gashed.

Joseph had been sent by his mother to call his father in from the upper pastures where he'd taken the old Massey Ferguson to mow the silage for winter feed. He had been late for his supper and he had always been a man of steadfast habits. Six-thirty on the dot, he'd appear in the kitchen, fling down his old cap, scrub off the day's toil at the sink, and sit himself down to tuck in to his feed. Spuds, bacon and cabbage. A glass of buttermilk and, as often as not, a bit of home-made apple tart and double cream. Paddy had liked his treats. And while Joseph would regale his father with tales out of school, Paddy would merely nod, sopping up his gravy from his big soup bowl with a slice of fresh soda bread, or frown if something met with his disdain.

If, however, Paddy was not in a good mood, both Joseph and his mother knew better than to interfere. He was the big man; even his silences could fill a room. Most nights, however, Joseph's door would creak open, often just as he was drifting off to sleep; a shaft of light would illuminate the dark and his father would tiptoe into the bedroom for a moment to bid his son goodnight. If Joseph was poorly or restless, Paddy would sometimes come and sit quietly by the bed. Just his father's breath above him, low and even, like the sigh of the ocean, had been the most comforting sound of his childhood.

When Paddy hadn't appeared and the sky outside had begun to darken, his mother had insisted he go fetch him. 'He's forgotten himself. Tell him dinner's waiting for him on the table.'

And here is where he'd come across the body of his father. Big Paddy must have been wrestling to control the tractor as it skidded down the steep slope and careered into the wall, tilting over and flinging him backwards against the stones. He would have lain there for hours as blood poured into his brain. Maybe still conscious 'til near the end, knowing that nobody would be coming to rescue him. Foolish to have taken the tractor that far up the hill alone. But that was Paddy. Loyal and dutiful to a fault. It was not in his nature to ask for another pair of hands. Joseph could have taken the day off school. He could have been at his father's side. Run for help.

He looks at his handiwork. It is crude. But the wall is repaired. The gap is patched up at last. His whole body aches but it will ease. There are some aches however that will never get mended.

'You are the wall that killed my father,' thinks Joseph, 'and now everything is broken.'

He gathers up his tools – sledgehammer, mallet, chisel – in the worn, leather toolbag that had been Big Paddy's – and slowly makes his way back to the house, as the streaks of salmon pink sky overhead turn to indigo.

Molly

Little one, little one
Where have you been
I rode a white horse
To meet with the Queen.

The skipping rope swinging faster and faster as she jumped and jumped and jumped shrieking with joy and laughter in a world of one long rapture at the wide blue sky and the endless summer days unfolding.

Days of light. Before it all came down. A world without adults. Without doubt or care. Just beetles and butterflies, thrushes and swifts tracing high arcs overhead, owls at dusk, earthworms, trout streams, badger dens and fox holes. Dark places where the wild ones lived.

Tell me my little one
What have you seen?
I saw the fine ladies
Who danced on the Green.

And always at her side in those long hot days, Rose. Molly would lie on her back next to Rose, shading her eyes from the sunburst of radiant butter-yellow between her fingers. Light, burning a hole through the day. Dandelion and buttercup, daisy head and cowslip. Chewing on a yarrow stalk, while Rose recounted the tale of ascending Icarus, the beautiful but arrogant boy, determined to out-race and out-shine the sun travelling across a pure Grecian sky, until his wings started melting like altar candles.

And they stared at that infinite, blue vault in awe, fingers entwined, imagining with delicious horror that frail body's final, terrifying, doomed plunge earthwards.

Life was always full of promise with Rose. They were an unlikely pair, the girl from the big house and the daughter of a tenant farmer. What did such things matter to them? What if the adults frowned on their friendship? She kept a low profile around Mrs O'Brien, Rose's mother, who looked down on her with an air of barely concealed condescension. Her own mother was thin-lipped and admonishing, 'Don't be getting above yourself, they're not like us.' Molly was a nobody. The O'Briens were descended from chieftains and ancient royalty. There were days when Rose would come to call and Molly would mumble, 'I can't today, I have chores to do.' She was embarrassed to be reminded of her lowly status, while Rose was forever free, her time all her own. The one spark in a house of forbidding conformity.

But, despite their differences, they'd been fast friends from the beginning. Molly was always happy to follow in Rose's wake. She'd instinctively understood that, beneath her gaiety, Rose felt lonely. Fearless, fun-seeking Rose. Game for anything. No corner of the estate, or the hills, fields and bogs beyond, was out of bounds to Rose. She needed some of Molly's quiet stability and good sense to stop her wildness getting out of hand. In the end, of course, you can't save someone from themselves, no matter how hard you might try. And Rose had tested her loyalty and friendship to the limits in time.

But for Molly – sitting alone now in the dark in this house of death, of shadows, of secrets and curses – for her, Rose would always be the girl in the dress of forget-me-not blue, tied at the back in a perfect bow, and matching sandals, standing at the great window overlooking the sweeping terrace and the multi-coloured flower beds.

It had been Molly's first visit to the big house. Her mother had secured the housekeeper's job and had brought young Molly along while she dusted and polished. 'You can make yourself useful about the place.'

In that first glimpse of Rose, her back to her, Molly, all of eight years old, felt self-conscious, overcome with shame at her patched grey frock with its curled, yellowing lace collar.

Everything in the room was interesting. The gold-framed pictures, the sideboard with its crystal decanters, the great fireplace, the mantlepiece of chubby, pink-faced china shepherds and shepherdesses (Meissen, her mother called them. 'Don't you touch them, one of them would cost a month's wages to replace.') but her eyes kept getting drawn back to the lovely girl at the window. And Rose had turned to see her standing shyly in the corner, and, grinning broadly, had announced, 'I'm Rose. Do you want to play outside?'

Molly did not know how to answer, and Rose, seeing the awkwardness, addressed her mother with supreme confidence, as if they were both grown-ups. 'Ah, Mrs O'Riley, you wouldn't mind me stealing your daughter here for a turn round the grounds, would you? I promise not to lose her.'

Her mother was equally flummoxed – it didn't seem right somehow – but she managed a frown and a brief nod.

'I suppose it can't hurt. Off you go now, Molly, and be good.'

A quick 'Grand' from Rose in reply, and then back to her with an outrageous wink, as though they were already co-conspirators, 'The holidays have been dreadfully boring so far, come on!'

Without waiting for an answer, she'd flung the doors wide and was already scampering down the terrace steps, yelling back over her shoulder, 'Mind yourself, it's a bit slippery.'

And that was it from then on. Molly and Rose. Rose and Molly. They'd had a perfect summer. As the years went on, their unlikely friendship endured. Molly would be the first person Rose would seek out after being away, first at the convent school and then at college in Galway, where she took a year's Italian course, 'for something to do.'

Then there'd been the local parish dance where Molly had met Paddy. Dressed in her finery, she'd known she was passably pretty that night, when so often she'd felt plain and dowdy in comparison with Rose's effortless glamour. She would never for an instant be able to outshine her friend. Lit from behind, Rose sometimes appeared as though the crown of her head might burst into flame. But Rose, seemingly indifferent to her looks, was forever passing down clothes she'd barely worn, with, 'Try this on you, Moll, it'll suit you so much better than me.'

On this occasion, it was a cinch-waisted, black-and-white striped, organza frock, way too stylish for a country dance. Its cut served to emphasise Molly's generous hips and bosom, the one area where she scored over Rose's slender, almost boyish, frame. Molly knew full well the lie behind the generous gesture and chose not to acknowledge it. In the end, like so much else, she had owed her successful courtship of Paddy to Rose and not just because of the head-turning dress.

For once, she had led the way, knowing they eclipsed everyone else in the drab dance hall, she and Rose, both looking as if they had just stepped out at the Ritz.

The spartan church hall – with its rusted tin roof, decked with a string of coloured bunting to offset the dingy off-white walls, and a large notice board announcing Novenas, pilgrimages to Knock and news of the Sisters of Mercy fundraiser for the Uganda mission school – was their ballroom of romance. Under the supervision of Father Diamond, this was the nearest they had to a formal mating ritual and courtship dance. But it was a serious affair and everyone prepared for it all week long, gossipy with excitement and anticipation. They'd all heard tales of dances in depression-weary America where couples danced for money until they collapsed with exhaustion. Father Diamond's cruelty didn't extend quite so far; on the contrary, he believed in keeping things short, with the understanding that matters began at six and would end at nine on the dot. 'You can have a bit of fun and then you'll all be able to get yourselves home safely while it's still light, and be rested and up for Mass in the morning.'

His superficial bonhomie was betrayed by a gimlet eye which kept a look-out to ensure that a pair of straying hands or young flesh pressed too close didn't let youthful excitement get the better of them. Still in their teens, the gauche, young farmers and labourers lined one side of the room and the young women primly arrayed themselves along the opposite wall. Between the two sexes stretched an ocean of desire which required an epic voyage by the boys to the further shore of possible coupledom and respectability.

The entertainer was a local boy, Eddie King, now reinvented as King Eddie and his Hot Trot Trio; they fancied themselves an American jazz combo of the kind that was becoming all the rage. A tureen of mild fruit punch and some bottled Guinness had been approved and, with a signal from the Father, the proceedings began. Nobody moved as the first bars played. Slowly, one or two lads with more courage than most stirred themselves and then a pack of young fellas bore down on their prey, like young wolves set loose on a flock of sheep. The atmosphere was suddenly charged with electricity.

Molly watched one, tall and awkward, his best suit not quite hiding his discomfort, approach her and Rose, stumbling slightly as though he'd suddenly discovered he had two left feet. At his side was a short, burly lad named Stoney, with a beetle brow and badly chopped fringe. To her dismay, Stoney was heading her way, while the taller one appeared to be intent on approaching Rose. Rose, who had spotted where Molly's interest lay, nudged her sharply in the ribs and whispered, 'Leave this to me.'

As the men came near, Rose deftly swapped places with a startled Molly and stretched an elegant arm out to Stoney who grinned like the proverbial cat who'd got the cream. The taller lad, who introduced himself as Paddy, swallowed any disappointment down and, ever the gentleman, gallantly offered Molly his hand. She took it. A spasm of electricity shot up her spine. Out of the corner of her eye, she caught a glimpse of the hapless Stoney weaving poor Rose round the floor like a bullock dragging a cart. They made for a comically incongruous duo. But Paddy, it turned out, was a surprisingly nifty dancer and they quickly synchronised into a comfortable rhythm, his steadying hand wrapped lightly round her waist. She could never say for sure if it was love at first sight. But it had certainly been love ever after. And something much rarer: a mutual ease and understanding from the very start that had built a solid foundation between them. Rose had intuitively understood what a good match Molly and Paddy would make.

Those were good days, the courting days. They were both shy. But Rose was always at her back, ready to steady her sudden flurries of doubt. 'He's a good 'un, Moll. If he asks you, say yes and don't be an idiot.' And ask he did, awkward and tongue-tied and heartbreakingly gruff, proffering a perfect, heart-shaped emerald in a pale Irish gold Claddagh ring, with the words, 'I got you a little something. What do you say? Shall we make a go of it?'

His almost handsome face was creased with anxiety. The ring was so exquisite, from an exclusive jeweller in Galway, that she had no doubt Rose must have had a hand in the purchase. She couldn't imagine how Paddy had paid for it and didn't dare ask Rose, though she knew Paddy well enough to know he would have been too proud to accept any help. He must have saved every last penny for months. His sincerity and the suddenness of the proposal reduced her to a fit of girlish giggles. Noticing his instant look of alarm and distress, she corrected herself quickly. 'Don't look like a great, sad lump now. You know I'll have ya, sure, who else would?'

When Rose appeared casually a few minutes later, laden with shopping bags, as though this was all just a lovely coincidence, Molly knew her friend had stage-managed the whole affair. Rose brought them to Sweeneys, a local photographer's studio, to have an engagement shot taken. Rose herself posed for a portrait in a stylish outfit and dinky little hat she'd just bought at Browne's department store in the High Street. Molly joked, 'It's time we found you a fella an' all,' and for a fleeting second spotted a look of sadness flit across her friend's face before the cloud passed and Rose announced, 'Too right. Maybe I'll try my luck with a few Yankee millionaires,' in a funny Mae West drawl and they all laughed and afterwards Rose announced, 'And now a small celebration for the happy couple. I propose afternoon tea with cake. My treat.' She shooed away their half-hearted protest.

'Yes,' thinks Molly. 'Those were the good days.' Then she remembers Rose sidling in to her kitchen one morning, looking like she'd been up all night, and, with no preamble, saying, 'Oh Moll, I've been the biggest fool, whatever am I going to do?'

Hawk

Hawk is drawn back to the sea, spiralling upwards on thermal flurries while below, the vast ocean is swept forward in its endless, tidal roar. Hawk is in constant battle with wind and water. Balanced, poised for flight in the stillness at the heart of chaos, she soars, then hovers, alive to every beat of the surf, and the threshing motion that swells before it cascades and crashes with curled foam upon the battered shore. The great ocean surges forth and draws back into itself.

Bogboy

His wounds are beginning to scab over. Jenks changes his dressings every couple of days, rubbing a dark, herbal tincture, thick as glue, smelling of honey and eucalyptus oil, across his back. Bogboy likes this ritual, the methodical way Jenks patiently completes the task, unpeeling the old bandages, cleaning the wounds with warm water, firmly rubbing his back in tender, sweeping strokes with a soft cloth, then applying the cooling balm. He enjoys the sensation, even allowing himself to drift and daydream, helped by the heat from the turf fire and the soft candlelight. Passive and relaxed, he holds his arms aloft to allow the fresh dressings to be wrapped around his wounds until 'All done' from Jenks and he is free to start the day afresh.

His new nest is the cosy alcove bed inside the kitchen recess, reached via a set of folding, wooden steps. He likes his home up here. Each morning, as he lies beneath the eaves, he can hear the scurrying of mice and the flurries and skittering of bird life. Often, without waking Jenks, himself an early riser, he can slip out at first light. Ned opens one lazy eye and pads over to be petted and then waits and watches patiently as Bogboy heats some ice-cold water, drawn from the well beyond the cottage, in the big, black kettle hooked over the turf fire he lights first thing. He watches the flame splutter into life. Next, he pours some of the water into a galvanised bucket and quickly swabs down his face and arms with a new-found fastidiousness because he knows that Jenks approves and, for reasons he can't fully explain, he likes the older man's approval. He likes to sit and sip the strong, black, morning tea, brewed from last night's leaves, and watch as the sky is streaked palest primrose, pink and blue.

In a remarkably short space of time, he has made himself at

home. With Tante temporarily vanquished (an astonishing turn of events he cannot fathom), he feels a new surge of independence. Jenks and he have found an unlikely companionship. There's a deep, layered understanding between them.

Now Ned whimpers and Bogboy lets him out. As usual, the dog scampers only so far, before turning as if to say, 'Coming?'

Bogboy steps into the day as though stepping into a temple of bright light. He used to hate the light. He craved the darkest of deep, dark places. The bog-lands. Earth and the lure of the underworld had been his element. The abode of the ancestors. For he, too, was nothing but dirt. But now the land is at his back, and before him lies the open expanse of the sea. Its tidal rhythms have become part of this strange new existence. He relishes its every mood. The dull thrum of the rainswept hills and sodden bog has been replaced by an unpredictable and expansive cadence of sigh and roar and slap and howl that stretches to the farthest horizon imaginable.

He follows Ned down the path that leads to the shingled shoreline. He catches sight of Hawk and his heart leaps in his chest. She skims across the morning tide, plunges and emerges with a flailing sliver of silver, talon-scooped from beneath the froth, and flies overhead, spiralling up and away.

His eyes track her as she heads back to a ledge in the cliff-face, where she immediately feasts on her prey. She tugs hard with her curved beak, stabbing into the soft innards and gouging out lumps of fresh raw flesh.

At the base of the cliff is an opening he hasn't noticed before: a fissure in the rock, worn by the flow of water forcing a passage through the stone. Ned is bounding forward, snuffling at a shallow, tidal pool, and Bogboy makes his way towards the narrow cave entrance.

Hawk has temporarily sated her hunger. She rises, calling excitedly, dipping and diving towards him. Bogboy is suddenly certain that it's she who has drawn him to this place. For a moment, he feels like the entire world has paused – frozen into stillness and silence. Then, he's aware again of the ocean at his back and he can no longer tell the surf roar from the thick pulse of blood in his head.

He squeezes through the narrow slit in the rock face and enters the darkness. The cave is deep and almost silent as the roar of the ocean and the wind's sigh both recede. He can hear nothing now but the rhythmic noise of moisture dripping from the walls. The roof curves, cathedral-like, far above him, and vaults way off into the darkness. He makes his way across the uneven floor, his feet scattering stones and pebbles which set up an echo in the chamber opening up around him.

All his senses are on high alert, but he feels no fear. He is startled by a shimmering glow, as though the sun's rays have slipped in through a crack to cast light on the strange markings, circles, spirals and geometric patterns, artfully arranged on the wall in front of him. It is as though he's staring at a map of the universe. Briefly, he hears again the triumphant shriek of Hawk.

Bogboy knows with calm certainty that this is the cave of the ancestors. It's like a place he's always known. The air seems to flow in and around him, and from the molten radiance a tall figure emerges, naked but for a necklace of shells and stones, and a mask of feathers, with a curved, sharp beak, that covers the top half of his head.

'Hawk King,' thinks Bogboy. Waves of energy pour from the figure and through the mask his eyes glitter. Bogboy and Hawk King stare at one another in mutual recognition. And now Bogboy knows who he is and why he has come here.

'You came from mud and dust and stone. You were born of transgression, of blood and pain and betrayal. Ask only for truth and you will always know. This will be your protection. Trust this. We, your ancestors, are with you from time eternal to time complete.'

Hawk King hands Bogboy a pale shell from his necklace and vanishes. Bogboy is left feeling a profound absence where before there was absolute presence.

When he comes to, he's lying on a pile of rocks which are digging into the small of his back. Ned is pawing at him, licking at his face and whimpering. Bogboy splutters and pushes the dog away from him. The day has turned cold. The sun is already beginning its descent into the sea. There is no sign of the cave or of Hawk, but he is clutching a beautiful, ivory shell in his palm. Somehow, he appears to have lost nearly an entire day. He rises, brushes himself down, whistles for Ned and makes his way back to the cottage, feeling more awake, more fully alive than he ever has.

He chants the song of Hawk, the song of the ancestors:

I am wave that rises, falls
I am rock, steadfast, still
I am sun, fire father bright
I am earth's dark womb
I am river, flow of life
I am sky, abode of light
I am mountain, cloud-capped peak
I am forest, tree and leaf
I am lover, chosen one
I am daughter, I am son
I am spirit, love that moves
I am seer, to all belong

I am cry of deer at dusk
I am wolf that howls at moon
I am warrior, I am king
I am soul of everything.

Molly

Molly resented the arrival of Michael into their private world. Rose adored her younger brother. In her eyes, he could do no wrong. It was astonishing to Molly how easily Michael could charm his sister and distract her. He made Rose laugh, often at the expense of poor Joycie, who tried so hard to get it right, to be the respectable one, to make a good impression in the world and uphold the family name.

Michael had destroyed what was special in their friendship. It wasn't jealousy Molly felt, so much as perturbation. To point out his casual cruelties would leave her open to accusations of oversensitivity or envy. He could charm the world, but she kept him at a cordial but polite distance.

She remembers the last days of fun and frivolity like they were yesterday. They would take the little boat and row it out to the middle of the lake. In spring, the trout, normally fat and lazy, would rise to the surface to devour mayfly that swarmed in clouds as the warm weather returned. Rose liked to do the rowing.

'Relax, Moll, leave it to me.'

Molly luxuriated in the first sun of the year. But Michael had taken to inviting himself along on their little jaunts.

Two daughters had not been enough for the O'Briens. A son had to be sired. Family pride demanded it. Rose gave the impression of caring not a jot; Jocelyn, the eldest, found it more difficult to hide her displeasure.

Michael had already assumed the mantle of crown prince as his by right. So, when the shadow times came over all of them, they came imperceptibly at first then more and more quickly. Assured always of his mother's indulgence, whatever scrapes he might fall into, he was always too fondly absolved. And it was that blind spot that doomed the family fortunes. Michael had no sense of proportion and not a humble bone in his body. All his life, he got away with transgressions his sisters would never have been allowed. At fifteen, he already had a reputation with the village girls: enough to cause embarrassed giggles at his brazen approaches. It was rumoured he'd been responsible for more than one deflowering but with the insouciant good luck of a serial heartbreaker, no unfortunate consequences had transpired.

So, to Molly's secret displeasure, instead of Rose and Molly, those last few weeks before Rose headed off to Italy, it was, more often than not, Rose and Molly and Michael.

They'd taken the boat out, all three of them, making for the floating pontoon in the centre of the lake. Although it was still early summer, the day was unusually warm. It would be one of their last carefree times together.

Molly had been up early as usual, bringing the herd in for milking, and starting the laborious task of butter churning. The morning warmth had kept building and the weather felt like it might break at any moment. The two young women lay stretched out, while Michael cavorted, jumped off the platform, then went ducking and diving in and out of the reedy edge of the lake, before gliding like an eel beneath the water for what seemed like minutes on end, reappearing breathless and triumphant. They were all in high spirits. It was a day for innocent, playful fun which made Molly feel like a girl again. But, despite the unexpected heat, the dark-green depths of the lake remained icy.

Rose, chic in a fashionable, lime-green, one-piece bathing suit she had no intention of getting wet, lay lengthways across the boards. She stretched her long, slender limbs, getting in practice for the Italian sunshine to come.

'Lie here,' Rose said, patting the space beside her and Molly allowed herself to stretch out alongside her friend, succumbing to the pleasure of having nothing she needed to do for once.

'My mad kid brother,' laughed Rose, as Michael performed a series of splashy dives followed by self-congratulatory he-man poses especially for their benefit. 'You know he's taken up a Charles Atlas body-building course? He bought himself a set of weights. Boys are such idiots. They're vainer than any woman, don't you think?' and she laughed with indulgence at Michael's foolish antics.

'He has a lot of energy, that's for sure,' Molly replied.

'He'll grow out of it, sure what's a young fella to do out here anyway?'

'Maybe he when he gets a proper job, he'll grow up a bit,' suggested Molly, knowing she was treading on dangerous ground but unable to stop herself.

Rose glanced over at her. 'He will run the estate.'

'And... you don't mind?' said Molly.

Rose frowned. 'Mind? Why would I?'

'Well, y'know, him being the youngest and all.'

'Sooner him than me,' said Rose, turning on her side away from Molly. It was a gentle rebuff and Molly knew it.

But something in her persisted. 'What will you do?'

'Me?' Rose turned back on her elbow to face Molly, clearly

astonished at the question. There was a brief, awkward pause before she replied, 'I don't know. Get married. I might teach, I suppose. In some nice convent school for girls.'

But her voice betrayed her lack of concern as she rested in that particular luxury of having no idea what to do with her life, afforded to girls of her class.

Molly felt a twinge of disquiet. She'd presumed too much on their closeness. Rose was about to head off to Bologna to stay with an Italian family and Molly sensed that with this latest development, everything between them would change.

She would marry Paddy, but the world lay at Rose's feet. Already, she seemed more sophisticated and soon physical distance would add to the growing emotional distance.

Jocelyn had gone to Paris for a summer art school, had become engaged to a handsome foreign count and, almost at once, sent word that she was married and heading to the far East for a long honeymoon.

Michael, having lost his audience, clambered back up onto the pontoon, rocking it from side to side for a moment, spraying them both with water. Eventually, all three lay under the drowsy heat of the day, drifting off into a comfortable, afternoon siesta.

At first, she thought she was dreaming. Some warm, strange creature was crawling up her leg. In moments, she was wide awake, aware that a hand was making its way upwards, where no hand should, by rights, be going.

Out of the corner of her eye, she could see that Rose was still dozing, oblivious to the shocking liberty that her brother was taking. Molly wanted to call out, 'Stop', or smack his hand away, but she could hardly believe what was happening, and feared Rose would accuse her of making it up. Michael must have taken her lack of resistance as consent and his exploration continued until he reached the top of her thigh, squeezed her flesh and then, to her horror, laid his hand upon her, fingering roughly.

It was as if this violation was being visited on some other young woman. To her disgust and dismay, she understood that knowing full well she was already engaged to Paddy meant nothing to a boy like Michael. Paddy was a farm labourer, and therefore of no consequence whatsoever.

Michael had in him the lazy sense of entitlement of his breeding, made worse by his evident charm and good looks. He didn't like to be left out of anything that might serve his turn. Molly was a game. Anything that Rose took pleasure in, Michael considered his also, by way of misguided sibling rivalry. Molly thought of her beloved Paddy, steady and reliable, whose physical prowess came from working the land and not indulging himself idly on an estate that he would one day simply inherit.

The hand itself, now squeezing hard, seemed like an alien creature with a life of its own, and it was only when he began to finger beneath her knicker elastic that she had the courage to push him roughly away. He withdrew at once, jumped up as if nothing untoward had occurred and dived splashily back into the water, spraying both herself and Rose, who yelped with annoyance at being disturbed.

Jenks

The stars are emerging. Jenks remembers one magical evening when he had stood with his father, identifying constellations. It must have been December – the rest of the year Jenkins senior would have been far too busy at court to spare time between studying briefs to keep his son company. On this night, his father had pointed the stars out to him with the scrupulous exactitude of a lawyer and it had become a memory game, until finally they'd recited them together in a litany. 'Orion, Taurus, Gemini, Auriga, Canis Major, Canis Minor, Carina, Eridanus.'

Now he's still scouring the night sky, imagining the worlds that might lie beyond. What life might be clinging to the surface of other planetary systems? On nights like this, a calm steals over him: a blissful quietude that feels deeper than mere skin and bone. He could safely say he is almost content.

Except he can't help wondering where the boy has got to and is trying not to be alarmed that it is already getting dark. Part of their unspoken agreement is that he is free to wander at will. To attempt to harness or corral him would be to subject him to the exact same restraint and lack of trust he'd broken free from at the big house. There is no sign of Ned either, which is both concerning and, possibly, comforting.

He feels such responsibility for the boy, who is unlike any other boy – more an untamed colt. And the boy is beautiful – he finally admits it to himself. He has exotic, delicately drawn features. He has what the locals refer to as 'a bit of the Black Irish' in him: the looks that speak of ancestors from the south, Spain or Portugal. And those exquisite eyes. Although not usually superstitious, Jenks senses that there is something magical about him. The feeling of tender concern is mixed with something he has hardly dared admit to himself. He knows only too well the vagaries of his heart. He recognised the look the aunt had given him when they had stared one another out in the battle for possession. But Bogboy isn't a possession. There'd been something shrewd and calculating in that look: weighing him up, assessing his 'type'. He's seen that look, with varying degrees of hostility, all his life from women who had figured out, with a combination of chagrin and disappointment, that they would be finding no romantic favour with him. The aunt's look had been very different, though. Searching, yes, but also it had held within it an immense sadness. She was doing her best to hide a sorrow he could only guess at. And something else. Pity? For him? For her nephew? For herself?

And Jenks isn't the boy's father. What could he possibly be? Friend? Mentor? Something else? Was that what the aunt had understood? Why would she have condoned the possibility? He had been as shocked as anyone when she'd turned the care of Alfie over to him without a fight. She was a woman clearly used to getting her own way. Why had she allowed it? He felt there was a motive missing – something hadn't made sense – though he had had no intention of arguing.

Therefore, the responsibility now lies all the more heavily on him and this disappearance is out of the ordinary. Whatever Jenks feels, he has a duty of care to protect the boy. For the first time since the war, he finds himself staring out at infinite space and praying to a God he is unsure he even believes in, to keep a young friend safe. It hadn't worked out too well all those years ago but Bogboy isn't Kenny, and this isn't a war.

At that moment, he suddenly sees Bogboy appear over the brow of the dunes below, radiant and glowingly alive, haloed by the last gleam of twilight. He is making his way back up the path to the cottage and Jenks's heart sings at the beauty of this boy on the cusp of becoming a man, a beauty graced with his own inner fire, and made more poignant by his total lack of awareness. Jenks feels his bruised heart open with pained joy, and understands that there is nothing he wouldn't do to care for and watch over him.

If he had any doubts before about the true nature of that

friendship, he has no illusions now. It causes him a sharp, physical pain that is, somehow, both grief and joy at once. The boy, noticing him, stops and tentatively waves. Jenks returns the gesture and smiles a welcome home, and Bogboy's whole body relaxes. His face breaks into an involuntary, broad grin for the first time ever in Jenks's presence. Ned runs forward to be fussed over, and in a moment of perfect stillness, there passes between the younger and the older man a current of energy so absolute and complete it feels sanctified by heaven.

Almost in a trance, Bogboy allows himself to cross the final few yards between them and half-stumbles, half-falls into Jenks's open arms. His body quietly shudders. Jenks wraps his arms fiercely and protectively round the weeping boy's bird-like frame and holds him safe.

Mickey

He doesn't think too much about the past. He doesn't like to reflect. That's why America had suited him. It was a forward-looking country. Fellas on the go, on the make. And why not? Life is for living, not wallowing in self-pity. Still, it is hard not to be coming home with a stash. No pot of gold to flaunt in front of the old crowd. He glances across at Carolina. A fine-looking woman. Nobody could doubt he'd done well for himself in that department, at least. And if their luck holds and bejesus it has so far, well, who knows? There might still be a pot of gold at the end of the rainbow. He laughs at himself, sounding like a real old culchie now. It's as if the Yanks have erased any pretensions to class he might have once had. When you've been reduced to sharing cells and filthy latrines with killers and other motherfuckers, there is no more room for folderol and la-di-da. Mickey knows all too well what he is, what he has been.

They'd negotiated a ride with a lad in an empty potato van heading back out to Galway. They'd met him in a bar down by the Monto that Mickey remembered from back in the old days. Still stank of stale beer, still the same smoke-filled fog with the watery, Dublin light fighting a losing battle against the gloom. A side-street bar like a hundred others, peopled by small men with big dreams. Bullshitters the lot of them. All big talk. He's seen it everywhere in the world. Bar-room know-it-alls. Losers to a man.

They're crossing a bleak stretch of flat turf bogs. One old cottage with a roof caved in. Famine cottages and then the ones that got caught in the troubles back in '21. You see them everywhere. Eyesores left to rot in the landscape. An image springs unbidden and unwanted into his head. Another thatch in flames, an old man staggering out from the burning building. No. Don't. Don't look back. He shakes away the vision.

He must have moved too sharply; Carolina has roused herself at last. She's been mighty quiet since they drove out of the empty Dublin streets through the better suburbs and onto the country roads heading west. Pulling her big coat round her like a blanket. She'd checked herself in the side mirror before they set off. She called it 'fixing her face'.

If the young lad has any opinion about the two of them, he is keeping his thoughts to himself.

'Back to the old sod, is it? How long's it been? Ah, nothing much has changed.'

He asks questions about New York, tells them about his cousin, Seamus, doing well in the NYPD. Not a topic Mickey cares to pursue. His opinions of the boyos in that particular organisation don't bear repeating. They are on safer ground discussing the upcoming Cork-Kerry match. There was talk that the Cork Athletic Grounds were to be demolished. No way, said Mickey, thinking he'd been gone too long. Everything changes. And yet some things never change. Football had always been Mickey's game; he's never quite reconciled himself to the wonders of baseball.

Carolina is nudging him for a cigarette. He pulls out his pack of Lucky Strikes. That's the last of them. Shakes one out for her. She swipes it elegantly and he offers one to the driver, Danny. Danny boy. He really wants to guffaw at the absurdity. Virtually homeless, with barely more than the clothes on his back, riding shotgun in an old delivery van with one trunk stuck in the rear: all that's left to show for nearly twenty years away. Chewed up and spat out again back where he started. Still, it wouldn't do to get gloomy.

'How are you doing?'

'I am fine. I have a… crick… in my neck.' She smiles at him. Sometimes he's aware that English isn't her mother tongue. That she takes pleasure in finding the exact right word and placing it just so.

'Want me to rub it for you?'

'Sure.' She glances over at the driver who seems preoccupied with the twists and turns on the road.

He starts to clasp the back of her neck.

'Gently.'

He softens his touch.

'Mm. Better.'

Somehow, she brings out a desire to… not hurt her… but punish her somehow. As though their lovemaking might, at any moment, erupt into violence. It seems to be part of their mutual attraction, this love/hate game of theirs. She's like a cat, he thinks. Soft and pliable when she's getting what she wants – sure, you can rub her tummy all you want – but cross her and the claws and fangs come out. For now, though, they are both happy to use and be used. It's her ill-gotten gains they are living off. Mickey isn't proud – he's lived off women in the past. But in this case, Carolina will be expecting some return for her investment.

He hasn't been entirely straight with her – all she knows is that there was money in the family. Sure, he'd run out on things when it all got too complicated, but family is still family; that much he knows. And Joycie – rattling around a crumbling pile that's falling around her ears as like as not – can hardly complain. The house is probably a gigantic headache for her. They could sell it off, split the proceeds. It is a perfect setting for a retreat – better still, a seminary. Just the ticket if you needed a glorified prison. The church might take it off their hands. They are as rich as Croesus. Always on the look-out for a bargain. The trick is to persuade Joycie to offload it. She could move into a cottage in the village or a small house in town, and he'd look around for a little bar somewhere. There are worse ways to die of boredom; sure, he's had enough excitement for one lifetime.

'What are you thinking?'

Carolina is looking at him with that quizzical stare of hers.

'Nothing.'

'You're thinking maybe this is a mistake.'

'No.'

'Well?'

Women. She isn't going to let it go. 'I was thinking about what kind of thatch roof our bar should have.'

She stares at him, then chuckles, which sets off her smoker's cough. 'Liar.'

'What?'

'You're nervous. You're thinking, 'What if they don't want to see me after all this time?"

'Something like that.'

She squeezes his hand. 'Don't worry. You have me, remember? We're a team. When you've dealt with the things we have dealt with, you can deal with anything. All we're asking for is what's rightfully yours. They can't argue with that.'

'I guess so.'

'I know so. Now, what's a girl gotta do for a rest-stop round here?'

Molly

Molly's mother had always had a soft spot for old Louis, an Irish widower who lived in a ramshackle cottage up a bumpy, weather-beaten track. He'd lost his soulmate, Mary Kate, a few years earlier and both he and his smallholding had fallen into disrepair. Many's the time Molly's mother had sent her daughter up the track with a pot of potatoes or a bit of thick stew and the words, 'Take that up to the poor old soul.'

Molly would lug it up the path, knock at the shabby door, be rewarded with, 'Is it yourself? You'd best come in and welcome. A sight for sore eyes and no mistake,' from Louis and an excited scrabble about from his old Collie. She'd carefully hook the pot over the open turf fire and, while it heated up, it was understood that she'd stay to keep him company. They'd sit either side of the smoky fire and she'd listen, the half-blind dog contentedly curled at her feet, while Louis played a tune on his fiddle or told her tales from the olden days.

Over the years, as she got bigger and stronger, she'd even go out onto the bog in summer and help the old man turn his peats. Once over six feet tall, but now bent nearly double from a lifetime of slicing his turf cutter into the soft, moist bog, he could no longer manage alone. Molly would be on hand to carry a load the two miles or so back from his bank of turf to the little, stone cottage, like a willing beast of burden, and would then help him stack his winter fuel against the gable wall.

Louis shared with her the poteen he brewed in a small still, out back. 'Don't be telling your mammy now. It'll be our little secret.' Which was unlikely since the whole district knew about Louis' poteen. The best for miles around, it was said: a skill his family had passed down through the generations. And it was known he regularly dragged a little cart with a clay jug filled to the brim to the back door of the pub after dark: no questions asked. The regulars were partial to a shot or two of Louis' potent special brew. He put enough of it away himself of an evening to ease his broken heart, and on nights when he was particularly deep in his cups, Molly and her mother would hear him strike up his fiddle and a plaintive lament would waft across the still, evening air before melting along with the twilight.

A quiet man but with a black temper if roused, Louis hadn't an enemy in the world. Except one. And that was Michael, a restless teenager, beginning to throw his weight around and expecting deference from everyone in the neighbourhood. There had been an incident that became the talk for miles around. Louis had come upon Michael pilfering from his hoard of poteen, stored in a big oak cask in his lean-to. Michael had given it a good lash and was sprawled on the ground, well and truly intoxicated. Careless of the fact that Michael was his landlord-to-be, Louis grabbed him by the scruff, took up a switch from the wall and gave him a traditional Irish thrashing, which sobered the lad up in a trice. Michael ran to his mother, but for once got nothing but a sound scolding and a lecture on the perils of the demon drink that had brought his father to an early grave. Word soon got out in the neighbourhood that Michael had finally got the come-uppance he'd long deserved. And thus, a grudge was born.

Molly, up at the big house with Rose, had had front row seats to the whole drama. Louis was the hero of the hour, the entire community enjoying the great craic, and Michael was left looking more foolish than ever. From then on, Louis kept the old dog out in the yard to guard his precious liquid.

'They have the badness in them.' That was how Molly's mother described anyone who had the temerity to cross her. She had a strict hierarchy of good and bad behaviour, and woe betide anyone who fell below her exacting standards. Life for a farmer's wife was harsh and unforgiving enough and, in addition, she'd supplemented their meagre income with her duties at the big house. She'd taken to her bed in her forties, worn thin and frazzled to the bone, before departing the cares of the world for good, leaving all her responsibilities to her daughter.

As for Molly herself, she has been hearing the evils of the world railed about from the Sunday pulpit for as long as she can remember. The first time she'd heard the word fornication mentioned in the same breath as temptation and thundered down upon the congregation by God's messenger on high like Moses hurling the tablets from Sinai, she'd had to ask her friend, Niamh, what on earth it meant.

'It's what your mammy and daddy do together in the dark after the children have all gone to sleep,' was Niamh's knowing reply, which left Molly none the wiser. It had taken until the incident on the lake with Michael for Molly to finally understand the nature of 'badness' in relation to men.

Mickey

The memories are pouring in thick and fast now, as though a sluice gate has opened. They've hired a local driver, Dennis Gillespie, a one-time school friend and drinking buddy, now running an ad hoc taxi service, to take them on the last leg from Galway to Coolhooley village, and the encounter with whatever is to come. Jocelyn's message had been terse and to the point and had ended, 'So come if you must, there are things to discuss, but expect no *céad míle fáilte* under this roof while I'm still alive – make your own arrangements in the village.'

He'd screwed her letter up. He hadn't shown it to Carolina.

And yet. Here he is. Back where he started, back where he belongs, for better or worse.

Dennis is a prattler, happy enough to carry on a one-sided conversation like a local parish newsletter.

'You'll have heard about Kevin O'Malley? Do you remember young Bridie? And you recall Mrs Brannigan?' Almost every name is followed by 'Dead.' A litany of human disasters, recounted with relish. Carolina drinks it all in with her usual air of high amusement. Mickey wonders if there is anyone left alive at all in the old country. He feels increasingly uneasy.

His mind swings back to the memory he's done his best to quash down beneath all others. He'd been young and the old fella was a nuisance, a bad-tempered curmudgeon fit for nothing and nobody. All he'd meant to do was to teach the old man a lesson, give him a bit of a scare. One he wouldn't forget in a hurry.

Like everything else about him, Louis' thatched roof had been in a poor state of repair. Mickey had overheard Devlin, the thatcher, boast that Louis had promised him a year's supply of best poteen in return for replacing his roof. Apparently, Louis had a nice barrel put by for the job. Devlin was on his way to order up some good, strong, reed thatch. Tommy McNulty had joked that if Louis wanted to attract another woman into his bed, he'd be better off starting with his own appearance before worrying about the state of his roof. Devlin had protested, 'Don't be going putting me out of a job now,' and everybody had laughed. And that was what had put the idea into his head. A stupid, madcap scheme.

He'd stolen across to Louis' place the very next night. He knew the old man went to bed soon after dark. His Collie slept outside but was only half-alive at the best of times and no guard dog. He'd brought a bone from the house and waved it in the direction of the dog, who'd snatched at it and retreated to his spot in the lean-to shed to gnaw at his prize. The ladder by the gable wall where Louis had been building his peat stack lay handily at the ready. Michael had stolen round to the back of the cottage and found the still. And a jug. He'd still been smarting at the memory of the hiding he'd endured in this very spot and that had spurred him into action without another second's thought. The night was black and silent. Carefully balancing, he'd hauled himself, the jug and its contents up to the roof.

Seventy percent proof should burn nicely, he'd thought, and poured the contents liberally across the straw. There'd been a good long spell of dry weather so the roof would be tinder dry. He'd nodded with satisfaction, all the while congratulating himself on his cunning. He'd lit a match and tossed it into the straw and followed it with a couple more, to ensure it caught properly. After a few seconds, it had started to smoulder nicely and he'd descended to watch the fun from a distance.

There'd only been a very slight breeze but by chance a sudden gust blew through the surrounding trees and caught the smouldering flame which now reared up. Michael had stood in the shadow of the trees, hoping to enjoy a prime view of his enemy forced from his bed to deal with the pandemonium. Well, old Louis had wanted a new thatch, so this was really doing him a favour, speeding up the process. As Michael stood fascinated by the dance of fire and flame against the night sky, there'd been an almighty crash, fit to wake the dead, and a rotten timber joist had collapsed inward, bringing a substantial part of the roof down.

Surely the old bastard must have heard that? Surely he'll come roaring out of the cottage at any second? he'd thought, with just a touch of exasperation. But no-one had appeared at the kitchen door and the dog, aroused by the smell of burning thatch and timber and the searing heat, started racing around the yard in crazed circles and barking wildly.

He can't be there, Michael had thought. He suffered a pang of disappointment that his nemesis was not there to witness the destruction of his property. Then a guttural howl had rent the night. A wizened, blackened, barely human shape, consumed by flames, had suddenly appeared at the door, clawing at the air, marching back and forward like a wound-up mechanical toy soldier, before finally winding down, and toppling over.

The last of what had been the thatched roof had caved in, demolishing whatever remained of the home of the feeble, juddering creature on the ground before him. And then there'd been another high-pitched scream, but from the opposite direction, and he'd swung round to catch sight of Molly, running, rushing across to beat at the clothes on the old man's back, to douse the flames, before cradling the fallen figure in her arms. Then, catching sight of Michael, the look on her face was pure and utter horror.

Molly

She would never forget the shock of looking up to see Michael. He was frozen to the spot, staring at the fire, his whole body tensed and radiating excitement like a tomcat that had just trapped a mouse. It was almost as if he was willing the carnage on.

'Michael, for the love of God, help.'

'What?'

The old sheepdog was howling, pawing desperately at the body of his master and she hesitated to push him away – his world too was going up in flames – while Louis was now being wracked in a series of agonised convulsions. A thick spittle frothed at the corners of his mouth. The old man's anguished eyes stared up at her.

Her voice hardened. 'Michael, in God's name, go now and fetch help.'

'Sure, what's the use? He's a goner.' He made no attempt to keep the callousness out of his voice as he moved to stand directly behind her. A chill went down her spine. She was only too aware of the threat in his stance. Despite his relative youth, he was already burly. The dog gave a low growl, a last, futile attempt to be the guard dog he was meant to be.

'Michael, did you… .?'

'What?' He defied her to say it, to complete the sentence. 'I was just out and about and heard the explosion. These old fellas' – and once again there was contempt in his voice – 'messing about in the back of beyond with the old fire water, sure, what do you expect? They've only themselves to blame if it all goes wrong.'

She knew the lie for what it was.

'You will go to prison for this.'

'Really? You saw nothing. It's your word against mine, Molly. Who do you think they'll believe?'

He was right, she could never prove it. Thatches caught fire and stills blew up all the time.

It was true that Louis wouldn't make it through to morning but there were still decencies to observe over the body and, with a final effort, she hissed, 'Go! Get help!' with a fierceness she had never known was in her. Without another word of argument, he vanished back down the path to fetch whomever he could find, and concoct whatever cock-and-bull story he imagined would serve his turn.

And now she was alone with the man who'd been like a grandfather to her throughout her childhood. The fire still raged, greedily consuming everything in its path. His home would be nothing but a smoking, burnt-out shell by morning. Nothing left of a lifetime.

A sickly, sweet smell like charred meat rose from him, and when she looked down at his face, scorched bright red, she couldn't contain herself and, to her shame, vomited violently to the side, bent double with the effort and desperately trying to avoid splashing him. She prayed over him with the old words that were instinctive, and, finally, she wept, partly in grief and partly in shame and frustration that she could find no more adequate means to ease his departing soul on its final journey. She cradled his body while she crooned, in between sobs, the words to *Roisin Dubh*, her heart and voice breaking with the effort. It had been one of the first songs he'd ever sung to her. She kept going, her voice tremulously threading through the night air, clearing the path for him to depart his earthly existence. When she next looked down, his body had stilled and she saw that it was done.

She looked up to the heavens, and understood that, just as there was real goodness in the world, so, also, there were acts of pure evil and that she had been witness to one that very night.

Mickey

It had just been a bit of a prank. All he'd ever meant to do was teach the old fool a lesson. How was he to know that he would be drunk as a lord and dead to the world? Old people should know better.

And, anyway, what kind of life must it have been, rotting away in the back of beyond, his woman gone, drowning his sorrows in drink? In a way, death had been a kind of mercy for him. Nobody could blame Mickey for it. He'd been young and foolish, no more than a boy, really. Even sailing the seven seas hadn't erased the memory of an old man in flames. It was no way to meet your maker, Mickey had to admit. Well, he'd paid the price, that was for sure. Life, that sour old bitch, had found a hundred ways to make him pay, and the cell block at Rikers had been far from the worst of it.

There'd been a huge turnout for Louis' funeral, he remembers; the entire community had wanted to pay their respects. The old man had been well-liked, it seemed – but those same people had more or less ignored him or made fun of him while he'd been alive. Hypocrites. The world was full of them.

And Molly. When had she earned the right to judge him,

look down on him, as much as to say, 'Call yourself a man, you're nothing but a cowardly boy!'? And she's still here, never moved so much as a mile away, now running the show, by all accounts.

He says the last out loud and Carolina asks sharply, 'What did you say?'

'Nothing. Nothing. Just thinking about the past.'

'I tell you it will all be fine. You'll see. Strange,' she adds. 'This place reminds me of my childhood in Jutland. The same' – she struggles for the right word – 'wildness.' But this doesn't seem to satisfy her. 'No. More than that. You can really feel it. A kind of sadness in the land, like it's seen too much sorrow and tragedy.' She gives him a searching glance and grasps his hand. 'And you, you stop brooding. There's enough of that out there. Remember. You're only here to claim what's yours. You have your rights.'

But does he? As the familiar landscape of moor and bog emerges, his whirl of emotions intensifies. Carolina is right, he has to stop brooding. He needs to keep his wits about him, get the lie of the land before he makes any kind of move. And there is the matter of Rose's boy, his nephew. The lad must be about the same age now that Mickey had been back then. Might he be an ally? Would he be happy to see his uncle? Maybe they could be friends. Anything is possible. That might depend on how much he knows about the past. What stories or lies has he been told?

One thing is for certain, two women wait for him up ahead, both of them ready and with good reason to thwart him: Jocelyn, implacable as ever, still blaming him for ruining her life. Well, she'd managed that all by herself. And Molly, interfering busybody.

So, to claim his rightful inheritance won't be easy; it is going to take a fight, he can see that. Well, so be it. Fighting is something he knows a bit about, and he can fight dirty if necessary. He'd been deprived of his dues way back; now it's time for him to redress the balance. He looks across at Carolina, drinking in all the surroundings as Dennis Gillespie's old jalopy jounces along a road that resembles nothing much more than a stony track. New York seems a long way away right now. He is back in this dung heap to claim his future. It has been a long time coming.

Bogboy

The first time he'd come upon a herd of Connemara ponies they had fled before he could get near them. This time, he comes better prepared and, after spending hours watching them quietly graze, he makes his move, proffering his gift. The leader of the herd, a chestnut-brown male, bolder and more confident – or more curious – than the others, comes forward to investigate. Bogboy holds out an apple, and the little creature loses no time in snaffling it. In seconds, the entire herd is surrounding him, eager for a similar treat. They are alert to his every move, closing in, jostling him, but he feels no threat from them. He is taken aback at first, then relaxes in the fierce pack energy they exude.

That night, Hawk King appears to him in a dream, riding out of the mist on a small but sturdy grey horse. He is naked, helmeted, and wearing an embroidered, leather scabbard with an elaborate, bronze-handled sword. Behind him rides a troop of equally fierce-looking warriors, also armed. 'The ancestors,' thinks Bogboy. They are riding across a flat, dry plain. Their faces are pricked and scarred and painted with indigo. The whites of their eyes glitter. Bogboy hears a deep, drumming noise and then the warriors let out blood-curdling cries that build in intensity and are carried by the breeze into the far distance, to the other side of the plain where an enemy army has assembled.

Hawk King stares straight at Bogboy and says, 'Join us.'

Bogboy wakens.

Something has been aroused in him that reaches back across time. The journey is deepening. Now, wherever he walks, he feels the shadows of the ancestors dancing alongside him, like those of scudding, summer clouds. He knows that, come what may, he has a warrior army at his back. And Jenks is there too, a quiet presence that helps still his uneasy thoughts. Sometimes, when the bad dreams return, he finds his way to Jenks's room and climbs into bed beside him. The first time it happened, it was almost as if he were in a trance. But Jenks was completely unfazed. He simply pulled the blankets aside and created room, and Bogboy clambered in and nested himself comfortably in the big man's arms until his panic subsided and he could drift back into a dreamless sleep. He loves the security of Jenks's presence. Simply being held. As though he were Hawk, allowing himself to be tamed. But, like Hawk, only as far as he himself permits. Once he feels safe again, Bogboy slips away as stealthily as he arrives, to reassert his independence, and returns to his own bed.

Jenks

One day, Bogboy arrives back at the cottage with a flat slab of limestone which he must have hauled up from the beach single-handedly. Under Jenks's half-amused, half-astonished gaze, he begins, almost defiantly, to assemble a shrine for the treasures he brings back from his walks. It takes up a sizeable corner of the small room. Jenks quietly observes, moved by the work and touched by the way Bogboy has taken ownership of his space.

He watches, fascinated, as the boy constructs his pagan altar of found objects: bits of fossil stone, coloured glass, eggshell, mosses, a sliver of bog oak, bleached bone. He places the big, pale-grey slab on a couple of sturdy, upright stones and the whole structure resembles an ancient stone dolmen. Jenks recognises also that it is an act of trust on Bogboy's part. That he is sharing a part of his world. And he notes, wryly, that it certainly makes a change from photos of the pontiff and gilt-framed pictures of the sacred heart of Jesus, lit by votive candles, which the locals all proudly display.

Jenks has a donkey and trap to get about in and for hauling modest supplies, but when Bogboy leads him up to meet the wild ponies, he has already decided it is time to invest in something better. The annual horse fair takes place in a couple of days; a bargain can be struck with spit and a handshake if you keep your wits and know what you are about.

Over an early breakfast, before Bogboy heads out on one of his wanderings from which he nearly always returns with some new addition to his shrine, Jenks casually asks, 'Want to help me buy a horse? It's about time we had one, don't you think?'

He is aware of the plural in the question. They have now started to take companionable walks together from time to time, each adapting, in their different ways, to the moods and rhythms of the other. Out in the open, where Bogboy clearly feels most at home, Jenks learns to read the youngster's changes of weather with the accuracy of a good barometer. There is something entrancing about the way he can shift from bright-eyed boy with eyes like a wide-open sky, to the dark storm clouds of an adolescent and, in an instant, transform again into a wise, old soul trapped in a young man's body. In truth, Jenks loves all Bogboy's quixotic moods and expressions, and the way, every so often, he will scour the sky with a look of longing, which Jenks assumes has to do with the affinity and otherworldly connection he seems to possess for the local birds of prey, and how he lights up with joy if one is circling overhead.

Bogboy's eyes shine at the prospect of the horse fair and he offers Jenks one of his sudden smiles, then indicates with a rapid display of their rough-and-ready sign language that he would be glad of company if Jenks cares to join him on his walk. Which is how they have ended up out here beyond the sky road, watching a herd of ponies in the distance.

It is a wilderness of gorse, bracken, blackthorn, crab apple and low shrub, with a few signs of what must have once been human habitation. Segments of broken wall that once marked field boundaries are now overgrown with mosses and lichen. Here and there, they come across a last remnant of gable end with a suggestion of rotted thatch: the ghost of a community lost to famine and emigration. It seems to Jenks that an air of deep melancholy hangs over the landscape, not helped by the overcast day and the damp in the air. None of this bothers the ponies contentedly grazing.

Today, the high-spirited boy is present, clearly in his element and unaffected by any thoughts of gloom. He suddenly lets forth a series of piercing, high-pitched whistles in the direction of the ponies, whose ears visibly prick. They are skittish and wary at first, but, as he approaches, they meet him without fear. He produces a handful of small apples from the little hessian rucksack he always carries; they come closer, sniff out his gifts and greedily eat out of his hand. He giggles as they nip at him. At that moment, the sun appears from behind thick cloud and gilds the entire scene in a golden glow and Jenks is reminded of a painting of the transfiguration of St Francis by Bellini, the face of the saint bathed in a holy ecstasy.

Now the ponies are nudging at Bogboy as he playfully dances about them, teasing them in a game of catch-me-if-you-can. One forward beast, a cheeky male, almost tumbles him to the earth. Instead, Bogboy produces one more apple which the pony snatches hungrily from his hand. He turns to Jenks and yells, 'See?' in triumph.

It is the first word Jenks has heard Bogboy utter since he brought him down from the mountain, and he answers quietly, 'I see.'

They hold each other's gaze for just an instant until, in the uneasy eloquence of the silence that follows, Bogboy turns away and begins to stroke the nose of the chestnut pony.

Tante

The ghosts around her bed are getting louder. Sometimes she wakes in the middle of the night and hears them chattering, as if they are at some dreadful celestial cocktail party and ignoring her, the hostess, completely. Rose is there, of course. Their long-suffering mother is there, frowning and casting disapproving glances at their father, who's already two sheets to the wind. And there's Alphonse with his pungent, French cigarettes, wafting the smoke away from her but then coughing and spluttering down into her face. Paddy, his head bloodied purple, and old Louis, nothing but a horrifying, charred mess. She wants to scream at the lot of them.

They're all long dead now, and she's next. She smells of death.

Her entire world has turned grey. It had started with her hair. Her best feature; Alphonse called it her *coroa de ouro*. Her crown of gold. And she had been a *princesa*. Now, she feels the lassitude of her days, shuttered in her room always in the dark since she can no longer bear the light on her eyes or the sun on her skin. Her nerves are shattered and jangled. Her voice, a whisper, has lost all its animation.

She'd woken in the small hours with the taste of strawberries on her lips. An intense memory. She had loved them as a child. Strawberries, fresh and ripe, the season's first and best taste of summer. Biddy would buy them at the local market. Big, juicy, fragrant Wexford strawberries from the back of a van. She had loved them until the day she had broken the cut-glass, fruit bowl. Rose was four and she was eight or nine. They had been playing on the lawn, barefoot on the grass, and had run into the dining room, just as the lunch gong had sounded. It was Rose who had spotted the strawberries first and yelled, excitedly, 'I want one.' There they were on the high sideboard, ready to be served as an after-lunch treat: a luscious, gleaming mound of fruit piled up in the Waterford crystal bowl, with a jug of thick yellow cream set beside them.

'We can't have them before lunch,' she'd replied, with sisterly good sense.

'I want one!' Ignoring Joycie, Rose had dashed to help herself but couldn't quite reach and had pulled the bowl too close to the edge. Joycie had called, 'Rose, don't! Let me.' As she'd stretched up to grasp one for each of them, she herself had tilted the bowl too far. It shattered onto the parquet floor, cascading strawberries all across the lovely red, cream and gold Persian rug. Shards of crystal, like diamonds in the sun, went everywhere. She had stepped backwards onto a sliver of glass which had pierced her heel. A bolt of pain had shot through her body. Her blood had welled up, mixing with the strawberries she was treading further into the rug. Even though she was both faint and nauseous, the look of alarm, then fury, on her mother's face, was unmistakeable. 'Don't move,' she commanded. 'Stay still. For goodness' sake, what on earth just happened here?'

Rose had pointed at her. 'It was Joycie. She did it.'

The tears poured down Jocelyn's face as she howled with pain and the sense of injustice.

'That's enough of that,' her mother snapped. 'Look at the state of the carpet.'

She had been lifted up roughly and bundled off to have her wound cleaned with iodine by Biddy. Afterwards, she'd been sent to her room alone for the rest of the day, 'to learn her lesson'.

The beautiful cream and red rug was stained ever after, like a constant reproach.

It was Rose's first betrayal and the first great shattering of Jocelyn's life. She had hated strawberries from that day forward and wouldn't have them in the house, not so much as a jar of strawberry jam.

'So, this is the end,' she thinks now. 'I was here. I existed. For what? I knew so little about life. I never really knew love. Who will ever remember me? Was this my life? This desiccated, dried-up husk of a thing?'

She had hardly scratched the surface of living. After the first betrayal, the line was only ever going one way.

She had a sudden memory of her first visit to Paris in the summer of '47, a summer of art galleries and Gauloises in the aftermath of the war. She had sat, transported, in front of a gargantuan canvas of Monet's water lilies. Time had ceased to exist. She was no longer observing but being. She was the lily pond, she was the paint strokes, each one a suggestion of a lily pad, her entire being had become suffused in the great painter's vision. People had come and gone around her until the gallery attendant had come at last to announce, apologetically, that they were closing for the day.

Why had she not pursued her creative dreams? She knew why. She'd been thwarted. Betrayed. Forced to be the dutiful one. Responsible for holding the remnants of the estate together. She'd been a martyr to her own bitter fate. And what about the boy? The wild, untameable spirit she had done her best to stifle? She must change that. Make sure that he would never run from his destiny, his dreams. She understood that now. Unlike her, he would claim: 'I came here and I existed and here's the proof.'

Her life is reduced to an old bedroom, lined with faded photographs. So often, I wanted to die, but more than that, I wanted to live, she thinks. Despite the pain. Despite the betrayals and the lies. She's startled at the simple, obvious truth of it. She had wanted to die for so long, and now that she is being granted her wish, she realises that actually she had wanted so much more to live.

Why had she settled for darkness and shadow? Why had she not flung open the shutters wide and flooded the house with light, like Alphonse had done in his Paris apartment on the afternoon of their impetuous marriage? There they had first made love. He had been so ardent and hungry, almost ridiculously so – she had held him off for weeks – and she had laughed at his passion as a way of covering her nervousness. He hadn't even been able to wait for bed. They'd rolled across the floor and she'd given herself to him, surrendering herself in dust and pain and a little spillage of blood.

Alphonse. Always too fast, always running. Running away or running towards. Perhaps both. Always eager for more. 'Greedy boy,' she'd whispered in his ear as he excitedly pounded at her, and then, 'You're too fast.' But speed was all he knew. It was the way he consumed life, the way he gulped down food, raced his beloved sports cars, strode through the days in search of the next experience. He was already too far gone in his own pleasure to care, fiercely kissing her lips.

He had roiled up her dress around her waist, snapped her stocking suspenders with practised ease, roughly torn down her satin panties and, in one powerful move, pulled her onto him and pressed himself deep inside her, piercing her violently. It had been excruciating, as though she had been both inside and outside her body. His gasped release announced that it was over. Then he had held her, and his kisses were soft and tender as if he had had to detonate a bomb inside him before he could be at peace enough to acknowledge the presence of another.

It's getting harder to stay in the light. Is he there? Will she meet him and Rose on the other side? What will she say to them, if so?

'I never knew why you betrayed me. I never knew I could feel such bitterness and rage. I never knew why we threw it all away. I never knew how jealous I could be. I never knew how lonely I would feel. I never knew how much I resented your beauty. I never knew how clever and cold and manipulative and self-serving you both were. I never knew how stupid and inadequate and outmanoeuvred I would feel. I never knew how much I wanted to hurt you both. I never knew how cruel and ironic life could be until I was left alone to bring up your son.'

And now Michael and his paramour are come to make mischief.

Bogboy

He's never seen anything like the fair. It is as if an entire city has appeared overnight in the middle of the countryside. His heart quickens. Everywhere he looks, there are horses of every shape, shade and size. He is barraged by noise, by colour, riot and throng; music on accordion, tin whistle and fiddle from various directions; an underlying rhythm of the tinsmith's hammer and the incessant cries of hawkers and traders. There are stalls selling everything from leather harnesses and saddles to porter cake and bottled beer. In one corner, blacksmiths are shoeing horses. But the most fascinating sight is afforded by the travellers. They have set up their caravans in a circle round the edges of the great field. Everywhere he looks there are traveller children, some coppery and others dark-haired and black-eyed. They exude a fierce, wild energy. He catches the eye of one of the lads riding past him on a huge, piebald mare and as the rider stares down at him, he feels a surge of electricity. The boy has a shock of black hair not unlike a horse's mane. Something about his pride bordering on arrogance and even contempt stirs up a deep response in Bogboy. The rider is like a young Hawk King come to life, and Bogboy is transfixed. He imagines leaping up behind him, holding him tight while they ride away into the distance together to set up their own special encampment beneath the stars. When he looks again, horse and rider have vanished into the crowd and Bogboy feels the residual trace of longing in his stomach, like a hunger he cannot put a name to.

Jenks smiles across at him. 'Why don't you go and have a look around? I can see you want to. Don't worry, it's still early. You won't miss much. Come and join me in a while, the serious trading hasn't really begun yet.'

It is true that the first horses are only now being brought into the field, led or ridden by traveller lads, most of them about Bogboy's age or younger and often wearing nothing but rough hessian pants, revealing taut, muscular bodies and nutmeg brown skin. But he keeps returning in his mind's eye to the first boy who had captured his attention, with those mysterious, dark, glittering eyes.

He takes off to wander the great, open field. A hurdy-gurdy man has placed a hat at his feet for passers-by to throw in coins while, nearby, a fiddler and accordionist are playing with a mixture of skill and abandon. Out of the corner of his eye, he spots a grizzled, old man, with skin like teak, helping a much younger man execute a series of impressive back flips and somersaults. The latter leaps and swivels in the air before landing perfectly each time with a flourish. Noticing Bogboy, he bows ostentatiously.

It is a rough, jangling and exuberantly alive world. He needs a moment to compose himself, and heads away from the throng towards the edge of the field. It is as if he is seeing everything in vivid colour, in contrast to the reality he has known for far too long. He loves the landscape of the bog, and has grown to appreciate the shore, but here everything is in high relief, larger than life, or at least the life he is used to. Jenks's kindly world seems tame in comparison to this wild drama.

He passes a brightly painted caravan set amongst a circle of other wagons, and is embarrassed to see a young woman suckling a tiny baby. He looks away but she calls out something to him, in neither English nor Gaelic, and when he turns back, she is smiling. He hurries off, even more embarrassed as her scornful laughter follows him. He is so used to solitude and his own private universe that this crowded, vulgar, all-too-human world leaves him reeling. He is almost on top of the large brown-and-white piebald mare with the handsome, bare-chested figure astride her before he stumbles to an ungainly halt. Again, their eyes meet. And hold. The young rider looks down at him with an unmistakable curiosity, as though weighing something up.

He nods, wheels his mount around efficiently and makes for a small caravan at the edge of the clearing. He turns around to see Bogboy's hesitation and tilts his head in a clear invitation. As if in a dream, Bogboy follows him to whatever fate has in store for him. He has no fear of being attacked, even though they are now headed away from the crowd. All he knows is that something new and extraordinary is about to happen

The boy stops near a caravan painted a blue that reminds Bogboy of starlings' eggs. The decorative, carved, wooden trim all around is primrose yellow. The rims of the big wheels are painted bright red and the spokes are a cheerful, apple-green., like the curved, narrow door. The older boy dismounts in one elegant leap. Bogboy comes forward and places his hand on the horse's muzzle. The horse calmly receives his touch. The older boy places his hand over Bogboy's and says, in a surprisingly deep voice, 'Don't be nervous. She'll like it more if you're firm with her.'

'This is Lily,' he continues. 'She likes you. She doesn't like everyone,' said the boy. 'I'm Shay – it means 'gift,' and he grins to reveal dazzling, white teeth with one gold front tooth that matches the small earrings that glitter in his ears.

Bogboy knows he is expected to say something and, half-reluctantly, replies, 'Alf. It's short for Alphonse. But everyone just calls me Bogboy.'

'Hmm. I prefer Alphonse. Alphonse, come.' He jumps up the

steps, lifts a decorated curtain and disappears abruptly through the frosted glass doorway. Bogboy knows he is expected to follow. His mouth is dry and his heart pounds in his ears. It feels like a turning-point: a decision that will change the way he will see himself and which will alter the course of his life forever. The moment of decision and hesitation seems to stretch out endlessly.

Beside him, the horse is contentedly cropping grass, clouds are scudding above swaying treetops; nearby he can hear the wood-pigeons' call and the clatter of their wings and, in the distance, the sounds of the fair meld into one low roar, carried to this peaceful spot on the breeze. He climbs the steps and follows his new-found friend into the caravan.

The interior is astonishing. A lavishly painted ceiling of gold flowers, strung with jewelled beads and pearls, including a mother-of-pearl rosary, is the first thing to draw his gaze. A small skylight bathes the whole interior in a diffused, amber glow that accentuates the golden panelled walls, the small, black stove and a number of intricately carved wooden cupboards. There is a woven rug with elaborate tassels. Another inbuilt dresser is stacked with plates and cups. Bogboy cannot help but think of the huge and austere mansion he has called home, and the simple cottage he shares with Jenks, and envies the life this exotic world reveals. At the end of the wagon hangs a series of ornate mirrors, large and small, in which Bogboy sees himself or, rather, several Bogboys, reflected. Shay has leaped up onto a narrow bunk bed, beneath which is a set of carved drawers. He sits enthroned atop the whole arrangement on a thick quilt, with large embroidered pillows piled either end.

'Welcome to my vardo, Monsieur Alphonse.' He pats the bed beside him and beckons Bogboy towards him with open arms, like a snake charmer.

'Don't worry, pretty little Monsieur Alphonse, Shay will take care of everything.'

There is a smoky, perfumed smell. Bogboy's head swims and he knows that he wants nothing more in the world right now than to be enveloped in the muscular, tattooed arms being held out to him.

He approaches Shay. Shay the gift. Before he knows it, he is being pulled up and held so tightly he can barely breathe. It feels like coming home.

And now he's Hawk: and the other is not other but Hawk too. He's flesh and no flesh. Separate and whole. Neither male nor female but driven by a deep urge to devour and be devoured. To dive into the lake which is the absolute surrender of self to the other. The mirror self. A union of opposites. It's a coming together and a battle of wills. Power and tenderness. Need and strength both. Conjoined and apart. Each moment is first and last. An explosion of light and flame through every cell. Thunder crack and lightning bolt and earth tremor and sea swell. He can no longer tell where he ends and Shay begins. The spasms of ecstasy engulf him like rolling waves until he's falling, falling, falling, breathless, into an abyss both miraculous and terrifying.

He's startled out of his trance to discover his ear is being nibbled. Gentle nips on the soft lobes, getting harder. 'Ow!' he protests and Shay just laughs.

'Where did you go, my pretty Alphonse? I thought you'd died for a minute...'

He can't explain where. When he opens his eyes, he's staring up into the mischievous, grinning face of his lover.

'You're a deep one, my pretty Alphonse.' He pauses and adds, 'You haven't been with a boy before?'

Bogboy hesitates. He can feel and hear Joseph whisper in his ear, 'Say nothing,' and he shakes his head.

'So, first time, eh? I'm honoured. My lucky day, then. Turns out you're my gift. You're a natural. You fuck like a wild, pavee boy.' The word lingers in the air between them and Shay pulls him up from where he's been lying underneath him. They sit face to face now, their bodies covered in fresh sweat and their stomachs sticky and beginning to dry. He doesn't remember tearing off his clothes, or being stripped bare, which is both alarming and oddly exciting. The entire mechanics of their pleasure elude him altogether.

He's too shy to ask how much time has passed but Shay answers his unspoken thought. 'I have to go soon. We've been here an hour. I don't normally have so much fun. I'm supposed to be helping with our horses.'

'We're looking for a horse.'

'We?'

'My... friend is.'

'It's good to have a friend.' For a moment, he hears the sadness in Shay's voice. 'We have to find our pleasure where we can.' He leans in and they share a long kiss, both deep and tender. Bogboy almost swoons again. But Shay interrupts his pleasure. He's discovered the scars all the way up and down Bogboy's back.

'What happened to you? Was it your friend?'

'No. No. He's not... no. I... can't say.'

'I understand.' And for a moment, Bogboy feels sure that his new companion does understand. Shay looks serious.

'We all have secrets. This' – he indicates the both of them – 'is impossible. Never happened. Best say nothing. Understand? It's never safe for our kind.'

Our kind? There's so much he wants to ask but he just nods.

'I'm not supposed to talk to you, let alone bed with you. Even so, first time calls for a celebration.' And Shay pulls a couple of engraved tumblers from the shelf and a glass-stoppered jug with a pale amber liquid, and pours out a measure in each. Bogboy accepts the offered glass.

'To the wandering tribe of boys who like only boys,' declaims Shay, downs his and refills it and holds it up to Bogboy, who takes it and sips. It's hot on his tongue, so he follows Shay's example, and almost chokes. It's like swallowing fire.

Shay laughs. 'Don't worry. A few more and we'll make an honorary pavee of you yet. You have the blood. I can tell. So, you're looking for a horse? I might be able to help you.'

He kisses Bogboy again, playfully. 'All part of the service. Clean up. Get dressed. Time to do business.' He throws a towel at Bogboy who dabs at the sticky trail on his stomach.

Suddenly, there's a loud banging on the door and an angry voice calling in the strange dialect he heard before. Shay mouths, 'Fuck fuck fuck,' under his breath and pushes him roughly into the tight space at the back of the top bunk. 'Quiet. Say nothing. Don't move until I tell you.' He shoves Bogboy's clothes hurriedly into the gap beside him. Say nothing. Say nothing.

Shay is at the door, trying to placate the caller. Say nothing. Say nothing, says the voice in Bogboy's head and it seems like the voices of everyone he's ever known are saying it. An angry, accusing mob chorus. And so Bogboy hides, and says nothing.

Jenks

Where the hell is Bogboy? Jenks had realised from the very beginning that the only way to keep the boy close is to leave him free to roam at will. Any attempt to cage him and he would break free of the jesses that restrained him like a semi-trained hawk. For he is, and always will be, a wilful creature, a wild bird at heart. Only if he feels truly free will he willingly return to the sanctuary of the roost.

Jenks doesn't for a moment believe the superstitious tales of vengeful gypsies and thieving tinkers abducting fair-haired children or substituting changeling babies in cribs like the fairy folk of old. Nevertheless, he cannot entirely quell his current sense of unease. Not that he is unduly suspicious of the surroundings, but it doesn't do to be unwary. There are light fingers everywhere at a gypsy horse fair. It is human nature after all.

Why hasn't Bogboy returned to check out the horses? He must have become engrossed somewhere else, but this thought doesn't entirely reassure Jenks either. It is hard to stay focused on the task in hand while he feels this niggling worry. The boy wouldn't get himself into a fight, surely?

Jenks forces his attention back to his reason for being here. The purchase of a horse. He has a wad of notes, secret and secure, tightly rolled up in a rubber band. He been looking forward to sharing this game of horse trading with Bogboy, but he decides to put his concerns to one side and concentrate on the creatures being paraded. Alongside him, in small groups, are keen-eyed, local farmers, many of whom are jotting down details in little notepads, nodding to each other and sharing sidelong comments on horses they either have their eye on or, possibly, have their doubts about.

Jenks recognises one or two: Hennessy, a bluff loudmouth of a man, who prides himself on having some of the best tillage in the neighbourhood; beside him, ferret-faced O'Donoghue, famous for his short temper and deep pockets. 'Sure, he's a fella who'd argue the toss with his own shadow, given half the chance,' one of his neighbours once observed, watching him beat a hasty retreat from the bar just as his round was coming into view. Jenks had managed to get on the wrong side of him mostly by virtue of being an Englishman. But both have now spotted him and send cursory nods in his direction. The whole business is a well-worn ritual of buyers and sellers and there are no better men at it than these farmers, excepting, of course, the travellers themselves. It definitely isn't an arena for the foolish or uninitiated.

Most of the horses are a tough, hard-working, cob breed much favoured by the travellers: lively but generally good-natured, bred for hard work. They have clearly been lovingly brushed and washed down, although they'd need checking by a good vet and probably worming. Most look strong at least: firm, high haunches and sturdy legs. Jenks has a sixth sense when it comes to reading a horse's character. To know one's way around the upkeep of dogs and horses is a basic requirement of being brought up a gentleman. If any of the travellers thought they could see him coming, they would be in for a surprise. But he'd wanted to share this experience. No. He'd wanted to be able to show off and he wonders why he feels this need to impress the boy. So, there is disappointment and irritation mixed with his anxiety. This was to be his gift to Bogboy, whose vanishing has taken the shine off the whole day.

A rough-looking, handsome young man catches his eye. He is loosely holding the reins of a placid, chestnut-piebald mare who stands patiently. Beside them is a lad of about Bogboy's age with a sharp, lively face. The younger one saunters up to Jenks.

'Is it looking for a good horse you were, mister?'

Jenks smiles at the directness and agrees to play along – 'I might be at that' – and the young man takes his cue and launches into his well-practised sales patter.

'Well, you came to the right place. We have just what you're looking for. Come. Come. I'm Shay. That's Lily. Not him – he's my brother, Billy,' and they all laugh, although Jenks notes the laughter doesn't extend to the eyes of the older brother, despite his show of bright teeth.

'I'm Jenkins, pleased to meet you.'

'English, are you?' This was Billy.

'Yes, I'm afraid so,' he replies. But he is met with a respectful nod.

'You'll be knowing a good horse when you see one. Lily here will see you right.'

Jenks examines her.

'She's been like one of the family. We'll be sorry to lose her.'

They haven't lied. She is well-proportioned, strong and well-muscled; her rear legs have the proper angulation for a good pulling horse, the front legs are clean and flat in joints and bone, and all four legs have healthy feathering, plus she has a generous, smooth, round croup on her. The brothers allow him to take his time. He leans down to examine her hooves. Lily offers no resistance. She seems free of any signs of fungal infection, as far as he can tell.

'If it's a ride you're after, she's as mannerly and manageable as you could want. Handles well. She'll give you no trouble. Take her for a canter round if you like,' offers the older brother, confident now he is closing in on a deal.

Jenks smiles. 'You wouldn't worry I might ride off with her?'

'You wouldn't get far.' The younger boy said, with a broad grin. There was no mistaking the intent behind the words.

'Shay will lead you to a spot where you can stretch her legs.'

'Why not?' Jenks says and with a 'May I?' and a nod of assent from Billy, he leaps easily and elegantly onto the horse's back, takes a comfortable, upright seat and a loose hold of the bridle and reins as Billy releases them. With a curt nod from the latter, Shay leads the way through the throng towards an open meadow of caravans and a distant line of trees beyond the edge of the fair.

They reach the edge of the encampment, where there are long lines of washing outside nearly every caravan. A couple of tinsmiths sit on stools in front of their vividly painted wagons, patiently tapping and cutting into the soft metal they are moulding into bowls and buckets. It is both peaceful and bucolic, yet Jenks knows that underlying the scene lie hardship and poverty, and his heart goes out to the multitude of young children. What life would they have? He knows mortality among traveller children is shockingly high, that travellers marry young and have big families. He is curious about Shay who looks to be of an age when he would soon be finding a bride.

The horse is a solid ride. Billy has spoken the truth. Why are they selling her? he wonders. As if reading his mind, Shay suddenly breaks the silence.

'You could let her have a bit of a run here round the perimeter. She'll show you her paces,' and suddenly bursts out, 'She's a good horse. Give her a good home, mister. You won't regret it!' and Jenks just has time to ask, 'Then why...?' before Shay chips in, 'We have cousins in Amerikay. Billy wants to join them. There's good money to be had out there they say, so...'

With a sharp 'Hup!', Shay gives Lily a mischievous slap on her rump and she startles into a trot. Is this a sly test to see how he will handle the provocation? Jenks is forced to assume control as she heads for the far end of the open common and the last of the line of caravans. Lily rides well and is responsive to his subtle commands. He allows himself to enjoy the sensation of being back on horseback; it has been much too long. As they reach the far line of trees, the door opens on a caravan set at a distance from the main camp, and out steps Bogboy, fully dressed but barefoot, holding his boots in his hand. He is seating himself on the top step, steadying himself to pull them back on, when he looks up and meets Jenks's astonished gaze.

Embarrassment, quickly followed by anger and then shame, flit across the boy's face. He scrambles up, his boots unlaced and runs down the steps then trips over himself, while Jenks calls after him, 'What's going on? Stop! Don't run.'

And Bogboy stops. The whole incident is as comic as it is bizarre. Shay runs across and catches up with them; Lily is getting skittish at the commotion going on around her and has to be soothed.

Just as Jenks is trying to make sense of events and piece together what is happening, Shay exclaims, 'So you're Alphonse's friend!'

Jenks observes and recognises the unmistakable current of energy passing between the two boys. A strange sense of desolation steals over him, followed by grief lumped deep in his throat. Alphonse? His wild bird has already begun to flee his nest. Turning to the gypsy boy, he says simply, 'How much for the horse? I'll take her.'

Mickey

'Jesus, Michael O'Brien, is it yourself? You can take the boy out of the bog but not the bog out of the boy, eh? The wanderer returns!'

The voice that greets them with easy familiarity as he and

Carolina step across the threshold into Seamus O'Rourke's bar belongs to none other than Seamus himself. The years fall away in Mickey's mind as the Irish pronunciation of his name rings across the nearly empty bar. A dark-haired lad, who is just on his way out as they enter, gives them both a shameless, almost disconcerting, stare. Mickey remembers how the arrival of strangers in the village had always been a subject for gossip and speculation, sometimes for days on end. He glances back and catches sight of the young man at the door, taking another curious look at them before he bolts.

Meanwhile, as if aware his initial greeting might have been an insult too far too soon, the speaker immediately adds, 'Sure, you're looking grand,' a blatant lie aimed at him with the practised insincerity of the professional Irish publican. Seamus and Mickey haven't seen each other in almost twenty years but they had been firm friends and occasional love rivals in their youth. Their drunken scrapes and romantic indiscretions had been the stuff of local legend. Now his one-time drinking buddy is a respectable pub owner, running his own bar, admittedly not much more than one step above a roadside shebeen, but which he'd wasted no time in naming after himself. O'Rourke's. It is the only pub in the village. Seamus now turns to Carolina, who is scanning the dim, cosy recesses of the bar with evident curiosity, and here his effusiveness seems utterly genuine. He aims at her a smile that is almost predatory, clearly making a shrewd assessment of how the land lies between his guests.

'You're most welcome, And who's this? Aren't you going to introduce us, Mickey? Most welcome – *céad míle fáilte*, as we say in these parts.'

'Still fancy yourself a bit of a lady killer, do ya?' thinks Mickey. 'Seamus, Carolina.'

'Charmed, I'm sure.'

Seamus had always had a competitive streak, even when they were boys and played on the local hurling team together. He'd always been a bad loser and if the game finished and he hadn't been top scorer or, worse still, had been on the losing team, he would be in a foul temper for the rest of the day and Mickey would have to accompany him to the pub so he could drown his sorrows and regale him – and anyone else who'd listen – with a blow-by-blow account of the match and where it had all gone wrong.

'Might you have a room for us, Seamus?' Mickey says, trying to keep the surliness in his mood at bay.

While Carolina might have a touch of class, there is no way of disguising that this is an inglorious homecoming – less Yankee swagger and more a desperate hole-in-the-corner affair. Mickey knows that Seamus is no fool and is already sizing up the present situation and puzzling out all the variables. Tearing his attention away from the lady in the room, the latter suddenly remembers he has a duty to perform as their host.

'We do so. Sure, it won't take long to get you settled in, Meantime, can I get yous both a drink? You'll be tired enough, I'm sure, after your journey.'

'A coffee would be most welcome,' says Carolina and gives Seamus her brightest smile.

'That's a fine lass you have there, Michael, me boy. Now, I shouldn't by rights be plying you with the demon drink at this ungodly hour, but seeing as this is such an auspicious occasion, what say you both to an Irish coffee?'

'I say, why thank you, sir,' is her immediate reply, and the two of them grin conspiratorially at one another.

It astonishes Michael that more than half a lifetime of travels to the ends of the earth feels like nothing more than a dream right now. Here in this tiny bar, it is as if time has stood still. His reverie is broken by Seamus.

'Don't be fretting, boyo. Sure, I was only codding yous. I have a fine seven-year-old Jameson's here you'll both like, I think. Just don't be saying anything to the Gard. He'll probably be by later.'

And, so saying, he takes down a half bottle from the shelf behind him and splashes them each a generous slug, plus one for himself, and announces, 'Get that down you, now. Here's to old times and new friendships.' They all raise a glass and, formal greetings and introductions over, Seamus continues, with a sly wink at Carolina, 'Talking of the demon drink, we used to have a fella around these parts who would stew up a bit of the old poteen for the whole village. Powerful stuff it was too. Would blow the top of your head off if you weren't careful. You remember, Michael? Old Louis? Of course, you do. Sure, one night yer man here decided to go and get himself spifflicated on the stuff. Got caught in the act, legless and drunk as a lord, and earned himself a good beating from Louis for his trouble. We all ragged him for weeks afterwards. So just be careful now, Carolina, this is the kind of criminal type you've got yourself mixed up with, eh?'

'Oh, is that so? Really, *Michael*,' she laughs. 'I'd have thought better of you.'

'Ah, well, we got ourselves into some fine old messes in those days, that's for sure. Wouldn't you say, boyo?' A wistful note creeps into Seamus' voice.

But while Seamus and Carolina have been amused at his discomfort, cold shivers have been running up and down Michael's spine.

'Are you doing alright there, Michael?' Having played his bout of mischief, Seamus turns solicitous. 'Why, man, you're white as a sheet. You look like you've just seen a ghost. Here… put some colour back in your cheeks.' Seamus tops up his glass and Michael isn't about to argue.

'I'm… fine. A-okay.' But he can feel the catch in his throat.

In the awkward silence that follows while he downs the whiskey, he hears Seamus' intake of breath.

'Jaysus, Michael, I was forgetting myself. You were there the night of the fire. I remember you running into the bar with the news. The place was packed solid. 'Course, it was still old Tommy Kennedy's back then. You looked nearly as terrible that night as you do now.'

By now he feels sick to the pit of his stomach. Will there be no end to this torture?

'The poor old soul burned in his bed. His still exploded and set his thatch alight. Michael here raised the alarm. You were lucky you weren't sniffing around the still again when it went up.'

And now Seamus addresses Carolina once more. 'Poor oul' cratur. It was a sad state of affairs. He was black as charcoal and past all hope by the time the Garda arrived. And by that time young Molly, from the farm up the road, had found him. She's the housekeeper now for your sister, Michael. You know that? You'll see her when you visit the old place.'

'I remember her well,' says Mickey quietly.

He can feel Carolina's eyes boring into him. He feels as though she is staring into his soul and doesn't much like what she sees there.

'But enough of all that doom and gloom. Here now, before I get yous both settled, I should warn you we're planning a bit of a session for you tonight to celebrate our prodigal son here. It'll be a late one, so don't you go expecting an early night, there's a lot of folks want to come and say hello. It'll be grand.'

'That sounds swell,' says Carolina, though it is hard to tell if she means it. It is, Mickey reflects, increasingly hard to tell what she makes of anything.

'Oh, and finally, before I forget, this came for you. The lad from the big house brought it over. That was him just leaving as you arrived.' Seamus pulls down an envelope from the bottle shelf behind him. 'Speak of the devil, he's Molly's lad, Joseph, the one who brought it over. He's off to pick up some supplies from the store. He'll be back shortly. Apparently, you're to give him an answer. And while you're reading it, I'll go fetch those Irish coffees I promised you. I'm a man of my word.' He pronounces this last with a shameless wink at Carolina, as he hands over the note to Mickey and heads into a back room.

When Mickey finally fumbles the envelope open, conscious that Carolina is observing him intently, and pulls out the notepaper, he recognises instantly the impeccable, copperplate handwriting of his sister. The contents are characteristically blunt.

Dear Michael,

I'm sure you will understand that personal circumstances make it impossible for me to permit you and your companion hospitality under my roof at present. However, you are both welcome to join me for a private rendezvous and an early supper tomorrow evening, should that suit your current plans. There will be an opportunity to discuss family matters and settle any outstanding issues between us. I will instruct Joseph to come and pick you up in the jaunt in good time. He will convey you back to your lodgings afterwards.

Cordially yours, Jocelyn

Not so much an invitation as an instruction. So, there is to be no forgiveness for the black sheep. But then, Jocelyn has always had a knack for holding onto a good grudge, whereas he's been inclined to let bygones be bygones and there, he thinks, lies the essential difference between them. But after all, it was the Irish way – a salvo in an unmistakable declaration of war. He looks up to meet Carolina's steady, questioning gaze.

'We've been invited for dinner,' is all he says.

Molly

The house has been in a frenzy since they got the news. In addition to her usual domestic duties and cares, she is now expected to organise an entire spring clean under the remote supervision of Madame. A village girl, Cassie, has been brought in to help with this. She is a pale-faced, lumpen girl with acne, but at least she's amenable and willing. Madame has ventured downstairs only the once, to explain in painstaking detail how she wants the dining room set up. Plates, china and glassware are to be immaculate, and the old Delftware brought out of a lifetime's hibernation. What puzzles Molly most is why Madame wants to impress the guest couple at all, given her antipathy to her brother and her professed contempt for his companion, a woman she hasn't met but has a decidedly low opinion of. To make matters worse, Madame has been even more imperious than usual, adding a highly-strung nervousness to her usual, complaining self.

Joseph spends his days muttering openly about 'The oul' bitch upstairs,' and Molly has given up going through the motions of correcting him. Nevertheless, once he'd been dispatched to hand-deliver the invitation and returned with a response, as instructed, he had been ordered to Madame's room to be grilled about the pair of them.

Molly is present as Madame fires question after question. 'Does Michael look well? How were they both dressed? How old is she? Does Michael sound like an American?'

Joseph mumbles his inadequate replies that lack all salient detail and therefore fail to satisfy. Madame finally bursts out, 'For goodness' sake, don't you have the slightest interest in anything?' to which Joseph fires back furiously, 'It's not my feckin' job to be your spy.'

In the shocked silence that follows, Madame merely waves a dismissive hand at them both which seems to indicate this poor behaviour and lack of respect is all that she expected. For once, Molly wanted to come to her son's defence at the injustice of the criticism, rude as he had been, but she bites her tongue. In fairness, she'd been as eager to hear her son's first impressions as Madame. Nevertheless, it's true: it isn't his job and neither is it hers to turn back the clock to create the illusion that the house isn't a virtual ruin. She has spent days dusting away a thousand old cobwebs, airing presses full of decidedly threadbare sheets and towels, despite the fact the pair aren't even staying, polishing the windows and every last surface with lemon juice and vinegar, and vigorously rubbing down everything from copper bowls to silver candlesticks with elbow grease and Brasso. The latter has turned out to be a job that seems to particularly suit Cassie, who has taken to it with surprising relish. She becomes particularly animated whenever Joseph walks into the room, though he remains totally oblivious. None of this changes the fact that the house is practically falling down round about their ears. All that effort to create a big fat pretence.

It is taking a heavy toll on all of them. Not to mention the preparations for the dinner itself. The list of provisions and proposed recipes are all written out in Madame's careful hand, along with daily additions and last-minute scratchings out until the original list attains the appearance of a barely decipherable, hastily dispatched battle plan. Well, isn't the whole situation a family war? A battle of wits and willpower? Ill as she might be, Madame displays an unusual level of engagement. In fact, Molly is driven to conclude that she is actually enjoying herself. Something about her suggests that she feels she has one or two trump cards still to play. Molly's suspicions are further confirmed when they receive a surprising visit from the family solicitor who spends an hour in private consultation with Madame. Nothing was divulged, but Madame was in a decidedly good mood for the rest of the afternoon.

In the early morning, with the first rays streaming through the dining room windows into what had once been the salon, all that remains of the splendour of the past is an air of shabby gentility. However, with bowls of purple phlox from the terrace garden and two Chinois vases of inky gladioli either side of the fireplace to match the dining table set with the lustrous, blue, Dutch chinaware, there is a certain elegance to the scene. A set of high-backed, Hepplewhite chairs has been brought out of storage from the back shed where they'd been dumped unceremoniously under tarpaulin years before. They have been grudgingly scrubbed and stripped back and had new layers of shellac applied by Joseph, a job which has taken him several days of constant grumbling. Now the newly varnished chairs gleam brightly in the sun. Madame appears to check on progress and, to everyone's amazement, finds little to fault. She looks frail, her skin chalk-white. The only things that seem to keep her upright are stern self-discipline and fierce pride. She praises both Molly and

Cassie for their hard work, noting that the tarnished silverware has come up beautifully, and informs everyone that the guests will be dining by candlelight. She even manages to praise Joseph for his splendid restoration job and for once he preens rather than bristles under her gaze. It is a peace offering of sorts.

But Molly also sees that Jocelyn's eyes are glistening. There will be no more suppers like this in the house while she is alive, perhaps never again. And the evening has little prospect of being a happy event, despite the efforts made to create a sense of occasion.

The one puzzle is why the dining table has had the leaves extended and been laid for twelve? Molly has been doing calculations in her head and can't for the life of her understand who will be present apart from 'The Yanks' as Madame insists on calling Michael and the mysterious Carolina. She is fretting that there won't be enough food. While Madame has insisted on the number, she has continued to remain tight-lipped about the guest list except to suddenly reveal, in passing, that one of the extra visitors will be Brendan Breen, the family solicitor. Whatever this evening is to be it won't lack for drama, thinks Molly, and in Madame's case, it has all the appearance of being a last supper.

As she leaves the room, her inspections complete, Madame turns back to Molly and confides, 'I do hope Michael behaves himself. Let's hope he's not planning on making a scene. There'll be an announcement and I need you to be present for it too.'

Molly opens her mouth, but Madame holds up her hand, more imperious than ever and says, 'All in good time. But you and Joseph have nothing to worry about, I promise.'

Joseph

'Fetch the Americans,' she said, even though Michael is her brother and the woman with him is from Russia or somewhere. 'And spruce yourself up, we don't want them thinking you just stepped out of the bog.' The cheek of her. Well, she is sick, sure enough, so you have to make some allowances.

'Try and be kind, Joe, she's not long for this world,' his ma had said one night when he'd come back from another dressing-down with a scowl on his face. Not long? The sooner the better as far as he is concerned. The end can't come soon enough. Then, maybe, there'll be some real changes around the place. He is sick and tired of living in a museum.

He'd taken the pony and trap, excited that something big was happening at long last. And despite his burning resentment at yer one, he'd run some Brylcreem through his unruly mop and plastered it down. First impressions matter and if Michael does take over, then who knows what opportunities might lie in wait? He looks like a real American, anyhow. Ma has shown him photos. In one, Michael is grinning at the camera, a young fella in a sharp suit and fedora, like a gangster in the movies and, behind him, Brooklyn Bridge. He can't wait to meet the both of them properly. Yesterday, when he'd called back for their reply, they'd looked tired and likely out-of-sorts with all the travel, and Michael had simply said, 'Tell my sister we'll be delighted to come to dinner.' It had felt tense. Today, he seems in a more relaxed mood.

'Hey, kiddo, you must be Joe? We didn't really have time to talk yesterday. A lot going on. Call me Mickey!' His words are followed by a hearty handshake. He notes the informality and thinks, 'Typical Yank.'

'Glad to see you, good of you to come fetch us. Can't wait to see the old place. I was just telling Carolina, here, it's a long walk otherwise.'

This comes out in a rush and gives Joseph a moment to appraise him. So, this is the notorious prodigal son. Far from impressive. Dishevelled, in a shiny, pale-blue suit that only an American would consider wearing. Nothing like the dashing young man in the photo. Joseph can barely disguise his disappointment. He attempts to smile at the man grinning at him. A man trying just that bit too hard with his 'hail-fellow-well-met' routine. Altogether too full of unnecessary swank. In an instant, Joseph sees just how nervous he must be. He is astonished to realise he feels sorry for Mickey, but the feeling is also laced with contempt.

Then Mickey indicates the woman.

'Carolina, here, is really looking forward to seeing the place too, aren't you, honey? She wants to know where this all began.'

He's gesturing to himself and laughing too loudly; neither of them is quite sure whether they're expected to laugh along with him, so neither of them does.

'So, Joe, allow me to introduce Carolina.'

She's something else. Equally overdressed but, somehow, it suits her. Around her neck is a deep, orange fox fur; it ought to look ridiculous out here in the back of beyond and yet, she's stylish, he thinks; there's no other word for it. And, in the next moment, wonders what on earth she's doing with Mickey. While he's thinking all this, she's turned her startling, blue eyes towards him, her carefully made-up, full-lipped face framed by dark, lustrous hair. It's impossible to tell how old she is. There's something ageless about her.

She presents her hand. 'Hello, Joe, it's a pleasure to meet you.'

He mumbles, 'Joseph, good to see you see too,' and takes her hand, while she, in turn, clasps his warmly. He's conscious of her soft, yielding touch and her hand lingers just a fraction too long as though she's trying to get the measure of him. A frisson goes up his spine.

Mickey interrupts with attempted gallantry, 'Say, honey, why don't you sit up in front with the young fella, and I'll sit myself down here in the back?'

They're standing next to the small jaunt, the only mode of transport the house still possesses, along with Bella, their ancient nag, who should, by rights, have been put out to pasture years ago. Still, it was Bella or the village's only taxi, which Her Ladyship has made absolutely clear she isn't prepared to pay for. Hence, Joseph, along with Bella and the cart, has been dispatched as the one meagre nod to Irish hospitality she has been prepared to concede. That, and the early supper that is to follow.

There's another awkward moment as Joseph helps Carolina in her short skirt and heels negotiate the step up to the front seat, which sets his imagination racing. Mickey has huffed and puffed his own way into the back. Joseph jumps into the driver's seat. Carolina's proximity is making his head swim, particularly the musky scent of her. He picks up the switch and swishes it with a 'Hup' at the horse, who jerks out of her doze and reluctantly sets off for home.

Hawk

Hawk hunger: black flame, craving, longing, raging. The all-consuming huntress soars on sharp-bladed feathers; scours expanse of rock, shrub, grass, bog. Eye of darkness, black hole, implacable tool of death. Taut sinew, raw power, lightning bolt plunges earthbound. Dives, dives, dives, sinks deep-tearing talon fierce into flesh. Sweet, tender, yielding body hot with blood pierced by beak. Pumping, quivering heart ripped apart, shredded and silenced.

Carolina

The landscape reminds her of childhood holidays in Northern Jutland where the family had a summer home and her father first took her sailing. She's always felt at ease in such places; they attune with her Nordic soul. Ghostly presences haunt them: bogmen and women buried beneath the soil.

She is exquisitely aware of the boy beside her, surely no more than eighteen. He would be quite handsome if it weren't for the permanent frown – and he clearly has no gift for small talk. A pleasant contrast, at least, to the constant stream of chatter from Mickey in the back, who seems compelled to provide some sort of nostalgic running commentary on every twist and turn in the road. She is highly amused at the young lad's attempts to look anywhere but in her direction. Men are so predictable, she thinks. They are all nothing more than boys pretending to be grown-ups, fondly imagining they rule the roost when, in truth, they haven't a clue about life. She wonders how Hollywood had come up with the notion of the charming, happy-go-lucky Irishman. Not by scouting around these parts by the look of it.

Suddenly, he jerks the jaunt to a halt, and points something out to her with a note of excitement in his voice, 'Look! There!' She follows his gaze. She knows immediately what it is. She's seen hunting eagles and red kites patrol the skies above the Vildmose.

It is a hawk, a female, the larger and more deadly of the species, readying herself for a kill. As if on cue, the boy exclaims, 'There she goes!' and they watch her plummet with ferocious speed. They all hear the terrified squealing. He is suddenly transformed: animated and – dare she say it? – thrilled. He turns to face her for the first time and his cheeks are flushed with genuine delight.

'Might be a rabbit or a leveret, there's a lot of them this time of year. D'you want a closer look?' He turns to include Mickey but they all know the invitation is really for her. It is a kind of dare, a teenage come-on, dressed up as a challenge.

'What do you say?" She, too, turns to Mickey, who seems strangely lost in his own thoughts. If he is still remembering the past, it no longer seems quite so golden.

'You go,' he says. 'I'll wait here.'

The boy grins broadly at her. He is now in his element. And she knows arousal when she sees it.

He leads the way. The raptor is already devouring its kill.

'She'll be eating it alive,' he says. 'They prefer it that way. She'll pinion the poor wee thing until it just gives up the fight.'

It is charming to see how eager he is to impress her. He slows her down with a wave of his hand but it is already too late; the hawk has spotted them, every fibre of her alert to intruders. They stand stock still and wait. The whole scene is like a tableau. Then Joseph breaks cover and the hawk loosens her grip on her victim and ascends with a screech. She hovers just above them to assess what kind of threat they present.

It is a truly pitiful sight. A young hare, its tiny body ripped apart, the soft underbelly exposed. All that remains is a bloodied mess. They can see still quivering innards and a faintly beating heart. Unbelievably, it isn't quite dead.

'Should we do something?' she asks, realising instantly how ridiculous she sounds, but it is almost unbearable to witness. He picks up a nearby chunk of rock and, without a moment's hesitation, smashes it down on the fragile skull.

He turns back to her with a look that seems to say: what else would you have me do? He's picked up a small, bloodied feather which he now holds out to her. The final dare. She takes it. 'That was very brave of you,' she says, and they exchange a look. Yes, he is on fire.

'We'd better go back,' he says, his ebullience dimmed again. And they leave the hawk to return to her feast.

Joseph

It was a big mistake to stop. His head is whirling. He can feel the veins throbbing in his temples. Why had he ever thought it was a good idea? He'd been looking forward to the arrival of the Americans for weeks, but this eejit playing the big man has left him feeling angry and disappointed. The long-anticipated homecoming is like nothing he'd imagined. It is as if Michael has betrayed him in some way. And in the heat of the moment, he had taken all his frustration out on the poor, dead creature back there. Let the woman think it was some kind of gallant gesture if she wants. Why not? She is the one bright spot in all of this. Had he imagined it or had she given him the come on just now? His mind is racing and he can feel the adrenaline still coursing through his veins.

Suddenly, everything is mixed up and, in his mind's eye, he sees himself smashing not a helpless baby hare but Bogboy; sees himself bringing the rock down on his skull over and over, while

Bogboy cries and holds his hands out pathetically to plead for mercy which just fills him with more rage, except now it isn't even Bogboy he is pounding but a creature with long dangling ears and Bogboy's face, one side of which is crushed and bloodied to pulp, and he screams in his head, 'Take that, ya fecker, ya filthy little pervert.'

When he comes back to himself, he sees that the woman is staring at him. He mumbles a quick, 'Sorry. We'd best get going again.'

Carolina ignores his offer to help her back into the front seat, where she sits, slowly twirling the bloodied hawk feather in her right hand and staring straight ahead. He's behaved like an idiot, and knows it. A feeling of shame steals over him. The horse stirs wearily back to life on his prompting and they head onwards, all three lost to silence.

Mickey

What the hell is wrong with the boy? He's his mother's son, that's for sure. She'd been exactly the same. Always watching and judging everyone and everything, and thinking herself a cut above. That was Rose's fault. Kind, open-hearted Rose, putting ideas in Molly's head. The son is cut from the same cloth. Looking down his nose at them. But he doesn't much like the way Carolina is playing up to him, either. He feels a stab of jealousy. It's as if she enjoys provoking him. She'd been the same with Seamus. Yet again, he feels rage building inside him and an urge to slap her, to remind her who is boss. But he isn't the boss, that is the problem. All of this is adding to his anxiety about the meeting with Jocelyn. As if he doesn't have enough on his mind without having to keep a wary eye on his woman as well.

He is distracted from his train of thought by the boy himself, who appears to be mumbling and cursing, and it occurs to him that maybe the lad is some kind of half-wit. That would make a whole lot of sense – he certainly hadn't appeared to be all there, right from the off. Mickey remembers vividly why he couldn't wait to get away from all of this in the first place. The poverty, the pettiness, the misery. Not to mention the priests and all that mumbo-jumbo that the faithful ingested like sheep. None of them with the wit or will to make something of their lives. How could he have forgotten?

Carolina looks tense, rattled in a way he's never seen before.

A few miles from the house, and making stately progress, a voice shocks Mickey out of his doldrums.

'Nice day for a visit to the old place.'

He spins round and old Louis offers him a toothless grin. 'I'd say that's a lively one you have there,' he adds, pointing a bony finger at Carolina who has now put noticeable distance between herself and Joseph and is perched uneasily at the very outside edge of the front seat. 'Oh yes, a lively one indeed. I'd say you'd need to be keeping a close watch on that one, alright. Before you know it, she'll be straying into some other fella's field.'

'What the...?'

'You have to show the skittish ones who's boss. Don't be taking any nonsense. It's for their own good in the end. They'll be running off, chasing after some young, hot-headed stud bull and before you know it, there'll be all hell to pay.'

The couple up front have clearly seen and heard nothing. Mickey chokes a scream and comes out in a cold sweat. He closes his eyes and tries to breathe in deeply, then slowly opens them again. Louis is still there.

'Keep your wits about you. I used to give my Mary Kate the run of the house, but I kept her on a leash all the same. I treated her like my queen but she knew her place and never gave me a day's trouble. You young'uns with your modern ideas should be careful. There'll be tears before the day's end. I'd say that young fella there has got eyes out on stalks.'

Mickey feels faint and his breath becomes more ragged. He understands he is in the throes of some kind of madness and this is all in his head, but the old man feels horribly, terrifyingly real.

'You can drop me off just here.' Louis looks around him. 'That's the track up to my place. Can't stay chatting. Must be moving on. Mary Kate will be wondering where I've got to.'

The old man rises and turns to face Mickey full on before stepping off the cart. And Mickey sees that while one side of his body looks passably human, the other has been charred black.

'Please, just leave me alone,' Mickey cries out, as his belly and chest begin to heave. But the apparition has already vanished.

'What did you say?'

'Nothing... honey. Just... nearly home.'

'Oh. Yes. Well. I've ruined my shoes. Some first impression I'll make with your sister.'

'It'll be fine.'

'Will it?' She turns to face forward again and her question hangs in the air between them like an accusation.

Jocelyn

The ghosts are back, crowding in on her. They almost never leave her alone. Mostly they're silent. They simply drift in and out of her room, suddenly appearing from out of the folds of the curtains or floating through the walls. Other times, she'll turn her head and one of them will be there, casually seated at her bedside, flicking through a magazine or just sitting in absolute stillness, staring straight ahead, presumably waiting for the ferryman to carry her across the River Styx to join them on the other bank. In the evenings, she can hear them muttering away to themselves or occasionally chattering to each other. She's become accustomed to their presence.

They come and go, different ghosts at different times. But always Rose. Often, she would be applying a deep-red lipstick, holding a gold, scalloped powder compact, a gift from Alphonse, up to her face, or painting her nails, and always in a hurry. Once, she had caught sight of Jocelyn watching her and apologised, 'Sorry, Jocelyn, I've no time to chat. I'm late already, the taxi's here. I'll see you when I get back.' Restless and fidgety, Rose constantly moves objects around the room.

After one particularly restless night of tossing and turning, she had woken to find Rose sitting at the bottom of her bed being fed strawberries by Alphonse. 'Mine, all mine,' she had crowed to Jocelyn, as she spat out the green calyces onto the bedcover. Another time, Alphonse was deep in animated conversation with Paddy. They appeared to be comparing notes on the cuts, bruises and gashes from their respective fatal accidents. Books had been scattered across the floor. Little china or glass bibelots had ended up on a windowsill or in amongst her bed covers or other mischievous locations.

Jocelyn is only too aware of how perplexed Molly is at how objects keep finding their way from one end of the room to another, but it would be difficult to explain. She wants to tell Molly, 'It's not me. My brain is as sharp as ever. It's the ghosts. The ghosts are real.'

She is sure that they will all be coming down to join the other guests at dinner, which is why she has made such careful provision for them at the table.

Jenks

The summons had come earlier in the week, via a rare visit from the local postman, Declan O'Leary, who had turned out to be a fount of gossip about the arrival of Michael O'Brien back in the neighbourhood and speculation about the current goings on at the big house. What did the arrival signify? Was he on a brief visit or coming back to stay? And why was he staying at Seamus O'Rourke's with his companion? A striking-looking woman. Foreign by all accounts. Why had they not been invited to stay with his sister? Was there still bad blood between them after all these years?

For once, Jenks had felt obliged to invite the garrulous fellow in for a mug of tea. It was clear that Declan O'Leary was hoping that Jenks would open his letter there and then, but Jenks wasn't prepared to be that obliging. Declan had to settle for tea and nothing more. Which wouldn't stop him breathlessly relaying a whole new layer of gossip to every eager ear he encountered on his further round. As soon as the insatiably curious Declan had been dispatched on his wobbly bike, Jenks opened the letter. Although it was couched as a request, it was clear that the embossed card, handwritten, was really an order to present themselves. After a cursory enquiry as to her nephew's well-being, Jocelyn informed him that she would be most grateful if they could both attend, as some news of great relevance and import to Alfie would be forthcoming.

Does Jocelyn want the boy returned to the big house? If so, how will Alfie react? What if he refuses point blank? The visit of his uncle from America is clearly a factor. There are mysteries here that Jenks can't yet fathom.

Since the encounter at the horse fair, which neither of them has cared to raise, the boy has retreated into himself. A coolness has come into their friendship, despite the fact that Jenks had always intended the horse as his gift to Alfie, bought her on the spot and paid way over the odds for her. He'd been so taken aback by the turn of events that he'd simply paid the brothers their asking price, simultaneously depriving them of the pleasure of haggling and lowering himself in their esteem. The last of his savings had gone in one fell swoop. After a spit and a handshake, the deal was done, and they'd ridden Lily home, or, rather, a clearly uncomfortable Alfie had, with Jenks holding onto him from behind, as an awkward gulf of silence had grown between them with each passing mile.

Now he has just about enough money left to get him through the summer. He will be reduced to dropping hints to his mother in his next letter home. Or hoping Jenkins senior's health has taken a sudden turn for the worse and that there will be at least a bare minimum bequest for him.

Alfie and Lily have bonded almost immediately. It isn't lost on Jenks that the horse also represents a link to Shay. The travellers are still in the vicinity. There are days when the boy simply disappears on Lily and doesn't reappear until well after nightfall. Jenks keeps his own counsel, although, he thinks sourly, as first loves go, the boy could have chosen more wisely. What if Jocelyn were somehow to find out, let alone Shay's brother or the other traveller families? Whatever they are getting up to breaks every taboo imaginable. But there is a new recklessness in Alfie, a kind of passionate madness. Jenks is helpless to guide or protect. He can hardly lock the boy up. So much for *in loco parentis*. If Jocelyn had seriously imagined that was the arrangement they'd tacitly agreed to, she would be disappointed. He's even considered the possibility of inviting Shay to the cottage. But his own feelings for Alfie are already too compromised without entertaining a couple in the throes of young lust. What are the chances that Alfie might attempt to run away with the travellers? It seems absurd to imagine such a possibility and yet…

The day of the dinner is fast approaching and finally he broaches the subject. At first, Alfie just stares at him and then simply answers, 'No.'

'I don't think you have a choice. Your uncle has arrived all the way from America. Aren't you at least curious to meet him?'

'I suppose. But I don't know him.'

'Well, isn't this your chance? You might like him. Plus, your aunt is your legal guardian. You're here at her concession. She can end this arrangement at any moment. Do you want that?'

The boy bristles. 'I'm not going to America with him. Anyway, she hates him. He stole a lot of money from us before I was born; that's why he had to go away.'

'I very much doubt that that's the idea. But it must be important. Otherwise, why would she have gone to all this trouble?' It is the most candid, adult conversation he's ever had with the boy.

'Alright. But I'm not staying.'

'Agreed.' Jenks smiles and receives the trace of a smile in return.

'Can we take Lily?' In other words, he would return to the big house only on his own terms, and have his own means of getaway at the ready, if matters were to get out of hand.

'Why not?'

Carolina

They are getting close. The road takes them through a spinney, the light pouring down through fresh, green foliage and huge heads of flowering, purple buddleia. The day momentarily darkens. She shivers, as though the fairy folk might suddenly emerge on their path and ambush them. But as the road narrows and climbs one steep, last rise, they pass an ancient churchyard, with a cluster of stone, Celtic crosses, covered in bright, orange lichen. There is a commotion – a horse at full gallop breaks through the trees just behind them and nearly swerves into their path, before the rider takes evasive action at the very last moment, turns the horse round in a half circle and, without stopping, shoots away into the distance ahead of them.

Joseph swears – 'Jaysus, ya little bastard!' – under his breath, as he fights to regain control of his sleepy nag who rears up with a startled whinny. He slows the cart to a halt. He is breathing heavily and his face has turned pale .

'Are yous alright?' He addresses her, only half-including Mickey, who calls back, 'A-okay back here, but who was that maniac?' Joseph looks like he might say something but then thinks better of it. As for Carolina, she'd only caught a glimpse of a young man with a red mane of hair and intense dark features. Joseph composes himself and slows down his breath, then urges the horse on: 'Giddy-up!' She merely gives an irritated toss of her mane and reluctantly begins to trot. And then, there, nestled comfortably in the small valley as it spreads out before them, is the house.

It isn't quite what Carolina expected. As the horse and buggy make the approach up the long, rough, gravel driveway, the kindest thing that can be said about the place is that it must once have had a certain elegant charm. The architect appears to have opted for a florid, Italianate style but lost his nerve at the last minute and switched to a more regimented, austere style. Perhaps the new owners had baulked at the expense. A mass of grey stone, badly streaked by rain, gives the overall impression of gloom. The building emerges out of a windbreak of Scots pine and copper beech, which does little to soften the air of sadness that hangs like a pall over the scene. The guttering and slate roof tiles are overgrown with moss and lichen.

She is tempted to drawl 'What a dump!' in her best Bette Davis accent, but thinks better of it. Mickey is already in such a weird mood, it doesn't seem like a good moment to provoke him any further.

Well, she thinks, this should be interesting.

Mickey

Here it is: the place he crossed oceans and circled the earth to get away from. Now he's back, like a beggar at the gate. Here, there's no escaping his past and he can feel himself becoming consumed by memories. He's reminded of a line by some American poet he once heard on the radio: 'Home is the place where, when you have to go there, they have to take you in.' And now there's a childish rhyme chanting over and over in his head.

Tinker, tailor, soldier, sailor...

There's the great copper beech. His earliest childhood memory comes flooding back. He was in his pram out on the terrace, watching light dance through the gold-rust leaves as the warmth of the rays embraced his entire body, leaving him in a state of bliss. A soft voice was pouring a lovely melody into his ear as the pram rocked. Rose. Her delicate, girlish tones sing along with a male voice coming out of the radio in the drawing room. 'I can't give you anything but love, baby...'

Rich man, poor man, beggar man, thief.

And now another picture comes back to him. He is watching two giggling girls on a perfect golden summer's day, from his favourite secret hiding place. Their thin, almost transparent, cotton frocks lift to reveal shapely, tanned legs, white socks and sandals, as they eat cherries and rhyme out on the terrace lawn.

Tinker, tailor, soldier, sailor,

Rich man, poor man, beggar man, thief.

He had been hiding in the branches of that old beech tree right above them, spying on Rose and her friend. Knowing that what he was doing was deliciously wrong. Knowing that a younger brother shouldn't be staring at his sister like that, but mesmerised, despite himself, by the swelling in her chest. The sun in the leaves was dazzling him; he felt safe and secure and thrilled in a way he couldn't yet quite fathom. He was rubbing himself excitedly a bit too hard against the smooth bark. *Rich man, poor man.* There was her friend. Molly. Equally tempting. *Rich man, poor man, beggar man, thief.*

Yes, he'd always been a thief. Stealing looks. Stealing hearts. Stealing innocence. Stealing the future from Rose and Jocelyn. Stealing away with shame like the proverbial thief in the night. And the girls had screamed as he'd leaned too far out, lost his grip, and slithered down from his hiding place, scraping arms and knees on his way down as he tumbled to the ground.

Rose's alarm had turned to fury at her little brother as he'd vainly scrambled upright and attempted to run, his cuts and abrasions stinging hard. Both of them had given him a well-earned pummelling across his back and shoulders and hooted with laughter as they let him go to limp painfully back to the big house, utterly humiliated, their scorn still ringing in his ears.

He's always meant to return one day. But somehow it has never been the right time. He might have come for Rose's funeral perhaps, but the black-lined letter with the news arrived weeks too late via a poste restante in Valparaiso. He might have come for Mama's. By this time, he had a semi-permanent address in New York. He remembers a series of increasingly frustrated telegrams from Jocelyn. Where are you? She wants to see you. But he still hadn't been able to face any of it. *Beggar man, thief.* And coward. He'd once heard a couple of his poker cronies discuss him in the men's room after the game, unaware he was on the john, and one had said, 'It's the one thing you can always rely on Mickey-boy for – he'll always let you down in the end.'

The lad helps Carolina off the side step as Mickey clambers down from the rear and turns to face the grim facade. They approach the entrance and Joseph steps forward and pulls the bell rope at the side of the double doors with their familiar brass knocker in the shape of a pair of hawk wings. As a small child, Mickey had loved to pound on them and hear the hollow thump they made as the sound reverberated and magically summoned someone to the door, which creaked as it opened. More often than not, Mama herself would greet him with her special smile and sweep him into her arms and shower him with loving kisses of welcome which made him giggle and squirm. But as he got older, the hugs got less frequent as her headaches got worse, and somewhere along the line he'd understood that he was a big boy now and too old for Mama's hugs and kisses. She spent more and more time in the drawing room, recovering from her migraines when not out on her beloved terrace, gardening, and he was instructed he must on no account make noise inside the house or disturb her, but should go round to the back kitchen door where Biddy would have prepared a glass of milk and biscuits for him. *Beggar man, thief.*

Then, one afternoon, Mama had sent word for him to come to her in the drawing room. She was lying deathly still on her big day bed. 'Come, Michael, lie next to me. There's plenty of room.' Biddable for once, he'd jumped up onto the chaise and she'd admonished him in a whisper – 'Gently, gently' – as he'd settled himself into the curve of her like a new-born puppy. She'd encased him softly in her arms and he'd been instantly and dizzily enveloped in her favourite scent. She'd shown him the bottle once, when he'd watched her lightly dab herself at her wrists and behind her ears, before setting off for an official dinner with his father's banker association friends. 'It's my favourite perfume,' she'd said. 'Here' – she'd held the bottle out to him – 'smell.' And for the first time he'd understood how wonderful she was, and he'd understood also that, in some obscure way, he was being offered a glimpse into the world of grown-ups. 'If you want to win a woman's love,' his mother had added, screwing the top back on the precious liquid, 'never buy her cheap perfume. Women hate a cheapskate.' It was a lesson in the power of seduction he'd never forgotten.

They hear the peal of the bell echo beyond the front door. Nothing happens. Nobody comes to greet them and they stand on the porch, an awkward little party of two. Joseph has disappeared around the side of the house. Two minutes pass. Carolina is compulsively adjusting her fox fur, and Mickey is tapping his right foot. They're both feeling the snub in their own way. At long last, footsteps approach. The door creaks open, first a crack, and then some more. Finally, she stands in the doorway, guarding the entrance like the hound of Culain, drying her hands on a long, kitchen apron. Molly. She's filled out like a true matriarch. She scrutinises each of them as they stand before her, waiting to gain admittance. He catches her eye, and eighteen years and more fall away. The accusation in her eyes is unmistakable. He remembers that look. Time hasn't softened her one iota.

'Jocelyn apologises but she's not quite ready. She's left drinks in the drawing room. You'll know where that is, Michael. If you and your lady friend would like to help yourselves, she'll join you shortly. You're very welcome.' All this is recited with shameless insincerity. Leaving them to it, she heads to the back of the house.

Carolina turns and raises one perfectly arched eyebrow. 'Wow. Welcome home, Mickey. I don't know about you, but I could sure use that drink.'

Ghosts

The ghosts have taken up residence. They carry their crimes and sins with them. They've all paid for their misdemeanours one way or another. And now all they can do is watch these new developments with interest. The house of dead things is coming alive with fresh intrigue. The ghosts watch with detached curiosity as the human comedy unfolds, and remember their own lives full of the same vanities, and the same hopes, dreams and fears. They too loved and hated, craved love or drove it away, betrayed or were betrayed. They are condemned to watch others fall into the same traps they dug for themselves. The disappointments, the shame, the futility. All that's beyond them now. The members of the ghost chorus sigh, roll their eyes or shrug their shoulders and take up front row seats to observe the conclusion of the story in which they all once had a part to play.

Carolina

It is definitely turning into a day of surprises. In the drawing room, there's a man and a boy in his teens, neither of whom seems particularly at ease. The boy has startling red hair.

Mickey looks furious. He just about manages to compose himself and holds out a hand. 'I'm Mickey. This is Carolina. You are?' And before either of them has a chance to reply, she interjects, 'It's a pleasure to meet you both.'

'Christopher Jenkins. Likewise.'

'And... you're a friend of the family?' Mickey is still clearly thrown and determined to find solid ground.

'In a manner of speaking. And I believe you must be Michael. Alfie's – Alphonse's – uncle?'

'Damn right, I am. So, you're staying here too?'

'No. Like you, we were invited by Alfie's aunt.'

'Ah, that's nice. Carolina, you won't be the only female apart from Jocelyn. Is your wife in the garden?'

'Not my wife. By 'we' I mean me and Alfie. He's been staying with me.'

Throughout the entire exchange, the young man in question has said nothing but has been staring at Mickey as though he were some kind of apparition. She cannot help but be amused. It occurs to her that perhaps their hostess has set up this encounter to contrive maximum drama and tension from it, though if so, it was a shame she had missed it.

'So, kid, I'm your long-lost Uncle Mickey. What do you say to that? I got a present for you all the way from New York City. Just wait 'til you see what I brought you, you're gonna love it.'

The boy appears fascinated, but still has no answer.

'So, cat got your tongue? You do speak, don't you?'

'Yes.'

'Great. You and me can get to know each other better. What d'ya think?'

'I suppose.'

'Hey. You don't sound all that keen. Me and Carolina here have come a long way to see you all.'

'Come on, Mickey, he's only just met us. Don't be hard on him. One step at a time, isn't that right, Alfie?'

'I don't know.'

'How come you're not living here? Place not big enough for you?' Mickey laughs like this is the greatest joke imaginable.

'Because I don't want to.'

There is an awkward silence. Jenks comes to the rescue.

'Alfie has chosen to live with me at present.'

'Yeah? Well, I'm still his uncle and I'm just trying to get to the bottom of things here. Maybe I've been too long Stateside but when something doesn't seem right, I speak up and –'

'Mickey, dear, why don't we wait for Jocelyn to explain?'

Michael is beginning to square up to this Christopher Jenkins; she can see that clear as day. They have taken an instant dislike to each other. The one, abrasive and direct to a fault. The other, she thinks, looks and sounds like he's just stepped out of a Noel Coward play. But she understands something else too, the source of Mickey's discomfort, which he can't articulate. It is hard to imagine that he had been born into this world, but at least he has come back now to reclaim it.

In the meantime, he appears to have missed the symmetry of Alfie following a similar path to the one he had himself taken, getting away from the oppressive life here. It is not the idea of escape that bothers him, but the manner of it, she thinks. No wonder he looks out of his depth. He no longer belongs here and yet the rest of his life has become an utter sham. And here he is, trying on the role of caring uncle for size and failing at that, too.

As for Christopher, she can see he is not a ladies' man. In contrast to Mickey, he has a calm, low-voiced charm and, while she appreciates that some men aren't necessarily bowled over by her, they always check her out. It is part of their nature. But this handsome Englishman shows not one flicker of interest in her beyond mere civility and good manners, and it is clear to her exactly why. And she can see that Mickey is reaching the same conclusion and doesn't like it one little bit.

How like actors on a stage we all are, she thinks. Supporting players standing around waiting for the appearance of the leading lady so the real drama can begin. Somebody has to take charge here. It might as well be me. I've been attending to men most of my life. Why stop now?

Their hostess has left out an array of drinks on an ornate French sideboard: a decanter of whiskey, Bombay gin, a good Côte du Rhône, and even a bottle of vermouth, and a jug of some kind of fruit cup, ice and lemon. She suspects that Mickey would have preferred a beer. Nevertheless, however austere their welcome has been so far, there's no stinting in the drinks department.

A gin and vermouth would go down nicely just now. 'Why don't I fix us all a drink while we're waiting?' she asks, brightly. She is about to move across to pour them when a voice behind her says, 'That won't be necessary. Molly here will take care of you. Thank you all for making the effort to come. It's such a pleasure to have everyone under one roof – old guests and new. You're all very welcome. Christopher. Alphonse. Michael, of course, and – Carolina, I believe? We've not had the opportunity to entertain in the house for such a long time.'

Here she is at last, the famous Jocelyn, an imposing figure in an elegant, oyster-pink dress which must once have been the height of fashion. Her hair has been swept up in a formal chignon held tightly by a tortoiseshell comb. She knows how to dress, thinks Carolina, admiringly. She really has stage-managed the entire moment.

'I trust you've all managed to make your introductions? At last, Alphonse and his uncle finally have the chance to meet. Family is so important, I'm sure you'll all agree.' And she smiles, as though at some secret joke. Molly bustles about, taking orders.

'We'll head across to the dining room very shortly, as I'm sure you're all very eager to know the purpose of our gathering.'

Mickey rears up, ready to have his say.

'All in good time, Michael, I promise. We'll catch up in due course.' Then she turns to everyone with that same amused smile, which, at the last moment, lingers on Carolina. It is as though they are the only two people in the room. Two women getting the measure of each other. Close-to, Carolina can see the immense strain and effort of will this is costing Jocelyn, beneath the carefully applied make-up, the social poise and hauteur.

'My dear younger brother, always so impatient.' This is directed at Carolina, while intended for everyone's benefit. Jocelyn continues blithely, as though nothing in the least out of the ordinary is going on here, 'Meanwhile, allow me to introduce our other special guest... a dear family friend,' and she stands to one side to reveal an elderly man in a formal, three-piece, tweed suit, brown Oxford brogues and gold-rimmed spectacles, who stands self-effacingly at her shoulder. 'This is Brendan, our family solicitor.' Straight out of central casting, thinks Carolina. And she understands that the whole thing is a set-up of some kind, an ambush.

'So bring your drinks and we'll head across into dinner.'

Ghosts

The ghosts have already gathered in the dining room. They too once ate and drank, danced and laughed and fought, schemed and plotted. Now they drift through eternity, drawn back in time and space to the stories that still belong to them, carried now by others, with their own secrets and desires. In each story, the ghosts come alive again. They rise from the dead and are present, remembered and felt. They are the ancestors now, part of the thread of life that stretches back all the way to before human memory. It's right that they are here to witness the present, for it was their actions that created it. Just as those here in this room will, in their turn, become the ghosts of the future, part of the eternal everlasting cycle of life and death, the great tide that ripples and swells out into infinity.

The audience has assembled. The players are ready. The curtain rises.

I always loved you
Why did I leave?
Too late
My lover
My destroyer
Cold too cold
So hot too hot
I'm dying
I'm burning up
Imposter
Why did I hate you?
Little tearaway
I'm on fire
Why did I deny you?
So cold
Why did I fail you?
Open a window I'm burning up
Lover
Liar
Loser
Gold digger
Where's the drink?
Ashes
Too late

Rose

There was beauty in your cruelty. Of course, you would say that there was cruelty in my beauty, that I used it like a weapon. Oh,

Jocelyn, always so self-righteous and proper, always judging the rest of us. Driving us all mad. Life is for living, a journey to the peaks where the oxygen thins and the rapture descends and you dance with the angels. You couldn't bear that in me. How you resented my happiness. I lived life to the full, while you chose a living death in this house you turned into a mausoleum. You punished everyone around you. You could never forgive that he came from my womb, could you? I was the thief. I stole what was yours by right. Why did I get everything and leave you the dregs of life? Because I went out and grabbed life with both hands, my dearest sister. I ate all the strawberries life offered. While you dipped your tippy toes in the shallows, I plunged to the depths and let the water wash over me from head to toe.

Jocelyn

She surveys the two couples – that is how she thinks of them – as they make their way into the dining room. How appropriate it should all end here. She will no doubt pay a price for the strain this is putting her under, but the chance to make amends and settle old scores will be worth it.

First in, Michael and the woman. Impressive in her way, Jocelyn has to admit. She presents herself well, with skilfully applied make-up which, no doubt, is designed to disguise her true age. With a shock, Jocelyn realises that, in the candlelight, Carolina could pass for an older version of Rose.

As for Michael, now she has a chance to study him more closely, the years have not been kind. Despite his best efforts, he just appears dishevelled and half-formed. The brother she remembers – the boy with confidence and flair to spare, born of utter self-belief in his own unassailable charm, and the destiny it promises to bring him – has long gone. This man has the puffy face of a common-or-garden alcoholic, strutting into the room with a would-be proprietary manner. It does little to compensate for the air of defeat that clings to him like the smell of cheap drink and stale tobacco. She hadn't remembered him being short and yet, next to the Englishman, he appears somehow physically diminished.

As for her nephew, he looks angry as he sidles in after them, with the mutinous air of a rebellious adolescent. Alphonse. Alfie. Conceived in passion; convinced he is unwanted. She has been unable for years to call the boy by his given name: the name she and Rose had finally agreed upon as Rose lay dying – a painful decision made in honour of the father he would never know. The name that breaks her heart again, every time she hears it. To her, he's always just been 'the boy'. Tonight, perhaps, she will make amends, or so she hopes.

'Bogboy,' she thinks, sadly. Is it any wonder he considers himself entirely alone in the world, in defiance of the background he despises? She sees his surprise at the state of the room, which shimmers in the magical glow of candlelight, creating an atmosphere both formal and elegant. Molly has outdone herself. Of course, the boy has grown up much too late to have seen the house in its glory days. The reason for this lies with his uncle, who has now discovered he won't be seated as an honoured guest next to her at the top of the table. Her solicitor is already sitting calmly in place there. Mickey is halfway down the rankings in the middle, flanked by Rose on one side and their father on the other, and looks ready to explode.

Meanwhile, the Englishman, bringing up the rear, strolls in like an afterthought, which, in a manner of speaking, he is, although he has made himself a valuable support to her nephew and thus earned his right to be here at the table.

She can't help but smile at some of the surprises she has in store for them all. She can already feel the presence of the others and, just for a second, shivers. It will be a family gathering for the living and the dead. The places have been laid out with that in mind. It is Michael who breaks the awkward silence. He is reading the names on the cards left at the different place settings, written in Jocelyn's careful, cursive hand. 'What the hell is going on here, Joycie?'

'You'll see.' Counting herself at the head of the table, she's ordered Molly to set places for Alfie at her right-hand side, Brendan to her left, then Rose and Alphonse; then Michael; then their father and mother, opposite whom she has placed Carolina, so her brother is both surrounded by those whose memory he has destroyed and separated from the living whose lives are still being blighted as a result of his actions. She has requested that Molly and Joseph join the table once dinner has been served and, next to them, at the far end, sits Jenkins, the outsider. He is there to bear witness as this strange family gathering unfolds. There is an empty place opposite him for whatever uninvited guest might turn up to make their own presence felt. Her intuition hasn't stretched far enough to know who that might be, but there are any number of candidates by her reckoning. She suspects she isn't the only one haunted by ghosts from the past. The symbolism of the thirteen is not lost on her and, as far as she is concerned, their betrayer already sits amongst them.

'In honour of my brother,' she begins, 'I have taken the liberty of creating the dinner we might one day have had as a family had fate not intervened. I'm aware that this is a far from conventional affair. But tonight, my intention is that we lay to rest some ghosts that have haunted all our lives for much too long. I ask you to indulge this whim of mine. It is not an idle one.'

Mickey takes his place, and Carolina, who has seemed highly amused and is evidently willing to play along, takes hers on the other side of the table, although she, too, is now beginning to look spooked.

When all is said and done, the past hangs over everything.

Bogboy

The atmosphere is charged with an undercurrent of tension between Tante and his uncle. He knows why, but witnessing their animosity is disturbing – and oddly exciting. 'This is the house I grew up in,' he thinks. Nevertheless, it seems different. And he's not the same person who left it. He's annoyed to be separated from Jenks who has been placed far away from the rest of them as though he were some kind of tradesman, or servant, and he's tempted to go and join his friend in protest. But Tante does something unexpected when she sits down after her strange little speech, having announced that the first course will be a modest potato and leek soup, a *vichyssoise*. She grasps his hand with her long bony fingers and squeezes it tight and holds onto it. He can feel how cold she is and that she's quivering. Suddenly he knows that he wants to stay by her side. It's as though he sees her for the first time not through a child's eyes but an adult's. He feels a compassion he has never felt for her before. He squeezes her hand back and she smiles and gently nods. Years of mistrust start to melt away, and all of this is conveyed in a glance between them in the space of seconds. Then another astonishing revelation comes to him: that she needs him as an ally and that, in the company of strangers, this is where his loyalty lies.

Molly and a plain, awkward girl he doesn't recognise wheel in an elaborately decorated soup tureen and place it on the table and bring a stack of equally pretty bowls from the sideboard. He had no inkling the place still housed such fine china. They begin to pour out the creamy, thick soup, and the girl places a bowl in front of him. He almost chokes to discover that it is cold.

Jocelyn

The atmosphere between the guests is even colder than the soup, which at least has the virtue of being delicious. Carolina gamely makes an effort.

'So, Jocelyn, the house is in a wonderful location. Mickey described it, of course, but I'd no idea it would be so impressive.'

Jocelyn turns a mirthless smile on the woman who, to her credit, stares calmly back.

'It was more impressive in the days when the estate could still pay for the upkeep.'

'Of course. I can imagine it must be hard these days to maintain these old places.'

'We manage.'

'Yes. And how long has your family been here?'

'We can trace our lineage in the kingdom back to the time of Brian Boru and possibly earlier. But the present house dates back to the 1800s – before that we had a tower castle house. There's an ancient family archive which documents much of the family history. But perhaps Michael didn't mention that. He never cared much for family tradition, did you, Michael?'

'Come on, Jocelyn, that's not fair. Times change. We couldn't stay stuck in the past forever and you know it. We needed to modernise.'

'No doubt. But it helps to know what you're doing first.'

'C'mon, let's not start all that...'

'This soup is wonderful – is it an old Irish recipe?'

'French. Our family has always had strong ties to France.'

'How fascinating... I didn't know.'

'No? Well, I expect there are quite a few things Michael hasn't told you.'

'For crying out loud, Joycie, Carolina's only trying to be friendly.'

'Of course. And your family are...?'

'Danish. From Eastern Jutland. Quite similar terrain in fact. Bogland. Without the mountains, of course.'

'Yes. Of course.'

'We were mostly seafarers rather than farmers. It's our Viking blood.'

'I think we would have classed ourselves as landowners rather than farmers. Regrettably, most of our land was entailed through the male line, with unfortunate consequences for us all.'

'Joycie. Enough.' Mickey looks ready to explode. Outside, the wind is rising and a storm is brewing. A fierce gust blows open one of the French windows and the room turns icy. The candles gutter and blow out as the big Bakelite wireless in the corner suddenly lights up of its own accord, and an announcer's voice says, over the dying chords of a sad country song, 'That was Hank Snow with *Nobody's Child* and now here's an evergreen favourite for all you romantics out there,' and at once a sweet female voice is crooning, 'I can't give you anything but love, baby...'

Bogboy

There's a subtle change of atmosphere, and time seems to spiral on its axis from present to past, passing back from the living to the dead. The wind is pushing everything sideways; a sleety rain is slanting into the room. There's a clatter of wings and a high-pitched scream. Somewhere deep within him, he's travelling with Hawk through an endless vortex of time and space. The armies on the plain are readying for battle. Along the horizon appears an overwhelming mass of black, feathered shapes with sharp-beaked helmets. More arrive, an ominous gathering: the mighty crow army. No quarter will be given. This is a fight to the death. Then comes the thundering drumbeat of blood pulsing in his temples. The wild hawk is skittering madly above him; he can feel her desperation to break free from this confined space. There's a war in his head. Now the hawk army rises to answer the call. Never has he felt such a power. From the darkest places comes the urge to lay waste to his enemy on the blood-soaked field. A thousand ancestral voices are screaming in his ear.

When he looks up, there is the candle-lit face of Joseph, and he is consumed by the longing to destroy the hated thing that has tried to crush him. He yells, 'I am the son of Hawk King and you will never ever tame me,' and he hears Hawk screech overhead, 'Kill. Kill.' He launches himself at his enemy who tumbles backwards and crashes onto the table, tipping over the tureen, spilling soup everywhere. His hands are suddenly at Joseph's throat, throttling him, and more plates are crashing all around them. The wireless is switching madly between stations and voices and music and static as though someone is trying to find the right frequency.

Suddenly, Jenks is there, holding him firmly, pulling him

away and quietly saying, 'It's alright, it's alright.' There is a woman crying and Molly is yelling, 'Stop this, please, stop.' Someone is laughing hysterically and a voice on the radio whispers, 'The past is rotting flesh, poisoning the ground.' He sees a grave with a vase of plastic roses and then it's a rose garden at dawn and the petals are laced with dew, and another, softer, voice says, 'The future is a gentle shower of rain and spring blossom.' He feels the rain on his face. Hawk flies in through the centre of a great rose window, crashing through the stained glass.

And then everything goes black.

Rose

My son. My son. My son.

Jenks

There is a massive roll of thunder and the terrace doors crash open onto pandemonium. Jenks rushes forward, ducking the wild bird that is swooping crazily above their heads, whirling in panic, looking for a means of escape. In a flash of lightning, he sees it clawing at the head of the American woman, who lets out a piercing scream and strikes at it as it tears her face.

He grabs Alfie firmly from behind to stop him causing any more harm. Alfie's body ricochets in his arms like a wild animal struggling to free itself from a trap, and he still holds on to the other boy's throat.

'It's alright. It's alright. Let him go. Let him go.'

Alfie stops. His entire body collapses and he passes out, but not before whispering, so low that maybe only Jenks can hear, 'He hurt me.'

A fully grown hawk lies on the dining table, feebly fluttering a damaged wing. Mickey is lifting an empty bottle of wine ready to smash her skull in, but Jenks stays his hand.

'No. There's been enough violence for one evening.' Their eyes meet in a brief contest of wills but, finally, Mickey concedes. Carolina's face is smeared with blood and mascara. Joseph, in his mother's arms, now sits upright, nursing his throat and glaring at Bogboy. Brendan is dabbing his mouth with his napkin, and has laid his other hand over Jocelyn's, for comfort. The window panes are rattling loudly and there is no sign of the storm abating. Nobody will be leaving the house tonight, that much is certain.

Tante's voice rings out across the room – 'Dinner is over. We will retire next door. Bring lights.' – as though nothing in the least bit untoward has occurred. Without so much as a glance at the injured Carolina, she adds, 'And can somebody switch off the wireless and do something to help that poor, damaged bird? Come, Brendan.'

She picks up a candelabra and imperiously leads the way.

Hawk

She is dying. The fierce, gold fire in her eye is diminishing. Her spirit is tuning to a new note. No need now for hunger. No more struggle. The infinite is calling her. Her wings are quivering and fluttering and her body is shaking, convulsing and dropping out of the light. Now she is a dead bird, alone in darkness, on a table of smashed crockery and spilled soup.

Molly

Oh my boy! How has it come to this? She tries to comprehend what has just happened. Two, seemingly random, acts of physical violence arose out of the blue, one after the other. She orders Cassie to fetch a couple of spare oil lamps from the cupboard under the stairs, and now the scene glows eerily, everyone's faces half-lit in the darkness. Joseph is back to his sombre and withdrawn self, and she would have loved to just pack him off to bed straight away but, whatever he might be feeling, they still have guests to take care of. It is the sacred law of Irish hospitality and there is nothing she can do but keep going. She waits for some instruction from Madame. Does she now need to fix up spare bedrooms for the night? There haven't been house guests for years. But Madame has enthroned herself on the ornate chaise longue that dominates the centre of the room and, apart from an instruction to the guests to help themselves to a drink – which they have all eagerly obeyed – she seems in no further hurry to take charge again. She has never appeared more inscrutable.

The American woman has taken out a small compact to check the damage and gasps at the sight of a deep gash on her forehead and a long scratch down her left cheek. Molly brings cotton swabs and antiseptic to clean out the wound and dabs gently at her face. 'Gee! That crazy bird. Do you think I'll end up with a scar? Perhaps I should find me a hotshot lawyer and sue somebody', she mutters, loudly enough for them all to hear.

There is little doubt for whom the threat is intended, but Madame refuses to rise to the bait and continues to sit upright, hands folded as if in prayer. Michael stands, drumming his fingers restlessly on the back of the winged armchair in which his companion sits, while at the same time helping himself to generous amounts of Jameson's from the bottle he's brought across to a side-table for his own private use. Just the same greedy, angry Michael that she remembers.

The French doors bang again in the dining room as Cassie breathlessly announces to Tante and the assembled company that it looks like the bird is dead and what should she do with it?

'We'll find a little box for it and bury it later,' replies Madame.

'We can't keep a dead bird in the house, Madame. It's terrible for luck.'

'You can attend to it later, Cassie,' Madame replies, sharply.

Bogboy, that wild one, is still groggy and half-asleep, on the velvet sofa, where he's been carefully laid by the Englishman who had carried him from the dining room. Both he and Madame seem protective of him, despite his brutal attack on her son. What is going on? Surely Madame and Bogboy hate each other? But here they are, while her son, the injured party, skulks at the back of the room in the shadows, as far from Madame and Bogboy as he can manage.

And where does that leave her? With her son? With Tante? Surely not with the Americans. Brendan sits quietly, opposite Carolina, in between the two camps in the one comfortable armchair available. He has said almost nothing throughout all the shenanigans, apart from remarking that it is unfortunate they won't now be able to leave tonight. It is still unclear to everyone but Madame why exactly he is here at all, but some kind of legal announcement must have been intended. All in all, he seems by far the least perturbed person present.

Why would Alfie attack Joseph? The sheer unprovoked ferocity of it makes no sense. A touch of madness? But it didn't seem like madness and she too had been close enough to hear

Bogboy when he whispered quietly, 'He hurt me.' Yes, she is sure she'd heard that right. Her mind goes back to the night Bogboy disappeared, how Joseph had returned late, even more distant and uncommunicative than ever. And then there was the scene at the Englishman's cottage when they went to bring Bogboy home. Molly remembers the look of terror in Alfie's eyes. She desperately seeks to subdue the memory. Meanwhile, the rain continues to sluice down, drumming on the roof tiles and cascading through the old cast-iron guttering.

Joseph

Just look at the oul' bitch, queening it over us all, guarding that little pervert like he's a bit of her best china. I'm the one who's been hurt, he thinks, aggrieved. Just his luck the bloody rain is lashing it down and all his ma can do is order him around, alongside that gormless girl, like he's just another household skivvy. Rage rises inside him. It brings with it a mental image that he'd rather not see, much less think about – Bogboy writhing and squirming beneath him. Slow down, boyo, no need for any of that. But it's too late, he's already remembering and, as he remembers, he wants to crush the life out of Bogboy all over again, as if that might erase the memory once and for all. He feels a surge of violent hatred for his enemy and the quare fella he's taken up with. What the feck is that all about?

Why is he being made the villain in all this? Tears of self-pity well up and he quickly wipes them away, glad that he's nearly hidden here in the dark. Fat chance any of them will have anything to do with the will, if that's what this evening is all about. There'll be nothing left by the time all the creditors have had their way. And what's left will go to these two in front of him – why else would yer one from America be over, sniffing about with his woman in tow, like a pig at a trough? The oul' bitch is on her way out, that's for sure. She's nothing now but a bag of skin and bone. And the Yanks will be getting the house, for what it's worth. Never mind that yer fella *Mickey* did the dirty on them all. Blood is blood.

And me and Ma will be turfed out on our ear without so much as a thank you note, he thinks bitterly, or maybe just a card and a jar of homemade gooseberry jam as a bonus to repay thirty years loyal and devoted service. That's how rich people do things. Why can't his mother see the truth? That she's never been more than a slave, just like her mother was before her.

Well, he is getting away from all the lies and rigmarole at the earliest opportunity.

Bogboy

He wakes. Or thinks he does. What is this darkness? This roaring in his ears? He was flying with Hawk through many dimensions. At the end of a long tunnel he saw a figure that might have been his father: handsome, and smiling at him broadly. And the figure pointed back the way he had come and said, 'You have a life to live, my beautiful boy.' And Bogboy had felt himself being pulled back by a force more powerful even than gravity.

Now there's the beginning of feeling and memory, a persistent sense of floating in a visible world of light and other presences, shadows becoming defined in space, faces taking on dimension and features. Now he's Hawk, ready to spread his talons and choke the life out of the flesh beneath; now he's Bogboy and his hands grip hard and know again pure rage, an urge to kill. The shame of it consumes him and a wave of grief and disgust sweeps through his body. He groans and the shadow shapes beside him stir. Jenks's voice brings him back to himself.

'Shhh. Take your time. You're safe now.'

'I did a bad thing.'

'Maybe yes and maybe no.'

Again, he enters a dizzying vortex, whirling him back once more to the violation of his body, which now starts to shudder uncontrollably. Jenks is holding him and Tante is ordering someone to bring brandy. Now he is looking down, with his bird's eye view on his own body, wracked and convulsed with sobs and Jenks is holding him tight and comforting him and saying, over and over, 'Shhh. It's alright. It's alright.' But it's not alright. It will never be alright and his howl fills the room and it's both him and not him, as though he's watching another Bogboy from afar, while all the other shadow figures are making a great commotion and his uncle is shouting, 'For Chrissakes, will someone explain what's going on here?'

Someone is pouring burning liquid down his throat and he splutters, 'Shay?' But it's not Shay, it's Tante. He chokes and coughs. He's just Bogboy again, lying on a couch with a room full of people staring at him.

Jenks whispers in his ear and he shakes his head. He won't do that. But Jenks insists, 'It's the only way.'

Hawk's fearlessness invigorates him. No enemy will have power over him ever again. He manages to get to his feet and shakily removes his shirt.

'Show them,' says Jenks, quietly.

Bogboy turns and shows the whole room his back, with its healed but still livid scars. He feels like meat, like an exhibit, a freak at a funfair, but there's relief, too, that his shame is exposed for the world to see at last.

'Oh, my God,' gasps a female voice.

'What the hell?'

Jenks turns him back to face the room. 'Now, tell everyone who did this to you.'

Bogboy points directly at Joseph, who yells, 'No. No. It's a lie. I didn't do anything. He's lying.'

'Where do you think you're going?' It's Jenks again, although he's not speaking to him but to Joseph, heading for the door.

'I don't have to stay here and what business is it of yours anyway? Your *friend* there just tried to kill me, the mad little bastard.' He doesn't even try to keep the sneer out of his voice.

'Joseph. You'll keep a civil tongue in your head in front of our guests.' Tante's voice cuts through the air.

'Why should I? He attacked me. You all saw it. He's not right in the head.'

'The young guy's got a point.' Michael has now joined in.

'You'll leave when I say it's time for you to leave, Joseph.' There's ice in Tante's voice.

'Joseph, do as you're told,' adds Molly.

Joseph hesitates at the door before going to stand, pointedly, beside Michael. They nod almost imperceptibly to each other.

'Listen, I don't know much about the law, but a fella's usually judged innocent until proved guilty, in my book,' says Michael. 'Where's the proof? Seems to me my little nephew here is throwing out some pretty wild accusations. It's just one guy's word against another.'

'Yes, Michael. Like the night you were at old Louis' cottage when it when it went up in flames with him still inside? "Your word against mine." Your exact words.' Molly rounded on him.

'What the hell are you talking about?'

'Oh, wow, chickens coming home to roost all round,' Carolina drawls. 'Quite a show you people put on for us tourists.'

'The ghosts have stirred,' Tante murmurs.

There's a smell of burning in the air. For a moment Bogboy's face and body feel unbearably hot.

Molly turns all her anger on Michael. There's no mistaking her contempt. 'You know exactly what I'm talking about. But that's between you and your God, if you have one. So, Joseph, my son' – Molly speaks low, but the pain in her voice is unmistakeable – 'swear on your father's grave that what Alfie says isn't true.'

'I never...' Joseph's voice starts to crack. All eyes are on him. 'I never... he started it.'

'Oh, Jesus, are we to be spared nothing in this house? This is not how you were brought up. If Paddy could only see –'

'Don't bring my father into this,' Joseph half-yells, half-cries.

'Started... what?' It's Jenks again.

'Looking... at me.'

'You did this because he was *looking* at you?'

Joseph's expression is a mask of venom. 'You tell them. Little sneak. Little pervert. Looking at... at... what you shouldn't have.' His voice sounds hoarse and cracked. Then he turns to everyone with new-found defiance. 'He's sick. He's just a sissy boy.'

'And you did this to him?' Molly's voice is hard.

'I didn't... I don't have to explain...'

'Oh, I think you do.' Tante brooks no argument.

'Fuck you all!'

Before anyone has time to stop him, he pushes past the Yanks, stumbles, and runs from the room. They all hear him fight to open the front door and there's a howl of wind and rain, and a loud slam as he plunges out into the night and the storm.

'Someone go after him. God only knows what he might do.' Tante tries to regain control of the room.

'I'll go.' Before anyone can argue, Jenks follows Joseph out into the darkness.

Jenks

Lightning zigzags the sky, and a barrage of thunder and torrential rain buffets all his senses as he plunges out into the elements. He has only intuition to guide him. He strains to hear some sound that might tell him the lad is near. Finally, he catches a distant, familiar whinny and he knows exactly where his quarry has headed. The big house still has the remains of a stable block, where Alfie sheltered Lily earlier in the evening. There is another neigh, louder now and with a note of anxiety in it. Jenks fights his way round to the yard at the back. Joseph is struggling to drag the horse out into the open. Despite the dark and the lashing rain, Jenks catches a glimpse of the white orbs of her eyes.

'Stop. Can't you see she's terrified?' Half his words are lost in the howling wind, but Joseph spins round for a second, just as Lily kicks out at him. This serves to infuriate him more and in a brash, athletic move he leaps onto her back, loses grip of the reins and can barely right himself before she bolts, with him clinging to her mane.

Whether by accident or design, horse and rider are heading directly for Jenks and he throws himself aside as they thunder past. His shoulder makes painful contact with the ground. Cursing, he levers himself painfully back upright, just in time to see Lily vanishing at full speed down the driveway. He stumbles after them, clutching his shoulder.

A low branch from the big copper beech that should have been pruned long before, brings the horse to a shuddering halt. Lily rears and tosses her rider backwards. Jenks sees the shadowy shape of Joseph arc through the air. The body hits the ground and doesn't move, and Jenks runs as best he can to the spot.

Joseph is sprawled in an unnatural loose-limbed pose. Jenks kneels down to him. The boy doesn't appear to be breathing and there is a trail of blood trickling from his mouth. Jenks lies him gently on his back and gets to work applying the kiss of life, methodically pumping the boy's chest with calm, practised strokes. 'Come on. Come on,' he urges, trying to infuse the body with his own life force. When he glances up, he spots Lily a short distance away, panting beneath an ancient oak tree. She seems like the only sign of normality in this bizarre drama. Through the curtain of rain, he is startled for a second to see what looks like the pale, glowing outline of a man, standing next to the horse, which seems in no way spooked by the unearthly presence. When he looks again, the ghostly apparition has vanished.

Still, he perseveres. Eventually, he is rewarded with a faint but unmistakeable stirring of life. A pulse flickers, along with a twitch beneath closed eyelids. Whatever state Joseph might be in, he is at least alive. There is also a lessening of the storm's fierceness, as though its energy, too, is spent. Jenks cautiously approaches Lily. She bridles, then calms as he gently whispers in her ear, low, soothing sounds and makes long, firm strokes down her neck and haunch to soothe her once again with his familiar touch. He draws her forward by the reins.

Yet again, Jenks is faced with a difficult decision. It is all too possible that Joseph has broken bones – even his back – but he needs to be inside, warm and safe, as a matter of urgency. There is nothing for it. But will Lily oblige? Jenks brings the horse up to the injured body and, with all his might, despite the stab of pain along his shoulder and ribs, lifts the young man and hoists him across her back. She patiently accepts this new deadweight without protest, and he is gratified to hear a groan from Joseph. Any sign of life is better than none. Carefully, he leads the horse back toward the house. Even amidst all that he has endured, he still has time to wonder what strange quirk of fate it is that sends him out, time and again, to become the saviour of reckless, damaged young men.

Tante

It has turned into the longest night. While they wait for the outcome of Jenks's search, she has insisted that Cassie transfer the rest of the meal – a *boeuf-en-croûte* and a *tarte tatin* – to the side-table in the drawing room for the guests to pick at if they feel so inclined. Unsurprisingly, nobody has much appetite for food, with the exception of Michael, who, she notes, has managed to wolf down a couple of portions of each course without slowing down any on his alcoholic intake.

She catches Brendan's eye and when he sidles over to her, whispers, 'It will keep until the morning. There's no rush now,' and he nods. She is immensely grateful for his professional calm at the minute. It is impossible to tell what he really thinks of the high melodrama unfolding all around him.

Molly is a different matter altogether. She appears possessed by a tumult of emotions, ranging from fear to anger, resulting in a state of high anxiety about her son. The best course of action has been to keep her occupied, and she is currently seeing to the makeshift guest rooms.

But when Tante suggests that people retire for the night, only Brendan acquiesces. Eventually, Carolina also allows herself to be shepherded upstairs, with barely more than a glance at Michael, who stays behind, which in itself is a telling state of affairs. However, within minutes, his head begins to loll down to his chest, and he collapses into the vacated chair and promptly falls into a drunken, fitful sleep, punctuated by a wheezing snore.

Alfie has sunk back into a restless, semi-feverish doze. Molly has brought pillows and blankets and helped tuck him up. Whatever Molly's private thoughts might be about what transpired between him and her son, for now it appears her responsibilities as housekeeper have taken precedence. But neither she nor Tante make any attempt to make Michael any more comfortable. Even Irish hospitality has its limits.

As for Tante, all the effort and tension she's been holding onto for so long is unravelling. Her fight is almost done. Rose is back. A distinct smell of Sobranie cigarette smoke, mixed with Rose's favourite cologne, wafts into her nostrils. Yes. Her sister is waiting too. Has been for a long time.

'Join us. You're not having any fun down here, that's for sure,' comes a familiar whisper, followed by a tinkling laugh. Even from beyond the grave, Rose is about to get her wish. As always.

And her sister is right. What on earth has she to hold on for anymore? Nothing – except for this – and she lightly strokes the warm forehead of the feverish boy who intermittently moans an incomprehensible babble. She moistens her handkerchief in the water jug and tenderly rubs his temples, as though with that one gesture alone she might erase his cares, along with her years of neglect of him.

Molly rushes downstairs to answer an urgent banging at the

front door, and Tante follows her. Molly's high-pitched howl fills the whole house as Jenks stands in the doorway, with the limp, almost lifeless, body of Joseph in his arms.

Bogboy

He's Hawk King leading his men to victory. The sky is blood-mixed-with-lymph-red and the sun blazes down on shield and sword. The plain echoes to the thunderous drumbeat of hooves kicking up dust as the rival armies approach one another with fearsome yells and whoops. It's the day of reckoning. There will be no retreat. The invader must be crushed and turned back to the sea. Hawk King's men are ready, warriors all, primed for the battle despite sweltering in the noonday heat. He feels the sweat dripping down his body. He steels himself to face his foe. Pitiless, black-hearted crow. Coward and thief. But now Hawk King is stronger, and his revenge will be all the sweeter. He has his tribe at his back. Tall in the saddle, he rides fearlessly forth. In this place, he is king once more. There's a roar from his men as he lifts his great sword, and a line of molten gold flows along its edge as he wields it high overhead, preparing to strike it down to bludgeon the skull of his enemy once and for all. There's a harsh clash of metal and a piercing scream.

Bogboy wakes. His body is soaking beneath the blankets. As he shakes himself back into consciousness, he sees Jenks enter the room with Joseph in his arms and hears Molly begging, 'Oh, God in heaven, tell me he's not going to die. He's all I have left in the world.'

In a daze, he stands. Jenks brings the body and lays it on the couch where only moments before he himself was lying.

'Is he...?'

'No. But he's in a bad way. He rode off on Lily and had a fall. I'm worried he may have broken his back. We have to get him to hospital.'

This is all quietly conveyed. Tante pours Molly a brandy and sits her down. But she won't be calmed and out of the blue she rushes across to Bogboy and slaps him so hard across the face that he stumbles backwards and nearly falls. Jenks catches him just in time.

'This is your doing. You and your filthy ways. You drove my boy to this! May God have mercy on your soul.'

In the shocked silence, nobody moves. Then a hoarse voice groans from the corner, 'What time is it? Any chance of a pot of black tea, strong, with sugar?' Mickey has woken from his drunken slumber.

Mickey

He can't quite remember how he's ended up here in the freezing kitchen. Somewhere, he's lost a few hours of his life.

He remembers how Molly's mother would always have the range laid with sticks and turf at the crack of dawn so the place would already be heated up by the time the rest of the house was stirring. Now, despite the cold, he must have drifted off for a moment, because when his eyes suddenly snap open again, his sister is sitting opposite him, staring silently at him. The boy is beside her, equally inscrutable. At the other end of the table sits Brendan, with a pile of documents in front of him. Somebody has made a big pot of tea which is placed in the middle of the table with a jug of milk and a bowl of sugar and there are cups in front of everyone, though nobody has bothered to pour. This used to be a comforting place.

It has all gone wrong. Even he can see the contempt in everyone's eyes. It has become only too clear that this had been his last throw of the dice.

When a woman turns on you, there is nothing for it but to quit the game altogether. His sister has been taking pleasure in humiliating him. He's walked straight into her trap. What had he been thinking?

The only option left is to let it fall out as it will, but he can already tell the result isn't going to be pretty. Whatever Jocelyn has up her sleeve, it is coming with a hefty dose of revenge – that much is clear. As for Carolina... that is on the outs, no doubt about it. You can always count on a woman to betray you.

There are no niceties.

'What were you honestly expecting, Michael? That we'd all just let bygones be bygones?'

He is stupefied.

'I used to carry you in here and rock you to sleep when you wouldn't stop crying and Mama couldn't cope with you. I was barely more than a child myself.'

He stares at her for a moment before answering, 'I don't remember.'

She smiles her older-sister smile, still so familiar. 'How could you? You were just a wee baby. We all adored you. Rose. Me. The whole family. But you were too much of a handful for Mama. She suffered terribly with her nerves after you were born.'

'I didn't know that.'

'You were meant to save her marriage, you know? She finally produced a male heir. We girls weren't good enough, you see. But, instead, things just got worse.'

'I'm sorry.'

'There's nothing for you here. You do know that?'

'No?'

'There's barely enough of an inheritance for Alfie.'

'I thought there might be something. When he comes of age. You said there was a trust fund. Surely it would be shared between the three of us, you and me and Rose – or Rose's boy.'

'There was a trust fund. I had to apply to the courts for access to it, to keep the estate going. There's nothing left of it now. And in any case, you weren't named. I never said you were named.'

'But I'm the boy. The male line, and all that. I thought there'd be something.'

'Have you forgotten this was Mama's family home, her estate, her money? She could leave it as she chose. She cut you out, didn't you know? Of course, you didn't, because once you'd ruined everything for us all, you ran away as fast as your legs would carry you. When your own sister died, you couldn't even be bothered to come back home for her funeral. That was the end of you for Mother. It was no surprise to me that you didn't come back for hers. You were always a coward, Michael.'

A picture comes into his mind's eye of peeking into the drawing room on winter and spring days while his sisters were at school and he was left at home with Mama, alone, always alone, watching her play her sad cantatas on the baby grand, a glass of gin and tonic to one side. He'd always been entranced, by the cascade of music, firstly, but also tense with anticipation that the glass might tumble and splash all over the keys. On good days, she might usher him in and sit him down on the piano stool beside her and show him the fingering of the black notes and the white, stretching his pudgy fingers to their widest extent to create the required sounds, and he'd laugh along with her, his chest bursting with joy at the notes he'd made that reverberated and vibrated in the air around them. But there were fewer and fewer good days in the end. And one day he watched her keel over at the stool – the gin had had the last laugh – before she pulled herself abruptly back upright and slammed down the lid. On another occasion, when she'd spotted him spying on her – he couldn't have been more than four or five at the time – she'd sent him off to the kitchen to get lemon slices to freshen up her drink. He could even remember the look on Molly's mother's face as she'd angrily sliced into a fresh lemon with the sharp knife that he was forbidden to go near and lain the slivers on a small saucer for him. He'd understood, from his earliest memory, the change that drink brought about in her. His father too had been a heavy drinker. But unlike his wife, he was a social alcoholic.

He'd taken after his father.

He can feel the presence of both his parents in the room, on either side of him. And what chance did any of us ever have? he thinks bitterly, but can only manage to blurt out...

'I... it's not true.'

But it is true. How can he explain the years he's spent trying to erase the shame and loss he'd felt? That he'd run away because it was the only option available to him. The only way he could save himself. Or so he had thought. But in the end, he'd always banked on an inheritance, however small, as his last resort.

'Why?'

'You really have to ask?'

'I made some mistakes but even so...'

'You signed away most of the estate on a foolish, criminal gamble... you ran away, Michael, and left the rest of us to clean up the mess you left behind. There are a couple of old documents where it looks like you forged our mother's signature, so I wouldn't go contesting anything if I were you.' And she stares across at Brendan who quietly assents.

'I tried my best, Joycie. I tried to make a future for us all.'

'You tried to make a future for you, Michael. No-one else.'

He can't think of anything to say.

'Molly is upstairs, lying next to her son, who may or may not make it. Christopher, Alfie's friend, has gone to Ballykineen for the doctor and an ambulance. Cassie's keeping an eye on Molly and Joseph, for now, while we deal with this matter. God knows what state Joseph's in or what care he'll need from now on, if he does pull through. But my will makes provision for her. And for Joseph. That's what Brendan was going to make clear before all this... stupidity... came on us. When I'm gone, everything else goes to Alfie. I've nominated Brendan as my executor, and he will oversee everything until Alfie comes of age. It will be up to Alfie then to decide what to do with the house and what's left of the land. So, you see, there really is nothing here for you.'

Alfie startled, looks up

'I don't understand.'

'You're the legal heir to the estate, Alfie.'

'All of it?'

'Yes. When Mother was dying, only Michael and I stood to inherit, but she'd seen how he squandered his intended legacy, which was nearly all the land, so in her will it was entrusted to me to take care of... on your behalf. That was the promise I made to your mother and mine.'

'How did I not know this?'

'That was very wrong of me. I'm sorry, Alfie, but I wasn't in my right mind for a long time.'

'But, anyway, you're still alive.'

She looks at the boy. Michael sees the penny drop for him.

'So, you see, you'll have to decide soon what to do. Brendan here will help you. He's always been a good friend to our family.'

'I get to decide everything?' There is a note of wonder in his voice.

'Yes. And there's more. But that's for later. Let's settle all this for now.'

As if in answer, Brendan gives a friendly nod in the boy's direction. It is as though they've already moved on and forgotten Mickey's plight.

'For pity's sake, I've nowhere else to go.' He despises the pleading he can hear in his voice. It's like sitting in this old kitchen has reduced him to the frightened little boy he's always felt himself to be.

'I'm sorry, Michael. That's on Alfie, here.'

There is an amused laugh from the doorway and Carolina enters from where she's been standing smoking and listening in, no doubt, the entire time. She's cleaned off the last of her make up. The left side of her face and jaw is badly cut and bruised. She looks shockingly old and haggard, as though she, too, has given up holding her mask in place.

'I have to say, you guys are just precious! Don't make a fight of it. I'd say she has you fair and square.'

'Why don't you just...?' It is out of his mouth before he can stop himself.

'What, Mickey? "Feck off", as you Irish so charmingly put it? Oh, don't you worry, I'll be doing that as soon as I can get a cab out of this God-forsaken bog. No offence, ma'am' – directly to Jocelyn – 'you've been very... surprising.' She stubs the remains of her cigarette out on a saucer on the table. 'I don't, as a rule, hold with hanging out with losers' – she turns her full attention on Mickey – 'and boy, you are one big fat loser.'

Alfie

So, this is it. He looks around the room he had once turned into his personal hideaway, as far from other humans as he could manage. He returns to find it untouched, festooned with cobwebs and dust, the decayed remains of his circles and the filthy bed on the floor. As he sets about clearing out his past, from top to bottom, he wonders who that person had been.

Before he left, Brendan had instructed him to be in touch. He has a future now. He has prospects. He has choices to make. People are talking to him as though he were an adult. His days are occupied with decisions. No longer can he wander randomly through a world that appears magnificent and terrifying at one and the same time. Now he can ride his horse across his estate, through fields that are rented out to local farmers and bring in a modest income. Tante and Brendan have shown him ledgers of accounts. They seem large sums of money. In reality, they explain, it is barely enough to pay the most basic necessities and upkeep. It is as though a whole secret world is being revealed to him. A world of figures and columns, monthly income and expenses, notarised in Tante's careful script. And there are even a few small investments, stocks and shares and bonds, that have been saved from the creditors who came calling all those years ago when Uncle Michael had gambled away the family fortune. Thanks to her general frugality and careful husbandry, they are not destitute. As for the house, yes, it is leaking in places and mildewed in others but, in many respects, it is a fine, solid property which can be renovated and restored with a not-too-sizeable bank loan. Brendan has promised to look into it for him and propose a plan.

He understands that he is being primed in the running of

the estate's affairs; that Tante is not long for this world, and that this is her final attempt to make amends. The revelation for both of them has been his aptitude for numbers. He is a quick learner and when she explains something – the maintenance of the garden, who owes what to the estate, when payments are due, what bills are ongoing and when they have to be paid by, the roof repairs, the problems with the boiler, or how often the septic tank needs emptying – he comes back with questions and wants more information. He can tell she approves. He shares with her a grasp of detail, added to his own natural curiosity about everything.

Now he has a destiny mapped out for him. He can be the one to bring new life to the estate, to restore its fortunes. To what purpose? The thought niggles at the back of his head and won't leave him in peace. He lies in bed in his small attic room, now spotless, and bare except for the big iron bedstead he's hauled in sections up to the top of the house with Jenks's help.

'You're sure you don't want to move into one of the big bedrooms?' his friend had asked. He was adamant he didn't.

'Same old Bogboy,' Jenks smiled.

But it is more than that. It is as if he is still resisting the final symbolic step of becoming that person: the landowner, the man of property. Something in him still baulks at – what? The responsibility? The certainty? The finality of it? Who would he become out here on his own? That is the biggest question of all.

But who would stop him if he chose to offer the travellers a permanent meadow of their own for their caravans? Even as he momentarily indulges the fantasy that Shay might be willing to come and live and work on his land, he knows how wild and impractical that idea would turn out to be. They had met up occasionally, when the opportunity presented itself, for brief and unsatisfactory couplings, which had none of the blissful transcendence he'd associated with their first coming together. Shay would simply turn up out of the blue – 'To see how you and Lily are getting on' – but they both knew the real reason.

As soon as he'd ensured the coast was clear, Alfie would lead Shay to Lily's stable, where he would find himself being pushed down roughly onto a heap of straw. So, this is sex? he'd think, as they grunted and groped towards some kind of mutual physical release, clawing roughly at one another's bodies in the hopes of working up a spark of genuine passion. Shay had appeared to be perfectly satisfied, at least, simply asking 'Did you get off?' But he didn't seem unduly concerned to get an answer and hadn't wanted to hang around, hurriedly dressing again without any gesture of affection, and vanishing as quickly as he'd arrived.

Another time had been even less edifying. Shay had appeared again, out of nowhere, to say that the travellers were moving on now, somewhere up north for the summer, and he thought he'd come and say goodbye. This led to a quick-fire exchange of mutual cock-tugging just out of range of the house in the big, back meadow and was no more fulfilling than a bout of self-pleasuring, not helped by the fact that as they approached a foregone conclusion, Cassie appeared, strolling along the driveway on her way up to the house. Spotting them both half-hidden beneath a flowering rhododendron, she had called out a cheerful, apparently guileless, 'Hiya'. Enough, as Shay laconically remarked, to put any fella off his stride.

Just as he's thinking of Cassie, she appears, breathless.

'Ma'am wants to see you. She says it's important.'

He is used to this by now. 'Another royal summons,' he responds, and is gratified to see Cassie's plain, serious face break out into a naughty grin and to be able to share a rare moment of complicity with her. She really is a sweet, good-hearted girl, he thinks. She deserves someone to love her, and he finds himself wishing that Joseph might still recover and maybe the two of them might find some comfort in each other. He is startled to realise that he now wishes only happiness for his one-time enemy. But Tante has called and it is time to answer.

Sometimes, Tante might remember some particular item of estate or household management she's overlooked – how to contact the hedger when the hawthorn hedges need hard pruning in early spring, for example, or the name and address of the best butcher in Westport. They are random sessions because they never know how well she will be feeling. Where once her inner sanctum had been virtually forbidden to him, now her sickroom has become an all-too-familiar sight. Her huge four-poster with its beautiful, chinoiserie coverlet that marks out the extent of her world – surrounded by her past, her beloved books and photo albums, plus a pharmacy of medicines and pills of every description in blue and green bottles, none of which appear to have much effect on her health, and boxes of papers, including the household accounts. Occasionally, there would be a tray with the remains of a frugal breakfast or lunch barely touched. That is the one thing that tends to make him sad. And yet her eyes still hold his, as steady as they ever did. He can see now what he has never noticed before: that her fierce gaze includes care, and, yes, even love. For the first time in his life, he feels himself willing her to live, to believe in her own future as well as his.

Cassie

Our Blessed Lady in Heaven, please save Joseph and make him wake up for his mammy's sake. I hope you will forgive me asking you for this special favour but you're the Mater Dolorosa and I know you understand what it means to lose a son. I know Joseph did some bad things in the past but if you can intercede with our Lord and help him get well again, I will say a decade of the rosary every day for a year and light a candle in your honour every time I go to Mass from now on, also for a whole year. And I know you can see into my heart, so please teach me to serve and worship you as best I can and to avoid all lustful feelings. And if you let Joseph get better, I promise to stay pure in thought, word and deed and to love and care for him like a brother. Amen.

Bogboy

Now his kingdom has a castle. His world, and everything in it, has been turned upside down.

The only other companion in the house, aside from Tante herself, and Cassie, who has shouldered the role of housekeeper while Molly is sitting in the Galway hospital at Joseph's side, is Michael, who spends the majority of his waking hours in his room, getting quietly drunk and listening to American sports broadcasts on the old radio, the excited voices of the commentators, crackling and distant on the airwaves. He rarely comes downstairs. Carolina has simply taken off without a backward glance.

With his enemies and adversaries vanquished, Bogboy discovers that victory leaves a bitter taste in his mouth and is not nearly as satisfying in reality as it had been in his dreams. He has no really satisfactory explanation as to why this should be so. If anything, he feels nothing but sorrow for them all. He feels as though his world of colour and flux and shape and pure sensation has begun to come into sharp-edged focus. He misses Hawk. Although he still takes time out to scour the heavens, trying to conjure her up, she won't appear, and he knows in his heart that she can't.

The only person who might understand is Jenks but now he too is talking of leaving, of going back to England – his father is seriously ill and his mother, who is in her eighties, wants him by her side. Everywhere Alfie looks, he seems to be surrounded by the dead and dying.

He and Jenks haven't spent much time together in the past few weeks, not since he moved back to the big house to be near Tante and keep an eye on her. He's ridden across on Lily to say hello a couple of times – it is part of their unspoken agreement that Lily is now his horse entirely – but it is as though there is a distance between them again, almost as if their closeness was only a temporary interlude and a polite, very English formality has once again taken its place. Neither of them seems to know how to reclaim the ease they once had in each other's company.

Meanwhile, he has decided to tidy up the old, walled, vegetable garden and restore it to its former glory. There is a glasshouse that has long been abandoned, so he's made the restoration of both it and the garden his first big project. And he has discovered he likes the work. It suits him to have a purpose. When Jenks found out what he was doing, he'd offered to come over and help. And it is while they are out gardening that they are finally able to talk once more as friends.

It is a warm, dry day in May, the first really warm day of the year. Both of them have begun to work up a sweat, have stripped off their shirts, and are enjoying the feeling of the sun on their skin. Jenks, in particular, has started to turn a healthy-looking shade of brown. It is good to be doing something physical and practical, weeding and planting out new beds and setting up plots for runner beans and tomatoes, sowing winter root vegetables – and they rediscover a mutually satisfying, quiet rhythm in the task at hand.

They are digging a long, deep trench for the potatoes and laying them in the bed of rich, moist loam. He loves to watch the ripple of Jenks's strong back muscles gleaming as he bends to his task of planting the small, chitted potatoes, that look like pale, white bones being buried in the earth, and carefully spading the soft earth over them. He hands them to his friend from the supply he's brought across in trays from the glasshouse.

'We'll cover them with a bit of straw, in case we get a late frost again,' says Jenks.

'Will you come back again? Afterwards.'

'I don't know.'

'Are you sorry you came here?'

Jenks turns fully to face him. 'So many questions, young fella-me-lad.' But his smile is warm.

'You haven't had much peace here. We caused you a lot of trouble. All of us.'

'True.' He straightens up and leans on his spade. 'But look, we got to know each other, didn't we? So, it hasn't been all bad.'

'I'm sorry.'

Jenks looks puzzled

'Sorry. Whatever for?'

'I haven't been a very good friend.'

Jenks studies him for a moment. A knowing look that is kind and sad at the same time.

'It's hard sometimes to know what true friendship means.'

Alfie nods.

'Anyway, I think you're becoming exactly who you need to become.'

He is being offered a blessing that he doesn't feel he deserves, but Jenks saves his blushes.

'Come on, we should finish this business here. Those clouds over there don't look too friendly.' It's true; there is a sudden chill in the air. And he can't now bring himself to ask the one question he most wants the answer to. 'Will you miss me?'

Because whatever the answer is, it will be the wrong one.

Tante

I didn't know how to live but at least I can learn how to die, Tante thinks.

'Rose? Are you there? Are you there? I know you are.'

And Rose *is* there, standing in her customary place at the foot of the bed, wearing a beautiful silk chemise, decorated with a print of blushing pink roses, and drawing on her Sobranie that looks more like a liquorice stick than a cigarette. Her skin looks pale, translucent, and she appears, surrounded by a glowing ball of silver light, like a fresh photograph that has just emerged out of the developer's tray.

These days, the ghosts are more real and more vividly alive and present to her than the living, certainly more alive to her than Cassie who comes most days now, except at weekends when she heads over to Galway and spends her time in silent vigil at Joseph's bedside, and invariably answers, 'No change, Ma'am,' when asked for a progress report. Tante can barely keep food down. A bowl of watery, chicken soup and maybe a small serving of mashed potatoes and carrots. Invalid portions.

'You're doing well,' remarks Rose.

'Stop it!'

'No. Really. You've done the right thing. At last.'

It is impossible to ignore the sting. 'Perhaps.'

'You have.'

'Yes.'

'So?'

'What?'

'Will you tell him the rest, now?'

She sighs. There is always more.

'You know I'm right.'

'Yes.'

Hers has not been a household where honesty reigned; hers has been a household of silences, thick with gloom and dust, filled with loss, regret and recrimination. But Rose isn't about to give up.

'This is not the place for him. And you know it. He was born for the mad, wide world. Don't let him be stifled. Not all laws apply to everyone.'

She can hear Rose's voice, loud and clear, quivering with feeling, the pure Irish lilt of it. There is a note of desperate pleading, almost fear, along with the anger. Rose vanishes into the ether again, her admonition still ringing in Tante's ears. Tante's breath comes rapidly. Her heart is fluttering. Suddenly, a polyphonic chorus of sound crashes over her: her own harsh breathing; the loud chitter of birds, cawing rooks, full-throated doves, a sudden flurry of pigeon wings; a courtyard, where feet shuffle and clatter across the mosaic tiles; the roar of the crowd at a *corrida*; young men driving scooters down narrow, winding mediaeval streets; the chant of children in the village school as their pure, young voices decline their ten times table; their laughter and scraping back of chairs as the day's lesson is done; the yowling of a lonesome dog, penned in a too-small yard; the tidal sough and swell of the Atlantic Ocean at Achill; a great tragedian holding his audience in the palm of his hand as the old king breathes his dying syllables; the train that whistles its approach down the distant track; the chord plucked by a street band tuning up their instruments, one string vibrating and lingering in the air; gossipy crowds of shoppers; the muezzin's call to prayer; the angelus bell; the outraged scream of the newborn babe; the first words formed in delight and wonder; the first lies, lovers' promises, the last outbreath of everyone dying at that particular moment.

Exhausted, she falls back on the pillows.

I, too, once had the world at my feet, she thinks. I, too, felt the call of the other: magic and exotic. When Alphonse left, my world became silence and darkness. But Rose is right. Alfie was born for the light and the noise of life. He has his mother's hunger and curiosity. Who am I to stand in his way? I might be old and dying but I can still find peace. No-one has any idea where a choice might take them and surely that is the beauty of it? And Alfie deserves to make his choice, whether it leads him home or into exile. If it means the end for the big house once and for all, then so be it. The price for saving it at all costs is too high.

It is time to reveal the last secret.

Molly

One agonising day stretches into the next and still he lies here, her beautiful boy, lost to himself, to her, to the world of feeling, attention and sensation. Her big, strong, galumphing son is now as helpless and fragile as a newborn baby again, kept alive with feeding tubes for liquids at one end and a catheter at the other. The sight of him has her heart torn in two.

He'd been a heavy pregnancy. She'd gone through so much pain to bring him into the world. Was it all for this? Surely God couldn't be this cruel? Was there even a God? She is beginning to doubt it. If there is, He seems to have a serious problem with mothers. Her prayers to Him feel increasingly empty and hollow. Even after the loss of Paddy, she has never doubted her faith, but now she wrestles with it every moment of the day.

She pictures herself as one of the angry Old Testament prophets, shaking their fists at a god who demands impossible personal sacrifice as a sign of faith. She is no Abraham; she is unwilling to sacrifice her son on that altar. In her darkest moments, she curses Alfie. If only he hadn't been determined to make a scene, none of this would have happened. Although she knows it isn't really that simple, true forgiveness is still a long way off.

The medics have placed Joseph on his own in a small, light-filled room at the far end of the ward. She has the Englishman to thank for saving her boy's life. If life it now is. By the time the ambulance had arrived to take him to Galway he had already slipped far away into the distant space he now inhabits. But she can't think about that now, won't allow herself to go to that place. The first few nights had been touch-and-go; it seemed he might well slip away altogether. But his condition has stabilised. She is grateful for that much at least. He still lives and breathes. The nurses are kind and turn a blind eye to strict visiting hours. Sister McDonnell had observed him soon after he'd been admitted and remarked, 'He's a fighter, that one. He's not ready to leave us,' and Molly was grateful for that kindness. Nurses see all kinds of patients, so wouldn't they have a good instinct for the ones most likely to survive? She finds herself grasping at every sliver of hope. She watches how they regularly check his airways for blockages and turn him on his side to ensure his lungs are kept clear; how they heave his dead-weight and reposition him again and again to avoid bedsores.

'Jaysus, he's a big lad, it's like shifting a log,' she overhears one of them cheerfully remark one day, as she comes into the room and they are changing his bedding. She actually finds their irreverence and black humour a comfort. They bring so much care and attention to just keeping her boy alive.

Dr Roach, the surgeon, had been gentle but firm with her.

'There's so little we know about the condition. He might emerge as right as rain but then again... all we can do is make sure he's as comfortable as possible and ensure his condition doesn't deteriorate. But he's young and strong. We can hope for the best.'

She'd pressed him further as to the outcome she might expect and encountered the reluctance of a medic to make promises. But, in the end, he'd admitted, 'With this degree of cerebral trauma, rehabilitation could be a long, slow process, even if all the physical therapies we try are effective.'

These are the regular stretches and exercises the nurses employ to ensure his muscles don't atrophy.

'But he is lucky that at least the fall didn't break his neck.'

She could tell he wanted to end it there, but she had to ask, 'So, what are his chances?'

His pause was enough of an answer, but he replied, anyway.

'Of a return to normal? Statistically, not great. There's maybe a one in five chance he might make a full recovery. It's more likely to be partial, with some impaired physical and cognitive function depending on the severity of the trauma and how it plays out when or – I hate to say this – *if* he wakes. The lapse of time between his accident and getting access to treatment probably didn't help. The fact that he survived at all is a miracle in itself. His system has undergone a severe shock. There's so much we don't yet understand about how that happens in individual cases. In the meantime, the brain is shutting down all but the most vital life functions while it tries to find a way to recover.'

She nodded. A one chance in five that her Joseph would come back to her. He might linger like this for weeks, months, years even. He might never wake up again.

Dr Roach was doing his best not to be brusque with her. And her son's life was to all intents and purposes in his hands. Dr Roach was the only God who mattered on this ward. It seemed to Molly that he held the power of life and death as he calmly monitored Joseph's pulse, reflexes and eye movements for new or further signs of recovery.

'I'm sorry I can't be more optimistic. However, we're learning more every day about the treatment of comatose patients. We'll continue to monitor his vital signs, and look for any evidence he's returning to consciousness. But, in the end, it's all a waiting game, I'm afraid.'

She is grateful, at least, that he hadn't tried to console her with false hope or talk down to her. But she doesn't dare even contemplate what it might mean if Joseph's condition shows no change or improvement over a much longer period.

The entire parish is praying for him. Praying for a miracle. There has been a collection. People have been generous, and Father Diamond has topped it up with a donation from church funds, which has helped her find a place to sleep in town. She is staying down beside the old Claddagh and her world has shrunk now to her rented room and the mile-long walk beside the river and past the university to the hospital. But, more often than not, she remains at her son's bedside through the night, sitting upright and slipping into a fitful sleep.

She is grateful to the night nurses. 'Stay as long as you need to,' one of them says, in passing, 'but make sure you get some rest yourself. You'll be no use to him if you tire yourself out.' They even bring her cups of tea, and extra pillows and blankets. It is most irregular, but then, some of them are mothers too.

And at night, with nothing but a small pool of bluish light from the bedside lamp and her son's almost imperceptible breathing for company, she imagines Paddy's presence in the room, watching over them. Fanciful as the notion is, it gives her comfort. Eventually, she finds herself talking to him as though he were sitting at the other side of the bed from her.

She imagines Paddy as clear as day, looking at her with the air of tender solicitude he always reserved for her in those times when her fears or anxieties would get the better of her.

'Our boy is strong. He'll pull through.'

'You think so?'

'He got help in time. Not like me. He was lucky that the Englishman knew what to do. I watched him.'

'You were there?'

'I've always been there for yous all. Sure, you knew that already.'

'Yes, I did... I do.'

'So, stop your worrying. It's all for the best.'

'It was a bad thing he did.'

'That it was.'

'Are we being punished?'

'Whisht, and don't be taking on so.'

'No… but I don't know how much more of this I can take.'

'You're doing the best you can. Sure, isn't that all any of us can do? And that's a grand wee girl you have there.'

It is her Paddy alright, although, admittedly, a more talkative version of the big man she'd known so well.

He is right about Cassie, who has turned out to be a godsend. So maybe there is a God after all. The one she was taught about at school that moves in mysterious ways. It was clear from the beginning that the poor, wee thing had a soft spot for Joe. Not that he'd ever given her the slightest indication that her feelings were in any way reciprocated. She has started to turn up unbidden, and it has become an unspoken agreement between the two of them that they alternate watches. That, as far as possible, one or other of them will be there to keep Joseph company.

She would make a good wife and daughter-in-law, thinks Molly. But most men have little sense when it comes to choosing a mate. She and Paddy had been the exception that proves the rule and now Joe might never even have the chance to find out. Her eyes fill with tears.

'Enough of that, now.'

It is Paddy again, scolding her, but with a soft twinkle.

'I'm sorry. I'm a silly, sentimental old woman.'

'You're his mammy. You want what's best for him.'

'A boy needs a father, too.'

It comes out as more of an accusation than she had intended and she regrets it immediately. Except, who is she talking to but herself, anyway?

'I know. I know,' comes the sad reply.

She's been managing for so long on her own that Cassie's love and loyalty is almost too much to bear. Dr Roach has suggested that the most up-to-date studies into care for coma patients indicate that, while the patient might appear lifeless, in reality they could be aware of much more of their surroundings than had previously been thought, so he recommends that she and Cassie read to Joseph, stroke him, and, above all, just chat to him as naturally as possible about anything under the sun.

Cassie can gossip for hours about all the latest goings-on at the big house, or down in the village, which has the added advantage of keeping Molly up-to-date. And she has an eye and ear for the most inconsequential details, which she relays with innocent enthusiasm. Which is how Molly comes to hear about Alfie's return to the house and his new-found role as Estate Manager. The Englishman is heading home, it seems. Oh, and Alfie has found a friend – Cassie giggles and clasps her hand to her mouth, blushing – she'd spotted him fooling around with a gypsy-looking fella one day in the tall grass.

For all her seeming innocence, thinks Molly, Cassie is a lot sharper than she needs to be. One day, she brings Molly an official-looking letter on headed notepaper from Tante's solicitor. It is clear and to the point. On Tante's death, Molly and Joseph will be provided for in rent-free accommodation in the big house, or elsewhere on the estate, as appropriate at the time, and an annual pension will be paid to her, 'in recognition of a lifetime of loyal service to our family, through good times and bad.'

It is a more than generous sum, she has to admit. Tante has added a shaky, handwritten note that simply states, 'You're in my prayers. We all pray for Joseph's speedy recovery. Ask for anything you need. You are family always. J.'

It is meant well. And a settlement in law is just and equitable. She wants to feel gratitude, but the attempted kindness leaves her with a hollowed-out feeling instead. Like so much of the family's benighted history, it has turned out to be too little, too late. A lifetime too late.

Jenks

He wonders if his life has been an utter failure. Cambridge blue, the war, art school and, finally, the life of a recluse. What has any of it amounted to?

Always on his mind: the troubled, difficult and dangerous young men he attracts – or is attracted to. The young men who conquer his heart but always leave, one way or another. What is he hoping for? Sex? Perhaps. A lover? Maybe. A partner? Possibly. Though he seriously doubts if he has the fortitude for all that the last entails. But a special friend and soulmate? Yes. Certainly that. Always that.

How far does he have to run before he accepts that nowhere is far enough to escape his demons and desires? Why couldn't he have simply settled for convention, like his friend Protheroe? A life of marriage, comfort and respectability, with perhaps an occasional furtive assignation in a basement club; the married man, always in fear of exposure and disgrace. This is entirely absurd even to consider as an option. But why had he insisted on the way of the outcast instead?

His mother's letters have become increasingly querulous and demanding. On the brink of widowhood, she is clearly struggling and his brother is of no use. As far as the family are concerned, he has lived for pure pleasure and ignored his duties and responsibilities with his refusal to settle down. In his last letter, his brother had been offensively direct: It's time you came home to give our mother a bit of love and attention. You've stayed away too long. You have nephews and nieces here who ask about their Uncle Clifford all the time.'

Robert has yet another big promotion coming up. 'So, who better to step into the breach right now?' is his concluding question. More than that, as Robert now controls the family purse strings, there will be no more life-saving cheques arriving from his mother to bail out his wild escapades. If he is still expecting an inheritance, then it will come with strings attached.

Is this the life he is doomed to? A pitiable and self-pitying sham of an existence without hope of reprieve. It just doesn't bear thinking about. The image he conjures up isn't so far removed from the truth. For all its tongue-in-cheek humour and love beads, England right now is not a comfortable place for men like him. And never has been. The prospect fills him with utter desolation.

He'd rather die, he thinks, seriously, than ever become that pitiful figure in the corner of the room, the bachelor uncle, enduring some respectable but dreary half-life. Better to accept his role of the black sheep and keep his distance. Let Robert deal with their mother. And if that leads to him being disinherited, so be it. It is an irony, he thinks, that just as Alfie is coming into his inheritance, he might lose the possibility of his own. But he isn't without useful skills; he'll get by.

Nevertheless, what is there to keep him here? One person. Alfie. His own sweet Alfie. Now that his future seems to be settled, he is a changed young man. Suddenly he is clear, direct and focused, with an astonishing level of energy and enthusiasm.

There has been no discussion at all of the dramatically changed circumstances of the past few weeks, but they have begun tentatively to explore a revised friendly accommodation

with one another. Dare he hope for a refreshed closeness and...
something more?

It is clear Alfie's aunt is in the final throes of her illness. If not
immediately dying, then the end is surely coming soon enough.
Why not stay and help him through the challenges that will
bring? Would Alfie ask? Should he offer? And would that mean a
final rupture with his own family?

He ponders these questions in the quiet, still hours alone
at home when his day's simple tasks are done. Even though he
now spends much of his time up at the big house helping out
whenever he can, he misses having his young friend around
at home, although it's clear to him that Alfie actually prefers
this new arrangement. Alfie's self-confidence has grown
immeasurably. He never suggests, for instance, that Jenks might
stay over, despite his long trek across miles of rough moorland
between the cottage and the big house, and that has nothing to
do with upsetting his aunt's feelings, Jenks is sure of that. There
is certainly plenty of room. No. It is something else. He senses
it clearly. The balance of power in their relationship has shifted.

He is taken aback to realise that not only is he deeply fond
of Alfie but also that he needs him, needs his friendship. Alfie is
always happy to see Jenks arrive but equally content to see him
go. As for physical closeness, that is clearly a thing of the past.
Suddenly, Alfie has the passion, fire and ambition of youth on his
side. From here on in, it is he, the younger party, who will be the
stronger of the two. There is already a streak of ruthlessness in
him. Would depending on a young man, who hardly knows yet
who he is, be any better a choice than returning to the bosom of
his own family, with his tail between his legs?

Which is why the invitation to a private tête-à-tête with
Jocelyn comes as such a surprise.

Tante

She shuffles her tarot deck and turns over the top card. Ten of coins. Legacy. Indeed; how appropriate. The time for settling accounts and making provision for the future is certainly long overdue.

There is a tentative knock at the door exactly on the hour she has requested and she calls for him to enter, which, after a brief pause, he does. He sidles into the room. Such a strapping, handsome man, she thinks. But so diffident.

'Welcome to my boudoir,' she announces, and regrets her levity immediately. 'Please forgive me. And don't be alarmed. I simply wanted a chat; perhaps friendly counsel, as well.'

His eyes narrow for a moment but he replies, with his customary good manners, 'That's quite all right,' and waits for her to explain.

She decides to come straight to the point. 'I thought we should talk as a matter of urgency about Alfie, since we're the two people in the world who care for him most. I need your help.'

'In what way exactly?'

'I want you to help me persuade Alfie to leave here.'

She watches him struggle to understand what she has just asked of him. Whatever he'd imagined this conversation was going to be about, this, probably, wasn't what he was expecting.

'I don't understand. I thought he was going to inherit the estate?'

'He is. I want him to give it up, or at least the running of it. I thought that might be where you came in.'

'You want me to manage your estate?'

'Well, yes, possibly. It had occurred to me that it might be a solution.'

'And what about Alfie?'

'I think it will be better for him to get away from here.'

'Have you talked to him about this plan?'

'Not yet.'

'Don't you think it might be more respectful to speak with him first?'

He has suddenly become heated; she approves the show of fire. He is defending his friend as a matter of course.

'Alfie's young. He's about to experience big changes and he's going to need older, wiser heads in his life. His uncle, as I'm sure you will have noticed, doesn't fit into that category, and certainly won't be in any position to provide guidance when I'm gone.'

'I'm still at a loss. Aren't you going over the ropes with him? Why do that if you don't want him to stay and run things?'

'It will be good for him to understand the exact nature of what he's inherited – less chance of him being cheated or bamboozled further down the line – but it doesn't mean he should get tied down by the responsibility of it.'

'Like you were, you mean?'

She raises an eyebrow. She finds she is enjoying herself. He might be a quiet man but he is a worthy ally.

'I think I felt more cheated than tied down, but maybe that's part of it, yes.'

'Why on earth would I agree to this?'

'Because you love him. You do, don't you?'

They look each other straight in the eye.

'Yes,' he replies, softly.

'Good. That's settled then. So, aren't you going to ask me?'

'Ask you what?'

'The real reason I think he needs to leave.'

'Alright. If you wish. Tell me.'

'Because, eventually all this could become a burden that would destroy any real chance of happiness he might have... and I should know.'

'Why do you think he would listen to me?'

It is the right question. She considers how to sum it up.

'Because he owes you his life. Plus, you've been like the father he never had... and he trusts you.'

'Is that why you chose to let him stay with me? Why you didn't order him to come back here after the attack?'

She smiles at him.

'He hated me, what would have been the point? And I could tell you'd be good for each other. And, yes, he'd grown up in a house of women and was running wild. He needed a steadying masculine influence. You came along just in the nick of time.'

She pauses. His gaze is rapt; she's won his entire attention now. It is her privilege, as a dying woman, that she can speak the truth with absolute conviction.

'And besides, where else could he have learned about his true nature? However, for his sake... and yours... it's important now you relinquish any claim on his affection.'

'How long have you been considering this idea of yours?'

'A while.'

'So, are you saying that letting him live with me was some kind of... audition?'

'No, of course not. But it gradually dawned on me that you could be the answer to my prayer.'

'And if I were to refuse to go along with your scheme?'

'Can you imagine both of you living here under the same roof? In some platonic or not-so-platonic state of connubial bliss? Come, come, Christopher. He's an underage boy. You're an older man. This is Ireland. We're run by priests and bishops. How long would it be before people began to gossip? It would lead to nothing but frustration. And, sooner or later, he would break your heart. Perhaps he already has.'

He simply stares. She knows she's hit the target and that he must already have considered all of this for himself. Which, of course, he has. Telling himself over and over that Alfie is an old soul in a young body won't justify an intimate relationship with him, even if he cares for one.

'And if I agree?'

'The offer stands. I think you'd make an excellent steward. We'd put everything in writing and, of course, it would have to be contracted through my solicitor.'

'I think I may have underestimated you.'

'I want what's best for all of us. You say you love him. What better way to show it than by helping to protect and preserve his inheritance, leaving him free to find his way in the world? Isn't that what a good father would do for his son? Please think seriously about what we've discussed. There have been far too many sacrifices made in this family.'

'One last question.'

'Please.'

'Where do you imagine Alfie will go, once he leaves here?'

'Leave that to me. Suffice to say for the moment that this is not all of his inheritance.'

'Ah.'

'He has other options to consider.'

'Which he doesn't know about?'

'Not yet. But he will soon. So, will you think about it?'

She watches him wrestle with all the implications of their conversation.

'You're asking a lot.'

'I'm asking you to do the right thing. Alfie needs you, it's true. Just not in the way you might have hoped or imagined. He needs an anchor in his life, but he'll always need to be free as well. It's wrong to cage a wild bird. You, above all, should understand that. Isn't that why you came here? Men of your kind will never find it easy to conform to the demands of society.'

She finds it hard to tell if his response is one of hostility or respect. Perhaps it is a mixture of both.

'You must think me a witch.'

Now he is smiling at last.

'Not at all. I think you're a very singular woman. Alfie is lucky to have you.'

'He may not always have thought so.'

'But I need time to think it over. Give me a few days?'

'Of course. Take as long as you need. Within reason. But bear in mind I'm not going to be around for much longer.'

Alfie

'This is him?'

'Yes.'

He's staring at the small, black-and-white photograph of his father in Tante's leather-bound album for the very first time.

A dark-eyed young man with slicked-back hair, in a white suit, stands before an ornate, tiled doorway surrounded by lush, semi-tropical plants. He's grinning at the camera, as though he's privy to an amusing secret. Next to him is a short but very striking woman with a sober expression, dressed all in black; her equally black hair is piled high. She's wearing a long, thin string of beads and holding what, at first glance, appears to be a fur muff until he realises she's cradling a small black cat in her arms.

'And that's my grandmother?'

'The Contessa Constanza, yes. She had already been a widow for many years when that photo was taken.'

'Is she still alive?'

'Yes. She wrote to me not so long ago. We've kept in touch.'

'And does she know about me?'

'Yes. She's often expressed the wish to see you, but it has never been possible.'

'And where was the photograph taken again?'

'It's called Vila Luz. It means house of light. It was the family's holiday home.'

'In... where did you say?'

'Estoril, Portugal. It's a fashionable resort by the sea. Near the capital, Lisbon. It's very beautiful. As is the Vila Luz.'

'How do you know? Have you been there?'

'As a matter of fact, yes.'

There are other questions now on the tip of his tongue, but he's trying to keep his thoughts in some kind of logical order. It's as if he's stepped into a mysterious, fairy tale version of his life.

'So that makes me Portuguese?'

'Well, partly. Your grandfather, Alfonso's father, was French. His French family called him Alphonse, but his mother, your grandmother, always preferred Alfonso. You were named after him, obviously.'

'So, which am I? Alphonse or... Alfonso?'

She's smiling. He can't help smiling, too, at the ridiculous situation and his equally ridiculous question.

'I think you can probably choose from now on, don't you?'

'I don't know what I am, so how will I know what to call myself?'

'You used to love playing in the mud, right from when you were tiny. Joseph joked one day that you were like a mucky little bog boy, and you liked it so much you kept repeating it ,and told everyone that was your name from now on. And it stuck. It was as though Alfie had disappeared and a new boy had turned up in his place. Like your uncle Michael, going to America and calling himself Mickey. So, you see, in the future you can be whatever you want to be. 'A rose by any other name would smell as sweet.'

'What's that?'

'It's from Shakespeare. A line from *Romeo and Juliet*. It was your mother's favourite quotation. Easy to guess why.'

'So, I'm a mongrel.'

'Mongrels are a lot healthier and stronger than pure breeds.'

'But I'm not even Irish anymore.'

'Of course, you are. Your mother was Irish. You'll always still have your Irish roots. You're a wonderful mixture, that's all. The Irish and the Portuguese have a lot in common. And the French and Irish always got on well, so you're an interesting mix. Unique. You should be proud. You have three different heritages.'

'Alfonso. Portuguese.'

'They pronounce it Por-tu-gaish.'

'Por-tu-gaish.'

He repeats the word after her, relishing the soft 'sh'. The taste of the word is a new, exotic flavour on his tongue. He likes it. It opens up in his head a world he never even dreamed existed. But then the spell is broken, as a new thought hits him.

'You lied to me all this time. You always said nobody knew who my father was. That my mother never told you. But you knew all along.'

'Yes.'

He senses her underlying weariness, along with the familiar

air of sadness that's always enveloped her, and the effort it's costing her to put up with his relentless interrogation.

'Why not tell me? Because I was born a bastard?' He spits out the forbidden word, but he feels no real anger, just a mixture of emotions too confusing to process.

'No. Nothing like that. You were a child born of love, that I'm sure of. But the whole situation was complicated.'

'In what way?'

She doesn't answer immediately.

'Complicated how?'

She suffers one of her sudden, disturbing coughing fits, all too alarmingly familiar in the last few weeks. She gestures for her inhaler, and he grabs it and hands it to her. Eventually, the worst of the fit subsides.

'Should I go?'

She motions no. When she speaks, her voice is weak, but she perseveres until it regains its strength.

'I was the one who loved your father first. We met in Paris while I was studying art there one summer. We had what was called a whirlwind romance. He was charming and debonair and I was young and naive. He swept me off my feet.'

He doesn't know what to say.

'He was an easy person to fall in love with. We married on a whim. We travelled the world. But then we came home, and he met my sister, your mother, and that changed everything.'

'But why...?'

'Rose was very beautiful.'

He's about to say, 'But that's wrong,' when he has a sudden picture of Jenks's face after he caught him slipping out of Shay's caravan; the look of desolation on his friend's face, and his own guilt that he had, somehow, betrayed his friend's love for him;

and he understands something new about life in general, and about himself in particular.

'You must have been very unhappy.'

'It nearly destroyed me,' she says, with neither rancour nor bitterness.

'I'm sorry.'

'On the other hand, if it hadn't happened, you wouldn't be here now.'

'All the same...'

'Anything else you'd like to know?'

'Yes. Tell me about him.' There's a moment's pause, before he adds, 'If that's not too painful.'

She ponders the question. 'Come,' she says, and motions him onto the bed. He settles alongside her, with the album still open at the portrait of his father and grandmother. They look at it together. She traces the outline of the white-suited figure, then begins to recite a description of his father, softly and dreamily, almost to herself, like an incantation. He listens entranced to the lilt in her voice and tries to imagine the mysterious, magical creature she's describing, as though between them they can conjure him back from the past and bring him into the room with them.

'He enjoyed life to the full. Turned heads wherever he went. Could charm anyone. He was very clever, worldly and sophisticated. He could be extremely funny, but also a little bit cruel with it. He had a beautiful voice. He loved to sing *fado*. They're Portuguese songs, very sad. He was full of madcap schemes, but when he sang, he was able to express something from deep inside his soul. When he serenaded me for the first time, we were standing alone together on the Pont Neuf, the oldest bridge in Paris, and that's when I knew I loved him. He could be wonderfully impulsive like that, but he was also too impatient. Always in a hurry. He loved fast cars. He raced them for a hobby. That's what killed him in the end.'

She snaps shut the album.

He'd continued to stare at the photo while Tante's hypnotic voice had relayed the litany of his father's qualities, good and bad. He glances across at her now and sees that, for her, his father is still very real.

'He died in a car race?'

'No... he and your mother had a big row and he drove off. He crashed his car into a ditch. He was going too fast.'

'Oh.'

'You weren't born yet, but your mother was carrying you. He wanted his family to bring you up but she wanted you to grow up here. He might have got his way in the end – she was already ill – but fate intervened for both of them.'

He tries to imagine this other life, this other version of himself growing up in a foreign land, but it proves beyond him. Would it have made any difference? Would he have been any happier?

'Are you sorry I told you?'

'No. Not really. It's a lot to take in, though.'

'Yes, I can imagine.'

'I'm glad you told me. Our family has too many secrets.'

'My fault, I fear.'

She takes his hands in hers and, despite her illness and frailty, he can feel the strength of her spirit. She motions to the record player that sits on a small table near the window with her collection of old records stacked beside it.

'Play it for me.'

'What?'

'You know.'

Of course, he knows. Many's the night he has lain in his room, unable to get to sleep, listening to the haunting refrain rising up through the floorboards and knowing that she too couldn't sleep. So, he finds the record she's asking for and carefully places it on the turntable. As it crackles into life, a powerful tenor, brimming with longing and regret, fills the room.

As Count John McCormack's operatic voice rises above a simple piano accompaniment and sings the words to *She Moved through the Fair*, he feels the depth of Tante's sorrow but also understands her pride.

The years of loneliness, the misunderstandings, the petty insults, the silences laden with resentment, all seem to melt away as they listen together. The singer's voice fades along with the dying notes of the piano and Bogboy lifts the needle and replaces the record in its tattered cover.

'You can ask them to play it at my funeral,' she says, and he nods.

'Do you understand?'

'I think so.'

'No matter what happens to you in life, the most important thing is to keep going as best you can, for whatever reason.'

'What was your reason?'

She merely gives him a look, and says, 'Don't be cute.'

She moves on, briskly. 'I imagine you want to know if you're like him?'

He's taken aback.

'I don't know. Am I?'

'You have his zest for life. And his melancholy streak. Plus, your mother's joy, and her beauty. Be careful. It's a powerful combination. You may break hearts without intending to.'

He'd never heard her speak in this way.

'How did you know?'

'I only have to look at your friend to know he loves you much more than you love him.'

'Will I ever be happy?'

Tante doesn't miss a beat. 'It's better to start by asking, 'Who am I meant to be?'. That's hard enough to answer for most people. Most of us get even that wrong.'

'I have no idea who I am.'

'All the more reason to go out into the world and find out.'

'You think I should go?'

'Why not? Maybe that will help to answer the question.'

'But what about here?'

'Christopher is willing to manage things here while you're gone. He just told me.'

'It doesn't seem very fair.'

'Why not?'

But he can't explain why.

'There's nothing to feel guilty about here. Go. Live your life. Meet Constanza. She's a remarkable woman. You saw the letter she sent?'

He had. It was in a thin, blue, airmail envelope postmarked Lisboa, with a set of stamps commemorating the Madonna in blue, sepia and mauve and the word Fatima underneath and the cost: fifty, ten and five *centevos*. Inside was a short note in spidery handwriting from his grandmother, with the invitation, 'Tell young Alfonso he's welcome to come and visit me any time.'

'You're right, it's a lot to take in. Maybe too much. But think of your grandmother. She's old now and wants to get to know her grandson before it's too late. Vila Luz was always where your father was happiest. If what she says is true, one day it will be yours. She says it's what your father would have wanted. You should write to her and introduce yourself properly.'

He wants to say, 'A remarkable woman? So are you,' but can only manage, 'Alright.'

'What?'

'I'll go but not before...'

'Oh, don't worry. That won't be long'

A stab of premonitory grief pierces him.

'Now go. I should rest. Ask Cassie to bring some of her potato soup, please, but no salt. She puts too much salt in everything.'

Cassie

'He moved. Jaysus, Mary and Joseph, he moved.' She is half-asleep and about ready to call it a night, so just for a second she can't tell if she has simply dreamed it. Between her duties up at Coolhooley and coming into town to be with Joe, she has barely a moment to herself these days and is bleary-eyed with exhaustion most of the time. It is impossible to say which job is the harder of the two.

As Doctor Roach suggested, she fills the silence with talk.

But recently, also, she has started to help Joe out. That is how she thinks of it.

When she was eight years old – such a good girl, everyone said – she'd been left alone with her brother, Feargal, while her parents had gone off to buy winter feed and visit relatives on the other side of the bay. Feargal, who was six years older, had protested loudly until their father had given him a good clout for himself and told him that he was keeping an eye on his younger sister whether he liked it or not, and that was an end of it. Feargal had looked across and caught her smirking, which had been purely a nervous reaction on her part – discomfort at seeing her brother put in his place – but it hadn't improved his temper one little bit. Once their parents had left, he had mooched about the farm, sullen and resentful, half-heartedly scraping the old flaking whitewash off the gable wall, a task he'd been left with as part-punishment for his intransigence. Cassie didn't mind his moodiness; she would forgive Feargal anything. She hero-worshipped him.

In particular, she loved to watch him at Sunday Mass in his red cassock and pristine, white undergarment, calmly and efficiently serving as the priestly acolyte during the service, setting the altar for the service, ringing the Sanctus bell at intervals to remind the congregation to stand or kneel and quietly, unobtrusively, presenting the priest with the brass thurible of incense for the consecration, or the silver paten and linen cloth in preparation for serving the host to the faithful of the parish. My brother, she'd think, her heart swelling with pride. He had a strong voice and could sing the whole of High Mass in Latin.

Their mother, Annie, who'd had both her children late in life, referred to his moods forgivingly. 'He's at that awkward age, sure he'll grow out of it, so he will,' adding with a laugh, 'but if only he wouldn't grow out of his shirts, shoes and trousers so quickly, not to mention eating us out of house and home.'

There'd even been talk that he might have a vocation. Father Diamond had been round to the house to discuss whether Feargal and the family might consider his training for the priesthood at the seminary in Maynooth; he'd most certainly be happy to put in a good word on his behalf with the bishop.

But now she and her brother were alone together, he'd ignored her, despite all Cassie's best efforts, turning his back on her coldly every time she had tried to talk to him, until, hurt and rejected, she'd gone back inside to play with her dolls. She'd spent most of the afternoon with her favourite, a wide-eyed baby doll that made lifelike noises, crying or gurgling or giggling depending how she pulled the elastic string on its back. She was delighted when, later in the afternoon, he popped his head round the door of the bedroom to ask, 'How's it going?'

'I'm just playing with Angela.' She pointed to the bright pink doll. 'I fed and changed her and told her a story so now she's tired. It's time for her afternoon nap.'

'Aren't you getting too big to be playing with dollies?'

She felt her eyes sting. How could she explain that her dolls were her friends and that most of the time she had no-one else to play with?

His tone softened. 'Ah, don't be starting the waterworks. I'm just codding with ya.'

'So will you play with me?'

'Sure. What do you want to play?'

She knew better than to suggest mammies and daddies or doctors and nurses with her dolls, but before she could think how to respond, he beat her to it.

'I have an idea. Why don't I teach you a game?'

'Yes, please!'

'Okay. But none of this baby stuff, d'ya hear? A proper grown-up game.'

And that was how she learned what big boys liked to do. He'd said they could name this game 'helping him out'. He had showed her his 'todger', and taught her how to hold it firmly and pull it, so it felt nice when it grew big and hard, and explained that the white stuff was where babies came from; none of that Virgin Mary nonsense. And that it was their secret, special game and no-one else must ever know, not even the priest in the confession box or she would surely roast in hell for all eternity, which would be like feeling burning-hot coals under the soles of her bare feet forever and ever amen.

'Isn't this more fun than playing with some stupid, plastic doll?' he'd asked, once the game was over.

'Is it a sin?' she'd asked, anxious.

'Not at all,' he'd replied and explained how it was healthy and good and natural, that everyone did it, one way and another. Even priests did it. This was truly surprising. 'How do you know?' she'd asked him, but he didn't answer and, instead, argued, 'And, anyway, why would God make it so pleasant if it was so wrong?'

She wasn't sure. It all seemed a bit messy and dirty. His face had screwed up in an ugly way and he'd made a funny, grunting sound when the stuff came out, and she couldn't really see the point of it, but he seemed happy enough after and she liked making him happy.

He pointed out she was the one who'd wanted to play with babies in the first place. All he'd done was put her right about how that happened and she'd agreed to help him out, so it was too late to be having second thoughts now. And that was how it had begun.

Then, two or three years later, the game stopped. Feargal started courting Kate McFeaney, from the next farm, and in no time at all was settling down. Kate had most certainly been with their first child by the time they headed to the altar, if you did the arithmetic, and most of the nosy neighbours in the parish certainly knew how to count, tut-tutting self-righteously all the while that neither the bride nor groom was much more than a child. But with a bit of arm-twisting, Feargal had been persuaded to do the right thing. They'd just about saved face. At least the family's honour had been preserved in public.

Her brother was now a respectable, married man with responsibilities: a father, with a second child on the way soon after the first, and another and another at regular, yearly intervals. And true to her promise, she had never told the priest or anyone else. 'Does that make me a good or a bad girl?' she'd often asked herself.

She didn't know what had first made her do it. Bored and tired during one visit and with nothing in particular she could think of to relate, in a moment of absent-mindedness, she'd pulled down Joseph's bedclothes, simply intending to admire him lying there and to drink in his beautiful innocence, face smoothed of all expression. But not so innocent after all it turned out. To her astonishment, despite his apparently oblivious state, he was sporting an unmistakable erection which comically tented his hospital-issue nightgown. She'd glanced around to ensure the coast was clear, although she knew the nurses wouldn't be in to check on him for a good hour yet, and then pulled up his gown.

It was utterly thrilling to be doing something so forbidden with the boy she loved, who couldn't resist and was totally in her power. More fun than playing with a doll, as her brother had said all those years ago. And yet, it was exactly like having her own living, breathing, baby doll at her command. Having broken the taboo, she had convinced herself that this too would help him in his healing. Surely if he could feel such an intimate, loving act, he could not be lost to her or his mother forever?

She understood only too well the consequences of being found out, and was careful to time such moments during lulls when the nursing staff would be most unlikely to intrude. She had been taught well. She knew how to be clever, patient and unobtrusive. She'd soon discovered that, spontaneous erections aside, he could also be stimulated into a state of arousal and took satisfaction in being able to manage that for him, too. It was part of his recuperation process. And now, here is the justification. He is returning to life.

She watches, fascinated, her excitement mounting. It is as if his body is being jolted by electricity. There is an odd rippling movement through his limbs and, although his eyes are still closed, she can also see a rapid twitching motion behind his lids. She leaps out of the chair by his bed where she has spent so many hours and days watching, waiting and praying for this moment, her bright-pink rosary beads wrapped tight around her knuckles. Her prayers have been answered. Well, everyone's prayers, she has to remind herself, careful lest she fall into the sin of pride. Nevertheless, she thinks, this must have been exactly what it had been like when Martha and Mary in the Bible watched Our Lord raise up their beloved brother Lazarus from the dead.

Now she has been blessed to witness a similar miracle, and been the one chosen to relay the good news. Joseph's mammy will be arriving soon to begin her nightly vigil. Cassie can't wait to see the look on Molly's face when she hears. She has suffered so much. Cassie charges down the corridor to find someone to tell, brimming with excitement, only to bump into a nurse coming out of a side storeroom with a pile of clean sheets. The nurse gives her a glare like a teacher at school.

'Woah! Woah! Slow down and hold your horses. There's no running down the corridor in this hospital.'

'But it's Joseph. I think he's waking up.'

'Well, take your time and let's not be jumping to any conclusions yet. We'll go and check, shall we?'

'He's moving. I saw him.'

'You say you think he's waking up? What did you notice?'

'He's shaking around a lot.'

'Has he opened his eyes?'

'No. I'm not sure. I don't think so.'

They walk rapidly back down the corridor and back into his room.

Joseph is indeed moving. He is now thrashing about in the bed, flailing wildly like a newly-caught fish. In between times, he is also emitting little moans of distress.

'We'd better find the doctor,' the nurse says, at the sight of him.

'Is he not alright?'

'Let's just wait and see, shall we? In the meantime, don't do anything more. Just keep an eye on him?'

'But his mammy? She'll be arriving any minute. What shall I say?'

'Say nothing. All in good time.' And she was gone, leaving Cassie alone again with Joseph, beginning to regret that she might have jumped the gun.

Joseph

The universe tastes like raspberries.

Molly

Molly has been assailed by Cassie and a solemn-faced Nurse Dolan, and taken to the visitor's lounge. It is a depressing, scruffy room, painted an institutional yellow which does little or nothing to cheer her up. Is it good or bad, the news? The nurse can't say;

232

she merely informs Molly that Dr Roach is examining Joseph at present and will speak with her shortly. The numbness Molly feels most of the time is replaced immediately by terror.

Then Dr Roach arrives. 'This kind of development is not uncommon, I'm afraid, after suffering a massive head trauma.', he explains.

Joseph has been sedated. 'Basically, his brain is still dealing with all of the after-effects of the initial accident. Sometimes, that can take weeks, months or even years to play out. His seizures might be as a result of cerebrospinal fluid building up in the spaces in his brain, causing swelling and a breach in the blood brain barrier.'

Molly has a vision of a great tidal wave of foaming red blood, rising ever higher, and crashing down on the fragile sea wall that was her son's delicate skull, and she wants to yell, 'I don't want a lecture from a textbook, I just want my beautiful boy back,' but instead she nods dumbly, unable to speak. She resents how healthy the doctor looks. What right has he to be so vigorous, smart and full of life while her son continues to deteriorate in front of her very eyes?

She feels bad almost at once. He is still doing his level best to help.

'Is he getting better?' Cassie interrupts. Her eternal optimism grates on Molly's nerves today.

'Don't give in.' She hears Paddy's voice in her head. 'While there's life, there's always hope.'

'We just don't know at this stage,' Dr Roach continues. He has a lovely voice, she thinks. All the better to deliver disheartening news.

'What you and Nurse Dolan witnessed today was most likely what we call an episode of post-traumatic epilepsy. He still hasn't woken up fully to his surroundings, but his eyes are open and while he's still mostly unresponsive to the world around him, there's some indication that he's in a minimally conscious state.'

Molly had once read the story of St Teresa of Avila and been gripped by her account of the dark night all good Christian souls must face at some time in their lives. This is hers.

Michael

Was there ever a more cursed, unlucky family than ours? he asks himself. How has it come to this? What is he? An exile in his own country, a stranger in his childhood home. He catches glimpses of himself in the bedroom window or in the small mirror over the bathroom sink, and wonders who is this florid, full-faced man, with thinning hair, his rheumy eyes with their heavy shadows staring back at him? And what had happened to handsome, fun-loving Mickey?

When he was growing up, some of the local lads would dare each other to spend a whole night inside the remnants of an ancient, stone fort above the village that was said to be haunted by the banshees. None of them really believed it – it was all old wives' tales – but he and his mate, Tommy Ryan, took on the wager along with a few bottles of beers and a quart of whiskey, just for the craic one evening. They'd proceeded to get themselves well spifflicated, egging each other on with half-remembered tales of witches, ghosts and ghouls, before bedding down in the warm blankets they'd brought up with them.

'Don't you be getting yourself dragged down into the underworld by some beautiful woman who turns up in your dreams claiming she's the feckin' Queen of the Fairies,' he'd joked.

'Sure, don't you be worrying about me, boyo. We'll soon see who's the bigger man.'

And they'd both laughed, delighted with themselves.

He'd felt a wave of nausea as he first lay down on the ground. It seemed to be rippling beneath him and he'd regretted not eating something first to line his stomach before guzzling down the beer and whiskey. When the world had stopped spinning, he found himself gazing stupefied into the night sky. The stars were intense glimmers of light, as though the great, black void was one vast, cosmic mouth waiting to swallow them up into its dizzying immensity. He'd shivered as a cool breeze blew across the uneven ground. He'd attempted to share this rare moment of cosmic insight with his friend, except the words wouldn't come out right, and all he'd managed was, 'Look!'

'What?'

'The stars.'

'What about them?'

'Huge.' And frightening, he'd wanted to add.

'Is it all poetic he's getting now? Are you going to be reading me one of your love poems next and asking me for a big sloppy kiss under the stars?'

'Ah, feck off.'

'Feck off yourself. Enough now. Get yourself to sleep.'

Tommy had rolled away and within minutes was snoring, leaving Michael alone in the dark and awake for longer than he wanted. He started to imagine human shapes in the shadows, hearing nocturnal rustlings, bat flutters and the hoots of hunting owls before drifting into a restless, dreamless sleep of his own.

In the pre-dawn light, he'd woken with a start and seen the empty spot where Tommy had been lying. Then he'd caught sight of his friend a hundred yards away on the other side of the fort. Tommy, not usually a scaredy-cat, was hunched over in a foetal position, rocking back and forth. At first, he'd thought he was codding him. As he approached, Tommy was gibbering to himself and punching the air in front of him.

'Get those feckin' black crows out of my face.'

'Come on now, snap out of it, Tommy boy.'

'I heard her. The curse is on someone sure enough.'

'Don't be going on so.'

'I heard her. You didn't hear her?'

'No.'

'She's coming for someone, I tell ya.'

'Pay it no mind. It's all just blarney. You've a bad head on you, is all, with the drink.'

'Someone's in for it, you mark my words.'

'Stop it. It's not funny anymore, Tommy.'

'It's true I tell you.' His face was fierce with fear and fury. Suddenly, he recited a litany of names like a spell. 'Kavanagh, O'Grady, O'Brien, O'Connor, O'Neill. The cursed tribes.'

'Jaysus, Tommy...'

'She said they all have the curse on them.'

'That's enough now. Don't be trying to get inside my head, boy, or I'll land you one, just you see if I don't.'

He'd half-heartedly shoved at Tommy who'd walloped him back. Soon they were throwing wild punches at one another until he'd caught Tommy full on the nose, which started to bleed.

'Ya bastard. Look what you just did to me!'

'You started it with your queer fairy stories.'

'It's real. She was as real as I'm standing here.'

'It's enough. I don't want to hear any more about it.'

'Suit yourself. I'm off.'

Whenever he thinks about the endless run of bad luck in his own family over the years, Tommy's words come back to haunt him.

Well, what could they expect? Their great ancestral hero, Brian Boru, had been murdered in his bed straight after tasting victory over his enemy on the field of battle and they'd been an unlucky bunch ever since.

He thinks of his father dying suddenly of a stroke out on the golf course, then all his own financial disasters and the family catastrophe that followed in its wake, and then Rose's terrible final illness, leaving an orphan baby son, and their own mother's death, no doubt of a broken heart, nothing but blow after blow after blow.

As for himself, he increasingly feels like he isn't so much cursed as possessed, as though when he stares in the mirror, he sees not himself at all but a reflection of some shape-shifting creature, a pooka, perhaps, from one of the old stories, who has assumed human form – his.

So much sorrow and loss. And when Joycie kicks the bucket, what then? Jocelyn had wasted no time letting him know the Englishman would be running affairs from now on. As though stabbing him in the back hadn't been enough. He felt this final insult like a slap in the face. The thought of that upper-class, English fruit lording it over him is simply too much to bear. When Jocelyn had coolly informed him what to expect, he'd gone straight to his room to get blind drunk, then smashed his fist into the wall in a rage. He still has the bruised knuckles to show for it. It is a miracle he hadn't done himself a permanent injury.

Talking of which, it seems the lad, Joseph, is finally coming round from his coma but is, apparently, near brain-dead – half-witted at best – and Molly will be bringing him back to stay in the big house with that young servant girl in tow.

As for his nephew, Joycie was adamant. 'He won't be staying here. Why would he? There's little or nothing for him here. He'll be free to come and go as he pleases. And if he finally decides to sell what's left of the estate, he'll be at liberty to do so. But don't worry, he'll make sure you're taken care of. I'm sure he'll be able to find you a room with a pub attached.'

So, this is how he is to end his days: In a house that should be his by rights, run by some English queer, in the company of a woman who hates him, along with her cretinous son and that dozy village girl. If there truly is hell on earth, then surely this must be it. He takes another slug of Black Label and wonders how long it would take to drink himself to death.

Molly

Joseph is still sleeping most of the day, as though he's reverted almost entirely to babyhood, but increasingly he wakes from long naps and stares wide-eyed into the distance, as though he is trying to recall some vital memory, just beyond his ken. His head moves from side to side as she calls out his name repeatedly, but if his eyes meet hers there is still no recognition in them, and she tries to bank down her feelings of frustration, continuing to hold his hands in hers or gently stroking his skin along his arms and down the side of his face, murmuring soothing, encouraging words of mother love. And just like a baby he will often make little sounds, grunts or sighs of pleasure that tell her he can feel her touch and likes the sensation. It is as though he is under a wicked spell, like the children of Lir, transformed into swans by the enchantress, Aoife. Like them, he seems lost to the human world.

Two months pass. While the nurses continue his physical therapy, Dr Roach drops by regularly to monitor his pupil activity and other vital signs. Cassie is as faithful as a puppy, passing on all the latest gossip. The parish continues to pray for him.

Then, one night, a night like any other, the miracle happens. Just like a baby, he says his first word. She'd been gently massaging his chest with careful, slow strokes, something she'd done for him as a child with vapour rub. She nearly leaps out of her skin when his mouth contorts, a sound begins to emerge and he struggles to form a word.

She leans right over him to pick out what he's saying. He gives no indication that he recognises her, merely that he has an urgent need to communicate something and needs her to know it, whoever she is. His mouth is slack, and droops badly to one side, and he battles furiously to make the sound he wants, getting more and more frustrated with himself and her.

'Ear... ear... ear,' he yells.

'What can you hear?'

He clings to her arm, his face contorted by rage. 'Ear... ear.'

She is as desperate to understand as he is to make himself understood. Each utterance seems forced out of his whole body with a supreme effort, like a cry from the depths of his soul.

He mumbles, shakes his head violently from side to side, and purses his lips in one almighty effort that leaves him drained and exhausted.

Finally, she understands. He is struggling with the first explosive consonant.

'B... b... b... b..' A rapid series of popping noises.

She laughs with relief, until tears run down her cheeks.

Beer. He wants beer. Her boy is back.

Alfie

Dear Grandmother Constanza,

Hello. This is Alfie, your grandson. I'm very happy to make your acquaintance.

I hope this letter finds you well. I'm quite well, thank you, though we're all very worried about my Aunt Jocelyn, whom I call Tante, who is very ill at present. I hope to come and visit you so I can learn more about my father and the rest of my family history. It has all been a big surprise to me, as you might imagine, but not a bad one, I hasten to add. Some surprises are good ones. I do hope you won't be too disappointed when you meet me but for now, I will leave off by wishing you well.

PS. I'm sorry not to come immediately but I am helping to take care of my aunt, whom I don't want to leave just now. I hope you will understand.

PPS. And sorry for my poor handwriting. I never really liked school!

Yours sincerely,
Alfie

In less than a fortnight, a reply comes from the grandmother he never knew he had, inviting him once again to come and visit when he's ready. In the past year, his entire life, his existence, his very sense of self has been utterly transformed. It's settled. He'll leave, in due course, to stay in his grandmother's house by the sea. And she has told him that she also has a small apartment in Lisbon itself, so he might prefer to stay there some of the time.

'I suspect she means if things get difficult between you and her,' observes Tante, tartly, on reading Constanza's letter. She's not really being sour, he thinks; it's to cover her discomfort at the fact that they both know he will only leave to visit his grandmother after Tante's death, and that she feels anxious about sending him off on a journey with an uncertain outcome. Either way, it makes for a very mixed blessing.

Once again, he tries to make sense of all that's happening but fails utterly. He's about to lose the only mother he's ever known, who has barely adopted that role before preparing to leave him, and packing him off to a second family he didn't even know existed. He, who has almost never set foot outside the boglands of his childhood, is about to become a voyager to other lands. Like St Brendan, the monk from ancient times, who stood on the western shore and left behind his little stone cell to launch a flimsy coracle on the waves and set sail, trusting in providence to guide him. Or like the warrior, Oisín, leaping astride the great white stallion without a moment's hesitation to ride to Tír na nÓg, the land of eternal youth. Brendan and Oisín were both wanderers, restless individuals not content with sticking in one place. Is he destined to be a wanderer too? If he'd been asked a year ago, he would have denied it, but now he is not so sure.

One afternoon, Tante produces a much-folded, well-worn map of Portugal and spreads it wide to show him this kingdom of explorers and navigators that is his patrimony just as much as the known world of his childhood. He stares, fascinated, at the unfamiliar landscape: blue, winding rivers; brown, crinkled mountain ranges standing out in stark relief; lush, green coastal plains. As she points out places on the map, he repeats them back to her – Oporto, Estremadura, La Serra da Estrela, Braga, Coimbra. These lessons will be among their last together, he thinks, and he's eager to treasure them, every last word, determined to remember each detail after she's gone.

She begins by telling him of the tiny, wooden ships that sailed out from Lisbon, nestled in the open jaw of the Tagus estuary, to discover new lands and founded an empire that stretched from Africa to India to the Americas. She tells him of the spice merchants and traders who brought back untold riches and built themselves opulent palaces and elaborate summer villas, just like the one he would be staying in, located in the hills and along the coast, in order to escape the heat of the summer in the capital. It's hard for him to imagine, he who is more used to bitter wind and driving rain and a damp that seeps deep into the marrow, in a land where an occasional pale watery sun breaking through dense cloud is to be welcomed.

As she describes the history and geography of his soon-to-be new homeland, he can see also that what she's doing is describing the Portugal of her past, transporting herself back to a time and place of heat and colour and light. She's sharing her memories with him because they're the most precious gift she has left to offer him. This, she's saying, is his true inheritance. He wishes that they could have enjoyed this new-found kinship sooner.

And yet, somehow, it's right that it has been as it was. Their clash of wills, as he was growing up, has forged in him a steely resilience, not unlike hers. It felt like cruelty, but perhaps she always feared that if life was too easy, he'd become like his uncle: lazy and stupid. Maybe she was right all along, and it isn't necessarily such a good thing to have everything handed to you on a plate.

Uncle Michael, who started out with everything and who Alfie had fantasised for years was, if not good exactly, then definitely interesting and exciting, has turned out in reality to be nothing but a drunken old sot and a bore. So how can you tell, then, who is a good or a bad person, or who will turn out well or badly? Are there warning signs or traits to watch out for in yourself or others? Most of his life he's been convinced Tante was a bad person and yet, it turns out she's been good in her own eccentric way, has actually done her best to protect him and his future, even if he hasn't always known it. Jenks is definitely a good person, he thinks; probably the kindest person he's ever known. But sad.

That's the next problem, so far as he can see. Being good doesn't necessarily make you happy. And if being good doesn't make you happy, then what is the point of it? Anyway, he doesn't think he can be a good person. For most of his life he seems to have annoyed people just for trying to be himself. He already knows that he wants to love boys, which means the church thinks he's a bad person from the start.

When he'd asked Tante if he would ever be happy, she'd basically told him it was the wrong question. He'd asked Jenks, and all his friend would say was, 'I think you have to find a purpose in life.' Which isn't a lot of help either, since he doesn't yet know what that might be in his case.

He and Jenks are continuing to repair the kitchen garden, fixing broken walls, terracing and planting, repairing storm damage on trees, pruning and lopping back branches where necessary. It's hard graft, and he likes it because they can work side by side in pleasant silence. The question 'What is love?' seems too big a question to answer and 'Does it always have to hurt this much?' is too hard to ask. In some ways, it was easier in the past, when he was just angry, lonely Bogboy.

One of the very first tasks they've embarked on – and have been working on for weeks now – is to restore the old fishpond and then plant it with water lilies. It is Jenks, of course, who points out the remains of the pond, the outline hidden by years of neglect and colonised by undergrowth. Once they cut back the weeds and dried grasses choking it, they see that it is still structurally sound. Then Alfie happens to mention in passing his aunt's love of water lilies. And Monet.

'Water lilies. Hmm. Might work.' Jenks ponders the ratio of effort and cost against possible success: the pond would need relining, plus a freshwater supply to aerate it, and then it would have to be stocked with young fish, before adding the lilies. Finally, he nods. 'Well, why not? It's certainly worth a try. Y'know they're among the most exquisite of blooms? Yet they emerge out of the slimy depths, just like us humans.'

Now it's starting to take shape; the lilies have just been planted, and Jenks and Alfie are waiting in trepidation to see if they'll unfold. 'Don't be fooled by the pretty pictures you've seen of lily pads. They're hardy blighters. It'll take more than an Atlantic gale or two to kill them off, just you wait and see,' Jenks said, as they waded into the water to put them in place. Whether Tante will live long enough to see the pond attain its full glory is doubtful, but it will be a living memorial to her and continue to bloom long after she's gone. Molly and Cassie and even Uncle Michael have started taking an interest in the works. They've all been sworn to secrecy for now, as regards the pond.

Molly approves of the kitchen garden. She's always deferential around Jenks, but there's still an awkwardness between himself and her and they've not really talked properly since the night of the accident. Joseph has been back at the house for almost two months and has come out of his coma. He's started to walk slowly with the help of a stick, and Cassie has moved in as his unofficial nurse. She seems to be the only person Joseph allows to take care of him. Nobody has intimated if this will be a permanent arrangement. He's suffered some brain damage. How bad or how irreparable it will be is still uncertain, but it's affected his power of speech and he mostly communicates with hand signs and a variety of grunting noises, interspersed with the occasional unexpected word which only Cassie seems to know how to interpret. It's as if they now have a language all of their own, which even his mother isn't a party to, particularly when he gets angry and frustrated, which is often; then he lets forth a stream of incoherent sounds, usually including a couple of choice expletives, which are among the few words he seems to have no difficulty articulating. Watching Cassie with him is like watching a mother soothe an oversize baby. His actual mother is back to housekeeping duties. If anything, she seems relieved and grateful to have Cassie take responsibility for her son, who now appears to adore the girl as much as he once despised her. She evidently dotes on him as much as she ever did, despite his invalid status.

He has difficulty eating solid food. When Alfie comes into the kitchen, he'll sometimes interrupt Cassie spooning what looks like baby food – mashed potato, carrot and turnip, stewed apple, bread soaked in milk or thick, vegetable soup – into Joseph's partly dribbling mouth, while providing a running commentary: 'There y'are now, one last big spoonful, isn't that lovely?' It turns out, fortuitously, that this is also the ideal diet for Tante, whose appetite has dwindled.

Whenever he catches Joseph's eye, there's no real look of recognition, so for now he doesn't press the issue. Cassie relates Dr Roach's plans to arrange remedial speech therapy to them one night when they all end up by chance in the kitchen together; all except for Uncle Michael, who is becoming more and more of a recluse.

On the whole, Alfie tries to avoid Joseph. But even with Molly doling out helpings of her delicious Irish stew to Jenks and himself from the pot that's been simmering on the stove most of the day, Joseph seems indifferent to everyone else, and only has eyes for his beloved Cassie.

Nobody knows what to do about Uncle Michael. It's a worry, alright. He takes his meals in his room, takes solitary walks around the estate and avoids the rest of them as much as possible. Other than that, nobody has much idea what he does with himself, aside from drink. 'Perhaps he's writing his memoirs,' says Molly to the rest of them on another evening when his name comes up in conversation. 'My life as an out-and-out rogue.'

It's as if they are all tiptoeing around each other, trying to work out their place in the greater scheme of things. They all know Tante won't be around much longer but neither Alfie nor Tante have mentioned that he is going away. So far, Jenks is the only other member of the household who knows. And Jenks is diplomatic with everyone, particularly Molly, to whom he is always careful to show respect, deferring to her greater experience and understanding whenever necessary. At first, there's a certain coolness whenever Alfie's around Molly, until one day she stops him in the hall on her way back down from helping Tante with her morning ablutions.

'A moment, Alfie. I'd like a quick word, if you don't mind.'

What now? he wonders, immediately expecting the worst.

She coughs awkwardly and dries her hands on her apron.

'I've been meaning to catch up with you, but with one thing and another...'

'I understand.'

'No, but that night' – her distress is evident – 'you know I wasn't in my right mind...'

And it comes out in a rush. 'I'm sorry, Alfie, I should never have said and done what I did.'

'Yes, well, that's alright. We were all a bit upset,' he replies.

'Yes.' There seems nothing more to be said. 'Well, I suppose I'd best be getting on.'

He likes that Jenks is planning for the future and not just the immediate present, that this neglected, overlooked patch of ground that they're tilling is slowly being returned to abundance.

Now they're measuring out and seeding a botanical garden of healing herbs. Following Molly's example, Alfie finally decides to pluck up his courage and confront a subject they've both been avoiding for far too long.

'I'm sorry.'

Jenks straightens up from where he's been putting tiny stakes in the ground, to mark which herbs have been planted where, and stares at him, puzzled.

'Whatever for?'

'Leaving.'

'But why?'

'Because I can't be your special friend.'

'Ah.' Jenks is silent for the longest time, then says, 'It would always have had to happen sooner or later, Alfie. You have your whole life ahead of you.'

'Yes, but...' He doesn't know how to say it. 'Won't you be lonely without...'

'You mean, will I miss you? Yes. Of course.' Jenks is looking him straight in the eye, but he's beginning to smile. 'I'll have plenty to occupy me here, so don't go worrying. You know when I said you need to have a reason to live? Well, this is it, right here right now, for me – thanks to your aunt, I should add. I can do this for you. On your behalf. So, you see even when you're far away, I'll still be able to be your friend.'

'Really?'

'Of course, silly.' He's smiling broadly now and it's as if a weight has lifted off both of their shoulders.

'Always?'

'Don't push your luck, young fella-me-lad.' They both laugh, 'Yes, always. Or as long as you want and need me to.'

'What about your family in England? Don't they miss you?'

Jenks frowns. 'Sometimes the best family is the one you make, not the one you're born into.'

It's the closest either has ever come to a declaration of love. And it's enough. It's as though he now has a foundation stone in his life to anchor him, once Tante is no longer there.

Another person can be a reason to live, he thinks. Isn't that what Jenks is saying in his roundabout way? Until recently, he doesn't feel he's ever had a person to really care about him or to care about in return.

But even that's not accurate. He never knew his father, but Jenks has become like a father to him in so many ways. He never knew his real mother, the beautiful and mysterious Rose, yet Tante has brought him up and, between her and Molly, he's got this far in life. But real love for another is a new feeling. He thought he might have found it with Shay but, of course, that was just sex, a fantasy, nothing more. He knows that now. With Jenks it's not sex but a whole lot more. Will he ever find both in one person? Is that too much to ask for?

A few days later, Jenks brings him a present, a small cloth-bound book, and says, 'Have a read of this if you get the time. It might answer a couple of questions.'

He glances at the cover. Plato: *The Symposium*.

'Thank you. I will.' He devours it from cover to cover that very night, believing that if Jenks has offered it to him then it must be important. He appreciates hardly any of it on first reading but understands that Jenks is answering the question he's been posing: that love between two men can be the deepest, most profound path to wisdom when freely entered into as a selfless act that doesn't involve lust but a recognition of beauty as a reflection of the highest good. It's exhilarating to enter into the debates of these clever, witty philosophers from two thousand years ago.

In the notes, the translator explains that in Greek society it was the greatest honour, in fact a sacred duty, for an older and wiser man to love a beautiful young man; to take it upon himself to educate and elevate his companion and guide him across the perilous terrain that separates boyhood from manhood.

That same night, he makes his way from his room to the hallway below and slips into Jenks's bed once more. Before, he had come to Jenks as a wounded puppy, needing comfort and protection. But this is different. This is a choice and not about need. Something has shifted inside him. Jenks wakes immediately as he snuggles in. There is a glimmer of moonlight bathing the room in its pale glow. He stares into Jenks's eyes, two shining orbs of quicksilver.

'Hello.'

'Hello again.'

They smile softly at each other. Both of them understand that nothing sexual will take place, whatever the temptation, which, admittedly, is great on both sides, because it would most likely destroy what is precious about the love between them. The act of lovemaking would take them to a place of appetite and hunger which would never be satisfied. This was about another love, pure and simple – given, received and shared equally as friends. It's sometimes called the love that dare not speak its name. Maybe that's because to try and explain it only diminishes the truth of it.

They're holding on tightly to one another. Man and boy. He loves the sensation of Jenks's warm, naked body against his skin. The weight and solidity of it, the musculature that is both strong and firm, yet tender and yielding as they enfold one another in each other's arms. This is home, he thinks.

Jenks is shaking. He's crying; his whole body is convulsed by a shuddering sob, and then another and another. And Alfie just continues to hold him while wave after wave of grief rises up from the depths of Jenks's being to find long overdue release. And he finds himself whispering, 'I know.'

And he does. He knows that just as he's still a boy and Jenks a man, so the opposite is equally true. That men are also lost boys. That he is already in spirit the man he will one day become in fact. And he feels the atmosphere in the spartan bedroom change; he can sense he's not alone but that he has an army of ancestors at his back. They are present with him and part of him and always have been and will be while he still has breath in his body until he goes to join them in his turn. He has been asking himself for so long, 'Who am I and what will I become?' And now he has his answer. He knows who he is and who he is becoming. Hawk and hunter. Warrior and king. Gardener and wanderer. He can and will be all of these things in his life. He is being offered a gift. He simply has to trust it.

Now it will be possible to talk to each other about anything, he thinks.

Jenks's sobs have subsided. His stormy sea is calmed at last. They're damp with each other's tears; he's aware now that they're each giving off a body odour, which is earthy and not at all unpleasant, a smell like loamy soil and deep roots and tree bark after rain.

He imagines their pale bodies entwined in the moonlight,

two beautiful water lilies unfolding in a dark pool of tears.

'Shall I stay?'

'Would you like to?'

'Of course.'

'Then stay.'

They sleep together like brothers.

Dr Roach

His arrival causes quite a commotion, which affords him great amusement. He doubts if any of them would have expected their specialist doctor to come roaring up to the front door on a Triumph 650cc 6T Thunderbird, spitting gravel in all directions and startling a pair of noisy rooks who rise up, complaining loudly at being disturbed. He thinks, as he removes his goggles and leather helmet and glances around properly to gather first impressions, that the whole place has the air of some great gothic romance. The Brontë sisters would fit right in.

He loves his little Triumph, which is his greatest pleasure outside of his work, so it is really no inconvenience to ride out here, on these wild roads to the back of beyond, to check in on young Joseph, not least because it is quite an interesting case and he is keen to write it up.

Harry relishes his work, and his occasional spins on his bike on his days off, but he misses romance in his life. It has been much too long since his passionate fling with Dermot at medical college. Dermot is in London now, at a Charing Cross teaching hospital, and a snatched weekend once or twice a year is no substitute for a real relationship. Harry had got so desperate that he'd joined a local chorale, because he'd heard rumours that the men tended to be musical in more ways than one. But after ploughing through Purcell's *Music for the Funeral of Queen Mary* for months on end with a humourless, over-exacting choir master, the best he'd managed was to flirt with several merry widows, who were always up for a bitch and enjoyed a good laugh in the pub after rehearsals. Despite his best efforts, he still hasn't really come across anybody worth tempting into his bed. At work, there'd been a lovely male student nurse he'd had his eye on, and a married anaesthetist who'd shown a bit of interest, but it just seemed like asking for trouble, however discreet one tried to be.

A young man comprises the welcoming party. He is standing on the front terrace steps and taking in Harry's arrival with more than passing interest, a lively but quizzical expression on his face. As he offers his hand, which is surprisingly firm, Harry notices his beautiful green eyes, flecked with gold and amber, with long curling lashes any young girl would kill for. Harry introduces himself. 'Dr Roach. I believe I'm expected?'

The young man smiles shyly. 'Of course. Hello, I'm Alfie.'

A current of recognition passes between them, followed by the unmistakeable knowing glance.

Alfie's nervousness makes him appear even more charming, but he can't be more than seventeen, thinks Harry, appraisingly.

'They're expecting you in the drawing room. I'll show you the way. I think Molly's making tea, unless you'd prefer...?'

'Tea will be fine, thank you.'

He winks at the boy who looks startled for a moment and then grins uncertainly. Harry loves to flirt; he can't help himself. When one spends so much time witnessing life-and-death struggles on the wards, as he does, one learns to appreciate the gifts life offers even more keenly. And at that moment, just as he is being ushered indoors, as though the gods have planned it, another striking figure, older and very distinguished-looking, strides around the side of the house and calls out in a plummy English accent, 'Alfie, that old lead guttering will need replacing before we get any more heavy rains.'

He stops short, noticing the visitor. 'Oh, excuse me. You're here already. Dr Roach, I presume?'

'Harry... please.'

They share a manly handshake. They've begun to size each other up even before Alfie steps aside to allow this greeting to take place.

'It's very good of you to come all the way out here to see us. I'm Christopher Jenkins. But everyone calls me Jenks. Sorry I wasn't here to greet you, but I see Alfie's taking good care of you.'

Things really are looking up.

There follows an awkward three-way dance at the doorway with its own strange little undercurrent. The moment is held just a fraction too long, until it is mercifully broken by Alfie who babbles, 'Actually, I should go and check in on Lily right now. She's my horse. Well, our horse. Jenks bought her at the fair. She's the one Joseph fell from. It wasn't her fault, obviously. Jenks will take you through to Joseph, is that alright?'

He is growing pinker.

'No problem,' says Jenks, finally.

Alfie turns, but now he's started he can't stop himself. 'Oh, and why don't you get Jenks to show you the kitchen garden after you say hello to Joseph? We're sorting out what we'll do with the old rose garden next.'

And with that he is gone.

'Quite a remarkable young man.'

'When I first knew him, he literally wouldn't speak at all.'

'Making up for lost time then, I see.' They both laugh.

'It's a long story.'

'Another time, perhaps.'

Jenks allows the implication of that statement to sink in before he continues, 'Don't mind Alfie. There's no obligation to take up his invitation. What he didn't mention is he's more or less the owner.'

'Ah. I see. No. I'd love to. My mother's a very keen gardener. She'd love all this.'

'Well,'

'Yes, we should probably get on with the business in hand. And then perhaps we can see what the garden has to offer us?'

Despite the risks involved in being too direct, Harry finds it pays to strike while the iron is hot. He is immediately rewarded when Jenks has the good grace to grin.

'Goodness, you're a fast worker!'

'I suppose I am a bit. In my line of business, I get used to making instant decisions. It's why I like the bike. You have to operate on pure instinct.'

'Would you say you have good instincts then?'

'About people? I'd say I do.'

'You're right. About gut instinct. I remember that's exactly what it was like during the war. One wrong move and it was all over.'

'Did you see a lot of action?'

'Too much.'

'Right you are. Sometimes an operating theatre can be a bit of a war zone.'

Jenks changes the subject. 'That's a beautiful machine you have there.'

'Isn't she? Care for a spin later?'

'Slow down! I'm a bit out of practice at this sort of thing.'

'I'll let you into a secret. I'm rusty as hell too. Still, it's just like getting back on a horse I find. So, what say you we go have a look in on Joseph and afterwards you can show me this famous garden of yours?'

And it is plain sailing from there on in.

'I hope it won't be a disappointment after the big build-up.'

'Something tells me I'll love it.'

'Shall we go in?'

'Lead on.'

The assessment of Joseph is equally successful. He has a way to go yet, but Harry is going to pull some strings to get him specialised speech therapy. He will continue to monitor the young man's progress, which will clearly necessitate more visits out to Coolhooley estate on a regular basis.

So, it is a most satisfactory outcome: the arrangement to check up on Joseph each month, and, more importantly, the unexpected meeting with the handsome Christopher. Yes, if things develop further with Jenks, he'll have more than one reason to be getting to know all of them a lot better in the near future.

He has a definite sense that their encounter could grow into something significant, but he reminds himself to be patient. As Jenks had pointed out, as they'd strolled through the garden at the end of Harry's visit, 'Anything worthwhile takes planning and a lot of patience.' Well, time will tell, but he has a strong feeling that everything in the garden is definitely coming up roses. He feels a renewed thrill of anticipation, throttles up a gear, and roars back down the driveway.

It has turned out to be a most interesting, not to say

rewarding, visit, he decides, certain that his exit is being as closely observed as his dramatic entrance had been.

Tante

This will be her last Christmas. The entire household has spared no effort for weeks on end to ensure this celebration together is as memorable as it can be. She's dealt her cards, and been satisfied with the outcome. More than that, she's been praying for the first time in years. 'One last Christmas, that's all I'm asking, let me get through to Christmas.'

But instead of a feeling of sadness, there is, for her at least, a sense of real jubilation. Something that even a few months ago would have seemed well-nigh impossible, is here at last and actually happening. That she has made it through to Christmas Day at all is miracle enough, but to be with family, however unconventional, and in her very own home, is something she could never have imagined. It is the greatest Christmas gift she could ever have hoped for. Because that's what we are, she thinks, looking closely at each and every one of them in turn: a family.

Seated alongside her is Alfie, then Jenks and his new friend Dr Harry, then Molly, Joseph and Cassie. Last, but not least, even Michael has put in an appearance. Here they all are, unlikely survivors of the flood, clinging to each other on their own little life raft. They are a unique clan.

This is a time of miracles, she thinks. Well, haven't we created one right here?

It is all thanks to Harry, of course. Dr Harry. He'd protested at being addressed as Dr Roach, but none of them had felt Harry quite respectful enough.

He is what they'd all been waiting for. No-one could have predicted the effect he would have on all their lives. He has Joseph's treatment in hand. Despite the cerebral damage, the young man is on the mend, with regular speech therapy and hydrotherapy sessions. 'Our miracle boy,' Dr Harry affectionately calls him.

As he greets Joseph on his regular visits, he invariably calls out, 'So how's our miracle boy doing today?' And Joseph looks up from his carving and grins. As part of his recuperation, he's taken up working with wood, again, on Dr Harry's recommendation, and has a remarkable gift for it. One of his first projects has been to carve a Christmas crib, which now has pride of place in one corner of the dining room, lit up with a string of fairy lights.

Speaking is still an effort, but he can approximate whole sentences with Cassie's help. She is infinitely patient with him, so he tends to get much less frustrated and use fewer swearwords. Molly observed to Tante, 'Sure all he needed was the love of a good woman to knock a bit of sense into him.' Another miracle. He would never be entirely quite right in the head perhaps, reflects Tante, but a softer, less aggressive version of the Joseph they'd known seems to be emerging day by day.

As for Cassie, there is an unmistakeable contented glow to her these days. When Molly lets slip that she's met Cassie's mother, and it looks as if a spring wedding might be in the offing, Tante just nods, sagely. There is definitely a feeling of new life in the air in more ways than one and if ever a young woman was born for childrearing, it is Cassie.

Alfie seems to have found his own way to make peace with Joseph, and treats him politely, with a kind of tender solicitude, as though Joseph were a sweet, somewhat simple-minded, older brother. In the more recent weeks of Joseph's convalescence, when he was not being wheeled by Cassie or his mother, Tante had spotted – and more frequently heard – him, racing excitedly around the lower house and grounds like a demon in his wheelchair, another of Dr Harry's handy hospital acquisitions, creating an entirely new household hazard in the process. Fortunately, as a sure sign of his improved physical strength and mobility, it remains more often than not now folded up in the hallway, as he is able increasingly to get around on his own two feet, including with Alfie, who takes him out on long walks round the estate. They seem genuinely to enjoy each other's company, as though they have reverted to their early years. It is as if Joseph no longer has any recollection of the recent past events and lives in a state of blissful amnesia. Though, as far as she can tell, Alfie is still careful to keep Joseph away from Lily.

'It's common,' explains Dr Harry, 'for the human mind to shut away things that are just too painful for it to process.'

When she'd casually mentioned to Dr Harry that he'd already become like part of the family, he'd laughed and said, 'Of course I'm family, dearest Tante. Aren't we all? The holiest imaginable. Sure, don't we even have our very own Joseph, the gentle carpenter?' And when she'd replied, in all sincerity, 'In that case, you're his saviour,' he'd simply guffawed and said, 'Nothing of the sort, my dear. Don't be giving me ideas above my station or I'll be convincing myself I can walk on water.'

In the corner opposite Joseph's crib stands a huge, beautifully decorated Christmas tree. Jenks, Dr Harry and Alfie insisted on a tree. She's started to think of them collectively as her boys, never mind that Jenks has years on her, and has said so, much to their evident delight. When she suggested that a tree was way too much palaver, Dr Harry simply said, 'Not at all. Leave it to us.' So, she did, and here it now stands. It has been the same with so much else over these past few months. Nothing is too much trouble. In addition to his crib duties, Joseph has found time to carve some lovely wooden candle holders and everyone has taken a hand painting them, and now the candles are lit and flickering in every corner, along the mantlepiece, and on the table, casting a warm amber glow over the entire room, and reflecting back at them in the crystal glassware and the tall windows. The Christmas tree is hung with baubles made from stiff corrugated coloured card. In addition, she's ordered pots of both red and white gardenias; their heady scent fills the room with a special fragrance.

As a last act of celebration, she's had them bring down a painting from the attic, and hang it over the dining room mantlepiece. It is a large canvas, six feet by four, in a heavy gilt frame, and she dresses it in sprigs of holly and mistletoe, with Alfie's help. Once it is hung to her satisfaction, she and Alfie stand back to judge the effect. She hopes he understands what it is she wants him to see. It is a formal family portrait, painted just months before her father died, by an up-and-coming Dublin artist. Her parents sit, regally stiff, in the centre of the pink and gold chaise longue in the drawing room: he in a dark-grey dress-suit; she in a frock of palest, diaphanous blue silk that pools over the seat. The artist had placed the two sisters rather daringly on the floor, on either side of their parents, on a patterned Persian rug, their casual pose contrasting with their formal party frocks, and their coronets of spring flowers. They crouch like presenting nymphs, each draping a casual hand on a parental knee for support: Rose on her mother's, she on her father's. Balor, the family wolfhound, takes up most of the space between them. Young Michael stands behind the chaise, in a tweed jacket, one hand on his father's shoulder, with just the hint of a pout. Already so clearly the young crown prince, he radiates an air of absolute confidence and unshakeable privilege. He would have been about twelve at the time. She was twenty, had already had a summer in Paris, and was hoping for another; the future looked full of possibility. All of them are staring fixedly out at the viewer with an unconsciously arrogant gaze, with the exception of Rose, who is reaching down to stroke the dog, so the viewer gets a three quarters' profile view of her, while Balor's head is turned, affectionately looking back towards his mistress. Rose looks as if she is about to break into laughter. The combination of landed-gentry formality and theatrical quirkiness is a perfect moment, captured before all of their lives imploded.

For years, Jocelyn had found it unbearable to look at, but, finally, this seems the appropriate moment and the right setting, to include Rose and her parents as presiding spirits of their celebration. It is also her way of passing on the family story. She is grateful that nobody, not even Michael, questions it or demands more of an explanation.

She's been appraising Alfie's reaction to it for several minutes, and she can no longer bear the suspense.

'I thought they should join us for Christmas dinner.'

'Yes.' He hesitates and adds, 'Everybody looks so sad.'

She looks away from him and back at the painting. He's right. She's never noticed it before exactly. But they do all look like unhappy people – all trying to live up to their assigned roles but actually wishing to be somewhere else.

'Except my mother,' he adds. 'And the dog.'

He's right again. Yes. Except Rose.

'Your mother had enormous *joie de vivre*.'

'I can see that.' He is clearly pleased. She tells him what he wants to hear.

'And you are your mother's son.'

'Then I'm lucky, aren't I?'

'I'd say so.'

'No. I mean, because in a way I've had two mothers. I've had the best of both worlds.'

She is rendered speechless. There is no implied criticism in his words. On the contrary, he is acknowledging a truth. It has taken two sisters to bring him to the here and now: the one who conceived him and bore him into the world and the other who brought him up. She suddenly feels faint and stumbles slightly. He notices her discomfort.

'Tante, are you alright?'

'I'm fine. I just need to sit down for a moment.'

He brings over Joseph's wheelchair, and helps her into it, and after she's recovered herself, she suggests, 'Perhaps I should go and lie down next door.'

More and more frequently, she spends her days in the drawing room on the chaise, which has now been transformed into a permanent daybed for her. It's the one immortalised in the painting. She has discovered, to her surprise, that she enjoys having bustle and activity around her for much of the time. When she first suggested it to Dr Harry, he immediately approved. And now he and Jenks and Alfie take it in turns to help carry her up and down the flight of stairs from her bedroom landing to the drawing room. At first, she had forcibly resisted the indignity of it until Dr Harry simply scooped her up in a fireman's lift, saying, 'And how else are we going to get you back at the heart of things?' and brought her from her bedroom down onto the chaise on the floor below before she could protest any further, after which there seemed little point in hanging onto false pride.

And now she is indeed at the centre of the action and finds it much easier to supervise all of the forthcoming arrangements.

The boys organised an evening of paper-chain cutting and the results are now strung out across the dining room and hallway. Leaping reindeer sleighs, dancing snowmen, a galaxy of heavenly Christmas stars and angels criss-cross the ceiling, adding to the festive atmosphere. Even Michael has made a contribution, arranging for a pal in New York to post over a box of special American treats: Hershey bars and Oreo cookies and a big jar of peanut butter and a jar of something called cranberry jelly. 'It's for making peanut butter and jelly sandwiches,' he explains, and proceeds to demonstrate.

'A jam sandwich,' sniffs Molly. 'Why didn't you just say so in the first place? There's no need to be sending away to America for those – we can make our own here.' Joseph begs to differ and now demands peanut butter and jelly sandwiches morning, noon and night.

When not spooning down portions of peanut butter, Joseph has been busy carving personal tokens for each of them to hang on the tree, and these now dangle from its spreading branches. Some he gives with no comment and for others he makes an effort to explain his gift in his halting speech. There is a beautiful Celtic cross for his mother, a miniature bottle of Guinness for Michael, a stethoscope for Harry, a trowel for Jenks, a little thatched cottage for Cassie, a winged bird for Alfie, 'because Alfie likes birds', and for her, an exquisitely carved folded rose on a stem 'with no thorns', while for himself he has carved a miniature toboggan, presumably in hopes of a white Christmas. Instead of an angel for the top of the tree, the boys have attached a picture cut out from a film magazine and pasted onto a thick piece of cardboard. She doesn't recognise the reference: a figure in a bright pink dress, with a wand. Dr Harry explains, 'It's Glinda, the good witch from the Wizard of Oz,' and when she still doesn't understand, Alfie adds, 'She's a friend of Dorothy', and then giggles along with the others like it is some terrific in-joke.

All three of them seem to bring out the best in each other, including an unexpected playfulness in Jenks. Despite the difference in their ages, they all have something boyish and mischievous about them, that isn't quite so evident in their respective natures when they are on their own. In isolation, they each have an air of restlessness, including in Jenks's and Alfie's cases, a tendency toward melancholy, but in each other's company, they are a gang and suddenly seem complete. She feels sure that is down to Dr Harry's influence. Despite the stresses of his work, Dr Harry manages to maintain a remarkably light-hearted approach to life in general. Jenks seems at least ten years younger in his company. Not wishing to be outdone by Michael, Dr Harry has ordered a big box of luxury Christmas crackers from a posh department store in London, and they are all now delighting in the fancy paper crowns, and opening their lucky bags of childish treats and toys, reading out what she can only assume are the world's worst jokes, all so bad that they become uproariously funny. Apparently, not even money can buy you better quality jokes.

But when she looks closely at Dr Harry, she can also discern the blue shadows of exhaustion under his eyes. He works long hours and drives himself much too hard. He's only been able to snatch two full days away from the Christmas roster at the hospital. Here is another young man who lives life too fast for his own good, she thinks. But she looks across at Jenks, who's swapped places with Alfie for a moment in order to carve the turkey, and she can see that he is the perfect anchor for the good doctor. One only has to look at the way Jenks gazes at his friend, to know that he is wild about Harry.

'Come along now, Stanley, chop, chop, there's a good chap,' begins Dr Harry.

'Pass down the plates then, Dr Livingstone, my dear fellow,' Jenks announces in his poshest English colonial voice, preparing to pile them up with perfectly carved slices of the Christmas bird.

'Right y'are, Stanley, me boyo,' replies Dr Harry on cue.

It is a kind of music hall routine they have going with each other, which she could not comprehend until her curiosity had got the better of her one day and she asked Alfie if he knew the significance of it. 'It's their private joke,' he'd explained. 'Before they met, they both felt like they'd been living in darkest Africa.'

Virtually all traces of the awkward restless child he used to be have vanished and have been replaced by an inner glow and a new-found confidence. He is ready to plunge into the choppy waters of the wider world, and navigate them on his own terms. Here, he is finally accepted unconditionally for who he is, and that has made all the difference to him. When she thinks back, she remembers that his father had always had an eye for beauty in all its forms, male as well as female, so that when she looks at Alfie, she can see traces of that indiscriminate lust for life in him too, mixed in with something darker and more mysterious. For now, Alfie sits comfortably between them both, looking totally at ease with himself. This family, too, is part of her legacy to him, or at least so she hopes. He will travel far to discover who he is, but he will always have this place to come back to.

They have been blessed with a mild Christmas, and the boys insist on taking her out to show her the garden. Everyone has remained uncharacteristically tight-lipped about the goings on out there for months, despite Tante's constant pressing for details. They swaddle her up in a cocoon of woollen blankets and push her outside in Joseph's wheelchair.

She can tell that all three are a little nervous of her possible reaction. They needn't have been. Her heart fills to overflowing at the sight of it. The kitchen garden is laid out in tidy rows for every conceivable kind of root vegetable. There are stakes and markers in the ground to show what would be on its way come the spring: from cabbage to carrot to swede to brassica and early potato; then varieties of lettuce and leafy greens throughout the summer months. The restored glasshouse is a nursery for all manner of exotic bulbs to germinate, for seedlings to be nurtured, for tomato plants to ripen their sweet summer crop and for golden pumpkins to burgeon in the autumn. Jenks points proudly to their herb garden in a shady corner, at this time of year, just rosemary and bay. The old brick wall has been repaired and restored and trellised and, in addition, there is to be a formal rose garden and a gazebo. They wheel her along a newly paved garden path to the archway and down to the old pond which had lain neglected since long before her time. It has been completely restored and water lilies are extending their tendrils, ready for the blossoms to emerge and unfold in the spring. In the dark waters are sudden glimmers of darting red-orange fins. 'Japanese carp,' explains Alfie, pointing excitedly into the depths below. 'I'm sorry you can't see it yet in its final state,' Jenks says.

It is more than enough. A labour of love far beyond anything she could have dreamed of.

Ever pragmatic, she observes that all this, impressive as it is, must have more than broken the annual household budget – no wonder they hadn't wanted to give away too many details. Jenks gives a small, embarrassed cough and mumbles that actually there'd been no expenses incurred because, on the death of his father, he had received a small legacy of his own. He'd had to go back to England for a few days, she remembers now, and noted at the time that it was a very short visit, more or less just for the funeral and back.

'It's a bribe so the black sheep of the family won't darken their doors again,' pipes up Dr Harry. Jenks jabs him in the ribs and tells her she is to consider this a gift to the estate for her many kindnesses to him. She could remind him that the estate owes him a great deal more than the other way around but chooses not to press the point. His evident pleasure in his achievement, the way he points out this or that detail or particular choice of layout and the reason for it, is clearly its own reward as far as he is concerned.

Then they explain their vision. What if part of the house could be open to the public? Dr Harry is sure they can raise funds to develop Coolhooley into a retreat centre, for patients suffering trauma of one kind or other. Peace and solitude; healthy, home-grown produce; walks in the reviving air. It is the perfect location and he is sure it will pay its own way in the long term, with proper management and a fully costed business plan. And it is a way to preserve the estate and keep the property intact to pass on to future generations.

'We want this to be our peace garden,' adds Alfie, indicating the pond and the surrounding space. They have already asked Joseph if he will create some simple wooden benches. 'Of course, it is all just an ambitious idea as yet, but what do you think?'

Of course, they don't need her permission. Alfie is the future. It will be up to him. Whatever he wants, he can make happen. No doubt Brendan will offer him sound advice along the way, if he asks for it. But that isn't the point of this exercise. What they want is her blessing.

She knows from conversations with Jenks that, during

the war, in London, homosexual men were able to enjoy unprecedented licence to meet one another and enjoy each other's company under cover of darkness. But those days have long since vanished, to be replaced by a frightening new crackdown by the authorities. Their lives will never be easy, but out here, away from prying eyes, despite the iron grip of the Irish clergy, maybe a different kind of freedom might be possible for men like Jenks and Dr Harry.

She gives her approval without hesitation. Of course, it is a wonderful dream.

'Thank you. I think we can go back in now,' she says. They are offering her the gift of a future she will never get to see. She suddenly feels very frail, exhausted by their passion and enthusiasm.

Back inside, as the Christmas festivities begin in earnest, it amuses her to see Michael's continued discomfort. In the house, the world of the boys is the inverse of society in general. Here, Michael's intolerant assumptions are completely upturned. Men like her brother will never be able to understand men like Jenks and Dr Harry, let alone Alfie.

It turns out that this Christmas might also be the last that Michael spends under her roof. He has found himself a woman: the village postmistress, Kitty O'Connor, a widow and one-time flame. Molly mutters, 'Dear God in heaven, what on earth do these women see in him at all?' The tenancy will soon be up on the village house, and Tante and Alfie have agreed Uncle Michael can have it in perpetuity, provided he doesn't blot his copybook ever again. Who knows? Maybe Kitty will help keep him on the straight and narrow. It is just a few doors down from O'Rourke's, which allows Molly the last word, as always. 'A house with a bar attached? Won't he just be on the pig's back for the rest of his days? Not that he deserves it, mind. And, married or not, I predict Kitty will be a widow again within the two years.' Although, in fairness, that might be wishful thinking on Molly's part.

At last, they arrive at the pudding stage. Molly has outdone herself and she and Cassie bring in a magnificent plum pudding, which Dr Harry proceeds to slather in brandy and set alight, and everyone spontaneously applauds.

After the chaotic and disastrously misjudged dinner all those months ago, she's finally got her perfect last supper. When the meal is over, and just before they retire to the drawing room to recover from their gastronomic exertions, Alfie taps lightly on a Waterford crystal glass and stands up, a little self-consciously.

'I'd like to propose a toast to my dear Aunt Jocelyn, Tante. If you would all kindly raise a glass...'

Joseph needs a prompt from Cassie, and Michael complies a tad grudgingly, but, once everyone's glasses are charged, Alfie begins, haltingly at first and then with growing confidence. Who is this remarkable young man who has replaced the semi-feral creature she remembers? She sees that he has a little piece of paper with notes in front of him and his hand is trembling slightly. Her heart goes out to him for this gesture, which he's clearly been practising.

'I want to acknowledge Tante, because without her, none of us would be here in this house today. It's thanks to her that we all can still live here.'

He pauses and looks directly at her. Out of the corner of her eye, she can see his speech isn't going down at all well with Michael, who looks as if he might actually get up and leave, but then seems to think better of it. But Alfie appears oblivious and only has eyes for her.

'I want to pay tribute to the woman who wasn't my mother,

wasn't even like a mother to me, but has been more than a mother; a woman who has allowed me to become exactly who I am.'

'Hear, hear,' Dr Harry chimes in.

'To my dearest Tante.'

They all now stand. 'To Tante!'

She rises, a little unsteadily, and bows graciously, like the queen she is. She wants to cry. She won't, can't, cry she tells herself, but a glistening tear rolls down her cheek and she lets it rest there, shining like a precious liquid jewel. After nearly a whole lifetime, she remembers again what it is like to feel joy.

Alfie

After dinner, everyone retires, bloated but content, to the drawing room and takes turns to sing carols and popular songs around the piano. Everyone, that is, but Michael, who complains he has a headache and feels out of sorts. 'I'm not surprised, with the amount he's put away,' Molly mutters, as they watch him stumble back to his room.

Cassie begins by singing *Silent Night* in a surprisingly sweet voice. Jenks contributes *Twelve Days of Christmas*, which, he explains, he'd once had to learn for a Christmas concert at school, and teaches them all silly actions and noises to accompany the words. Dr Harry surprises everyone by leading them in a few rousing choruses of old favourites, including *Danny Boy*, although they mangle most of the words and can't reach the high notes, and *Wild Rover*, to which they all clap along. Joseph becomes particularly excited and gets the clapping rhythm of the chorus hopelessly, hilariously wrong. They sing *Sweet Molly*

Malone, and when Dr Harry asks Molly if she'd been christened in honour of her fishy namesake, she protests, 'The cheek of it, that I was not, I was named after my grandmother', and tells him he deserves a good slap for himself. Dr Harry serenades Jenks with *You Are My Sunshine* and together they sing *I Can't Give You Anything but Love, Baby* to each other and to celebrate Cassie and Joseph. Molly leads them all in *Daisy, Daisy*. Even Joseph manages to contribute a verse or two of *She'll Be Coming Round the Mountain* for his beloved, with a little help from the rest of them, while Tante, enthroned once more on her daybed, simply beams at them all.

He can't imagine a time when there has been so much fun and laughter in the house. When it comes to his turn and everyone insists, 'Come on now, Alfie, give us a song', his mind mists over and he feels nothing but a terrifying blank until he remembers the one song that had once seemed to sum up his life. In a quiet, shaky voice he sings *Nobody's Child*, choking up towards the end. When the rest of them applaud his effort, he immediately adds, 'Of course, it's not true.'

Jenks smiles at him and says, 'It's alright, Alfie, we all feel like that sometimes.' Then Dr Harry says, 'Here's a song dedicated to us all', plays some opening chords, and begins in a strong, high tenor voice:

When you walk through a storm
Hold your head up high,
And don't be afraid of the dark...

It is the famous song from *Carousel* and one by one they all hum along or join in. As the final notes die away, it feels as if a healing angel, maybe Glinda the Good Witch, has visited the assembled company, and Tante says quietly, 'The ghosts have been laid to rest at last.'

Looking over, Molly says, 'We should get her back upstairs, I'll prepare a warming pan for her bed,' and Dr Harry nods and helps Jenks carry her back up to her room. Dr Harry can be heard softly serenading her with the words to *Goodnight Irene*.

The Christmas celebrations officially over, the party breaks up the very next morning. Cassie takes Joseph in the new pony and trap to meet her mother and actively discuss wedding plans. There is little doubt, thinks Alfie, how affairs in Joseph's household will proceed once they are married, surrounded as he will be by a trinity of Irish matriarchs: namely, his wife, his mother and his mother-in-law to be. Dr Harry returns to work and Jenks goes to stay with him in Galway for a few days, but not before checking they can all manage without him. Once assured, he is like a little boy let out of school, and can't wait to leap on the back of Dr Harry's bike.

'Taking his life in his own hands with that one,' comments Molly. Michael, who still seems awkward around the house most of the time, is also off, back to his widow in the village, having persuaded a reluctant Cassie and Joseph to drop him off.

With nearly everyone gone, the house is suddenly eerily quiet again. And, as if she has merely been waiting for the household to empty of guests and family alike, three days after Christmas, Tante's health takes a serious turn for the worse.

The crisis begins with a fever. Molly hears her restless cries and then runs back and forth all night long to wipe down the constant film of sweat from her brow and hold her hand and stroke her arm. She takes a moment to run up to Alfie's room, only to find the bed empty. She calls out for him and he emerges, bemused, from Jenks's abandoned bedchamber, clutching a pillow in his arms. 'Come,' she says, and he is at once fully awake.

He does his best to support her, bringing fresh towels, helping her change an undersheet that has got soaked through, fetching anything she needs.

He fills glass after glass of water for Tante to sip. The mild weather has broken and a cold front descends from the north, bringing icy winds and freezing temperatures and a promise of that rarest of events: snow. Tante continues to complain of feeling too hot. She is burning up. Her breathing has become harsh and irregular. Molly takes him aside and whispers, 'Dear God, I think this is it. The pneumonia has her in its grip. You'll have to go and fetch the priest.' He queries whether this is really what Tante would want, but Molly insists it is.

'What about a doctor? Could we get her to the hospital?'

'It's too late for that. And if we try to move her in this weather, that would kill off the poor creature, for sure. She always insisted she'd only leave here feet first.'

It is true. He'd been in the room one day while Molly was tidying up and heard his aunt say, adamant as always, 'Can you imagine anything worse than not being able to die in your own bed? In some dreadful convent hospital, for instance, being pawed over by the Sisters of Mercy, while they pray for your eternal soul and sniff at your chamber pot? No, thank you. I'll make my own peace with God in my own way, and die in my own bed at a time of my own choosing.'

Molly pleads, 'Fetch the priest. He'll know what to do.'

Lily is shuffling restlessly in her stall. One of Alfie's first tasks with Jenks had been to ensure the stable was mended and the rotten boards replaced and weather-proofed for her. Even so, it is chilly, and despite her winter coat she is shivering slightly. He feels sorry to have to take her out in this temperature, particularly as flurries of thick snowflakes are now falling from a leaden sky. She offers only the slightest tug of resistance as he brings her into the yard. He and Jenks have talked of setting up a carpentry workshop out here for Joseph, in the stone barn opposite, where he can start to make furniture. But, right now, the whole place just feels cold and cheerless and reflects his own feelings about this swift turn of events.

He's got so used to Tante's illnesses over the years, her endlessly failing health that, somehow, he's managed to put from his mind that there is only one sure and certain way it will end. That it looks to be happening in bleakest midwinter seems particularly sad and cruel.

He rides towards the village. He looks back, as they turn the curve in the drive that sweeps away from the house and, through the relentless snow, glimpses a lone, orange light glowing faintly in the corner bedroom on the first floor. The rest of the house is a block of shadow. Lily picks her way gingerly through the unfamiliar, white world settling in around her and he hasn't the heart to urge her to go faster, despite his anxiety that by the time they get back they will be too late and it will all be over.

They are in luck. Father Diamond has just returned from a parish visit to Mr Flaherty, poor faithful soul, his housekeeper explains. She is a thin woman; everything about her seems thin, including her sharp, pointed nose and drawn lips which purse ever so slightly on the news of Tante's condition. It has been several years since Tante ventured inside a church and Alfie has taken after her in that respect. On the few occasions that the priest has paid them a courtesy visit as part of his parochial duties, Molly has supplied him with tea and freshly buttered soda bread, but Tante made it abundantly clear she had little time for the faith of her fathers, and her nephew needed nothing in the way of religious education, thank you very much, so, this particular mission is awkward, to say the least.

Father Diamond appears promptly. Alfie asks if there is somewhere he can shelter Lily, and the priest offers to house her in the small garage next door, squeezed in beside his trusty old Ford. 'There. Snug as a donkey in a stable.' Once that is accomplished, they go indoors where there is a strong smell of beeswax and fried egg. Alfie glances around him as the old priest disappears to gather the holy oils for Extreme Unction. He is struck by how austere and chilly the room feels, which has nothing to do with the temperature outside.

Apart from the customary picture of the Sacred Heart by the fireplace, there is a narrow, copper bronze vase containing tall, white lilies, next to a fireguard and coal tongs, although the fire itself is out. On the opposite wall hangs the one concession to domesticity, a fine, needlework tapestry of the words God Bless This House, in a gilt frame. The housekeeper brings a tray of watery tea in a flowery cup and saucer, a jug of milk, a bowl of sugar lumps, and four thin, dry sweet biscuits on a small plate. 'That'll keep you going.'

Father Diamond returns, carrying all the items necessary for the sacrament, including a violet silk stole. He takes the opportunity to deliver a sermon, mercifully short. 'Dying is a serious business,' he says, fixing Alfie with a stern gaze, and pronouncing the fact with great satisfaction. He adds that he and his aunt have done well to turn back to the bosom of Holy Mother Church at their hour of need. 'The last rites must be honoured and observed with the holy sacrament to release all sinners from human bondage and back into God's grace.' Alfie doesn't consider it necessary to point out that the call is neither his nor Tante's idea.

They agree to go back in Father Diamond's car. Alfie will collect Lily later. The snowstorm is worsening, turning the world as white as a shroud. He suddenly wonders whether, if they slow down the journey long enough and never actually arrive, they might somehow delay the inevitable. It shocks him to realise just how unprepared for his aunt's death he really is. For years, he'd fantasised it was exactly what he wanted, that without her domineering presence in his life, he would be free. He sees what a childish illusion that had been. He knows now that her absence will be a huge void, and sees that, in some way, she had wanted to protect him from the terrible feeling of loss that is about to engulf him. Her own losses had crippled her. He has recently read *Great Expectations*, after she'd recommended it to him, comparing her life to that of the tragic Miss Havisham. 'What's the point of your life if you don't leave the world a better place than you found it?'

In the end, her legacy will be very different from that of Dickens's wounded character. Tante has done all in her power to ensure that the same fate that she had suffered will not befall him and that all those she leaves behind will have at least the chance to build a better future for themselves and find some happiness.

He feels the beginning of his grief. But it is too soon. There is more to do yet. There will be time for this later, he tells himself. 'Find out who you are and then you'll know who you're meant to be,' he hears her instruct him. And, suddenly, it is as though he is visited by Hawk no longer, but a holy dove, descended from the heavens. He hears another voice from even deeper inside him say, 'One day you'll tell this story,' and his grief instantly vanishes, replaced by an overwhelming sensation of certainty and calm, and he answers, 'Of course.' For the first time ever, the world makes complete sense.

Jocelyn

Pains in my joints. Voices in my head. Itches on my skin. I knew there would come a time when nothing more could rouse my body to action. When all roads would be exhausted except the one to oblivion. No twitch of pleasure or spasm of joy. My face is already my death mask. I taste my failures like ashes on my tongue. The weight of memory lies heavy on my head. My heart is hard as a walnut. You are the spectre that haunts my days. I can no longer remember what I liked about you.

She had foolishly imagined dying would be easier than this. You'd close your eyes to the world and let the final sleep embrace the mind and body, while you drifted off into a blissful state of nothingness. But, of course, she'd reckoned without the journey that must be endured before the destination is reached. Her spirit might be ready to depart, but the body, even hers, which feels as though it's already lived through a thousand lifetimes, is stubborn and has other ideas, and insists on clinging to life.

'The snow's settling,' she hears Molly say.

Then there's another voice in the room.

'Jocelyn, can you hear me? Would you like to pray with me?'

No, she would not. But she feels too enfeebled to protest.

'I think we should begin,' he's saying.

Begin what? she wonders, and feels herself drifting off to wherever the snow is settling. Random voices and visions are unspooling in her head. The living and the dead. Mostly the dead. They have more to say.

A hand – not Molly's, more masculine; the man's – is rubbing something unpleasant on her forehead, then on her nostrils, lips and hands. She can smell and taste some kind of oil. And she has a strange image of a cannibal preparing to cook and eat her.

'Through this holy anointing, may the Lord in his love and mercy help you with the grace of the Holy Spirit.'

'Amen,' say Molly and the male voice in unison.

Oh, that. The holy oils. The chrism. It had been the same for Rose at the end. So, it's finally time for all this rigmarole, is it? Is there really no end to the indignity of dying?

She's made her farewells. Her work here is done. She wants it to be over. Just let it all be over.

Alfie

'I think we should let nature take its course now. I'd say she's more than ready.'

'She waited until everyone left.'

'It's often the way. They hang on until they can leave with little or no fuss.'

He hates the way they're talking about Tante as if she is already dead.

'Well, young man, you'll soon be coming into a lot of responsibility, Molly here tells me.'

'I... yes.'

'You'll have to be the man of the house for everyone now and stay strong. Can you do that for us all, do you think?'

He chooses to ignore the remark.

'Well, I'd best be off, if I'm to get home safe tonight.'

'You're sure you won't stay over?'

'You're very good, but I have to be up for early Mass. The faithful will expect a service tomorrow, whatever the weather.'

'Thank you for all your trouble, Father.'

'Sure, it's no trouble. Let me know what else we can do to help and we'll talk about other arrangements when the time comes.'

It's all so clinical and matter of fact. Something inside his head explodes.

'You mean her funeral? You don't have to talk as if I'm not here.'

There's a moment's shocked silence. Molly stares at him, aghast at his rudeness. You don't insult the clergy whatever your personal feelings might be. The old priest gives him a long, searching look, then turns back to Molly. 'As I said, anything you need, the Church is always here for you in good times and bad.' As Molly shows Father Diamond out, Alfie hears him whisper, 'We'll talk very soon. Don't worry about the boy, he's naturally overwrought. He'll calm down once he's had a bit of a rest.'

They listen in silence as the car engine jolts and splutters noisily but fails to fire, until, after a couple of false starts, it finally coughs and wheezes into life and the car tyres crunch over the blanket of snow that's just beginning to freeze. And then there's just quiet between them.

He can tell she's burning to say something, but his heart is already full to the brim, and as she opens her mouth to begin, he simply wants to shout, 'No!' and flee back up to his room. That's what angry Bogboy would do. But he's not Bogboy anymore, he thinks, he's Alfie, who is loved and whom people care about, which means he can love and care in return, if he chooses.

'Come into the kitchen.' She motions to him to sit down, which, reluctantly, he does. Then she holds out her hands towards him, palms upwards on the table, which is so unexpected that he automatically places his inside hers. She closes her hands around his and strokes them.

'When my Paddy died, I just wanted to bite the head off

anyone who came near me for months afterwards.' He nods. 'Your aunt was the only one who understood. She never made a fuss about anything all that time. You probably didn't notice.'

'No.'

'What you saw at Christmas, that was like the real her, the person she was before all her troubles began. She could be a lot of fun, sometimes. You've seen how she is with Dr Harry. Your mother brought that side out in her. In all of us. But your mother betrayed your aunt, too. That was the other side of her. She had to have her own way. Some people just don't see the consequences of their actions. Or don't accept them. There's good and bad in all of us, Alfie. It's a lot harder to be good sometimes, but in the long run, it's better that way. Your aunt had so much to deal with and your Uncle Michael messed everything up, then ran away and left her to cope with it all on her own. Then you came along, and, finally, there was Rose dying. Everyone advised Jocelyn to give you up for adoption. Your grandmother was no help. The scandal nearly killed her. She only lasted a few months after that. Father Diamond had the bishop write to your aunt. They had a place waiting for you in a lovely orphanage run by the holy sisters, and said they'd find a good Catholic couple to bring you up. They nearly persuaded her. She went in to Galway to sign the papers. I went with her. I said to her, 'You're sure this is what you want?' Anyway, while she was in the bishop's office, she had a change of heart, there and then. Oh! There was a terrible to-do about it. They kept saying that she must sign, that she was in no fit state to bring a child up, that she was making a terrible mistake, that she was ruining your life. They all pressured her. The bishop, the nuns – Father Diamond was there too – but she wouldn't back down. They even brought me in from the next room to help persuade her. But I could see her mind was made up. She'd made a vow to your mother, you see, and she couldn't go back on it. It was never easy for her. But she forgave. Keeping you was her way of forgiving, do you see? Whatever happens in life, you must always learn to forgive, Alfie. I have.'

'I know. Is that why you stayed on to help her?'

'Sure, what else could I do? She wasn't cut out to be a mother. Some women aren't. I already had one little boy – what difference would another one make?'

'I used to think she hated me.'

'She never hated you. She just didn't know how best to bring you up. She wanted to be an artist when she was young. Instead, she found herself trapped out here, a spinster with a falling-down estate, landed with a baby. You weren't easy, you know. You were wild and wilful from the very first. You were your mother's son, alright. Jocelyn tried to protect you as best she could. She was terrified you'd hurt yourself and she'd have to answer to your mother in the afterlife.'

'I'm sorry.'

'Don't be. It's no matter. She always knew you were somehow different. She sometimes laughed about it. 'I have a fairy child. They came in the night and left me a changeling.' Well, anyway... she and you got there in the end.'

'Thank you.'

'It's enough. Drink up your tea and we'll go check up on her. Then you should sleep.'

'What about you?'

'Don't worry about me. I'll keep an eye on her tonight. You can take over in the morning for a while. It won't be long now, I'm thinking. We'll just try and keep her comfortable as best we can. Father will notify the undertaker for us as soon as it's necessary.'

Tante

Tante wakes from her long sleep. Is she still Tante? She feels empty. She is poised between nothingness and the ten thousand things. Alive and not alive. Dead but not dead. Neither flesh nor spirit. It's not yet time to rise and soar. But soon. Very soon.

Bogboy

He wakes. It's still dark. And cold. For a moment he can recall nothing. Then he remembers. Can life seem both more real and less real at one and the same time?

The moon has risen. There is a sprinkling of stars in the clear sky. All is snow glow. Is life like this? he wonders. Just like snow? Both solid and transient? And is he Bogboy or Alfie right now? Or neither? He doesn't feel much like anything. Hollow.

He has a strong impulse to go downstairs and see Tante. He dresses rapidly and pads down to her room. Molly is sitting upright at the bedside. Faithful to the very end. She has her back to him and hasn't yet heard him come in.

There's the faintest sound of breathing, a chesty wheeze in the air like the sound of surf that rises, then sighs away again.

He places a hand gently on Molly's shoulder. She gives a start and looks round at him.

'Jesus, you gave me a fright. I thought you were a ghost.'

'I can take over for a bit. You need to sleep as well.'

'You're sure?'

'Yes.'

'Well, maybe just for an hour or so. I could do with putting my head down. She's peaceful now. She drank some water and went back to sleep again almost immediately.'

Molly slips from the room, and he goes over and glances out of the curtain at the first hint of pre-dawn light and then comes to take his turn at Tante's bedside. So, this is what her life has been reduced to? he thinks, amazed. This is her final deathbed journey. Is she at all conscious? She's catching at air: tiny, laboured, raspy breaths that gurgle in her throat, little whimpers of distress. Her chest barely rises and falls. At first glance, she could already be dead. There is a strange intimacy to this moment, alone with her, sharing her last hours on earth. Witnessing her succumb, all sense of self draining away. She's no longer a daughter, sister, lover, friend... or mother. Her body is closing down on itself, fluttering and shuddering in a series of involuntary spasms. He's counting her last precious breaths, sighs, heartbeats. She is doing the work of dying which nobody else can do for her. He thinks, I must remember this, as he takes in the face he's loved and hated, pleaded and fought with, kissed and insulted, craved and ignored.

Her eyes are suddenly open, glazed and uncomprehending. As his gaze meets hers, he takes in at the same time the fine hair on her scalp, now moist and straggled; her mouth, pinched with sorrow and disappointment, a gaping, creased hole like the void she's being sucked towards; the sharp, stubborn ridge of her jawbone and, where she's pulled the sheet away from her, her emaciated breastbone beneath the flimsy material of her nightgown. Yes, he thinks, I will remember all this too.

He strokes her cheek and she reaches out to him with her claw-like grip, the back of her hands purple-black and bruised.

Does she see him? He can't tell. It's not important.

He's Bogboy. He has work to do. A journey to take with her. But first, he goes to the window again and, this time, pulls the curtain all the way back to let in the dawn light which is now beginning to illuminate the sky. Next, he climbs into bed with her and settles himself alongside her, holding her close to him, with infinite care and tenderness. 'You don't have to do this all alone,' he tells her. She emits a plaintive, drawn-out cry, like she's trying to call out a name but can't quite shape the sound of it.

No matter. He knows who he is. He's pure spirit, leading hers towards the light, the spiral nebula, to unimaginably far distant galaxies beyond. He's Hawk, the trailblazer, beyond space and time, king of infinity, leading her up and away beyond the darkness and the shadow places.

He leans in and whispers in her ear, 'It's alright, you can let go now, you can go towards the light.' And she does. Now, finally she can be Hawk too, soaring, ascending, letting earth slip away far below her. The moment of her death is almost imperceptible, a single, involuntary spasm of her jugular vein as the weak blood flow stills and settles and her faint final breath evaporates into the ether. It's over.

There are figures waiting for her, ready to welcome her. He can feel their powerful presence all around him. The entire room glows with their radiance. As he watches, holding her body in his arms, the sun rises up over the ridge of the mountain and the new day begins.

Acknowledgements

There are so many people I have to thank for enabling me to bring *Bogboy* to life because, like most creative endeavours, it would never have happened by my efforts alone.

First and foremost, I need to thank my extraordinary mentor and friend, Claire Steele, who, more than anyone else, inspired me to believe that I really am a storyteller. At Constellations Press, she and Jill Glenn patiently guided me through the process. I am so grateful to them for their scrupulous editing skills, their attention to detail, and their endless faith in the project.

My thanks also go to:

My mother, Bridget, from whom I learned that anything can make a good story if you have a love for words and know how to use them.

My Uncle Harry, the adventurer, whose faith in me made me believe that whatever I dreamed of achieving was possible.

My English teacher, Mr Parsons, who first encouraged me as a shy, bookish teenager to write stories and then took seriously my fledgling efforts.

Tom, who was one of the first people to tell me, 'You should write a novel.'

The amazing writers in my writers' groups, including Sharon, Shelagh, Cath, Heidi, Sue, Jeannie, Gemma, Holly, Alison, and Coco, each of whom inspired me with their individual brilliance, while, at the same time, offering generous support for my work.

All my gay brothers at the various gay men's retreats I attended, where I nervously recited excerpts of *Bogboy*, and who all immediately demanded to know when they could read the rest of it. Here it is, guys!

The wonderful VG Lee and our LGBTQ+ writers' group in Hastings, for reminding me that our stories matter and need to be heard now more than ever.

Harold, who has always been there for me and who gives me space to confide my darkest moments. He helps me to find the light again whenever I lose faith in myself.

Athena, who is as practical as she is wise and talented, and a true friend.

My dear friend, Catherine, who is the best cheerleader anyone could wish or hope for.

Dan Fauci and The Actor's Institute, where I first learned what true creative risk looks like.

Bruno, who, over the years, has shared his impeccable taste and wisdom with me, and who has made me appreciate the beauty of economy.

Fuzzy, who makes me laugh – and who doesn't need that, in these dark times of ours?

Frances, because everyone should have a friend in life who anchors you, keeps you honest and knows where true north lies.

And, finally, my brother, who reminds me that I do have a family, and I do belong, and that kindness and loyalty make all the difference.

And last, but not least, this is for all the Bogboys of the world who wrongly believe they are worthless, because no-one has yet revealed to them the light they carry inside.

Constellations Press is a small independent press
committed to publishing works of fiction, memoir and essays.

We publish books that boldly reimagine society and
celebrate our diverse humanity, adding to the
total sum of the world's beauty.

constellationspress.co.uk